DREAM UNCHAINED

Paranormal Romance by Kate Douglas

Demonfire
"Crystal Dreams" in *Nocturnal*
Hellfire
Starfire
Crystalfire

Erotic Romance by Kate Douglas

Wolf Tales
"Chanku Rising" in *Sexy Beast*
Wolf Tales II
"Camille's Dawn" in *Wild Nights*
Wolf Tales III
"Chanku Fallen" in *Sexy Beast II*
Wolf Tales IV
"Chanku Journey" in *Sexy Beast III*
Wolf Tales V
"Chanku Destiny" in *Sexy Beast IV*
Wolf Tales VI
"Chanku Wild" in *Sexy Beast V*
Wolf Tales VII
"Chanku Honor" in *Sexy Beast VI*
Wolf Tales VIII
"Chanku Challenge" in *Sexy Beast VII*
Wolf Tales 9
"Chanku Spirit" in *Sexy Beast VIII*
Wolf Tales 10
Wolf Tales 11
Wolf Tales 12
"Dream Catcher" in *Nightshift*
Dream Bound

Published by Kensington Publishing Corporation

DREAM UNCHAINED

Kate Douglas

APHRODISIA

KENSINGTON PUBLISHING CORP.

www.kensingtonbooks.com

APHRODISIA BOOKS are published by

Kensington Publishing Corp.
119 West 40th Street
New York, NY 10018

All Kensington titles, imprints, and distributed lines are available at special quantity discounts for bulk purchases for sales promotion, premiums, fund-raising, and educational or institutional use.

Special book excerpts or customized printings can also be created to fit specific needs. For details, write or phone the office of the Kensington Special Sales Manager: Kensington Publishing Corp., 119 West 40th Street, New York, NY 10018. Attn. Special Sales Department. Phone: 1-800-221-2647.

Aphrodisia and the A logo Reg. U.S. Pat. & TM Off.

ISBN-13: 978-0-7582-6935-5
ISBN-10: 0-7582-6935-8

First Kensington Trade Paperback Printing: November 2012

10 9 8 7 6 5 4 3 2 1

Printed in the United States of America

This book is dedicated with great appreciation to my agent, Jessica Faust, for her amazing ability not only to see the potential in my totally off-the-wall ideas, but then to convince an editor that I can make it work. Really. She does that!

And to my editor, Audrey LaFehr, who gives me the freedom to take those ideas into uncharted territory. I've never once been told, "No, you can't do that." As a writer, knowing my editor and publisher are behind me no matter how far out I manage to go on that proverbial limb is beyond price.

Acknowledgments

My thanks and appreciation to Martin Biro, my editor's intrepid assistant, who magically makes things work. I really don't want to know the details, because then I'd be wallowing in guilt for all the trouble I cause the poor man, but, Martin, thank you. I remember when Audrey hired you—she said you were going to do a terrific job. She was right.

Kensington's production department and art department, the publicists and IT people, marketing and sales—everyone has a role to play from the time a proposal is accepted to the final moment where I'm holding the printed book in my hands. Thank you all. You've given me an opportunity unlike anything I ever imagined, and I'm thoroughly enjoying every minute.

As always, my sincere thanks to my talented beta readers. Camille Anthony, Nicole Passante, Rhonda Wilson, Jan Takane, Rose Toubbeh, and Lynne Thomas do their best to keep me from falling flat on my face. Any stumbles are entirely mine, but these ladies are terrific, a small but important part of the village that brings my stories to life.

1

It wasn't until a tangerine slice of sunlight flashed above the sharp edge of the plateau that Mac Dugan realized he'd spent almost the whole damned night on the deck outside his bedroom.

Sitting in a hard, wooden Adirondack chair, freezing his ass off while the woman he loved and his best friend were curled up together in the big bed in the room behind him.

He imagined the two of them—snuggled warm and cozy in a tangle of twisted bedding—and didn't know whether to laugh or cry at the visual. Dink, all long, well-formed male with a sexy mat of dark blond hair across his chest, washboard abs, and a strong, sharply masculine face darkened with morning stubble.

And Zianne? Fluffy little gray squirrel.

Last time he looked, she'd had her tail curled around the top of Dink's head and one tiny paw resting on his ear.

It wasn't supposed to end like this.

He took a deep breath, pushed back his fear and the sharp burn of frustrated tears, and focused on what they'd shared last night. Mac, Zianne, and Dink, together again as they'd been so long ago. Zianne had held on to her human shape long enough for them to make love—the three of them connecting in a way they'd not been able to do since her abrupt disappearance so many years ago.

Twenty fucking years. Twenty years wondering if she still lived. Worrying whether or not all of his creative energies, every spare penny he'd been able to raise, and the combined technological advances of the entire research and development team at Beyond Global Ventures would be enough to rescue Zianne and the few surviving members of her people from slavery.

Twenty years, sixty million dollars, and a lifetime of focusing on an impossible rescue would all come down to the next thirty-six hours or so. Fewer than two days for Zianne to live or die, for the few remnants of the Nyrian people to survive.

Or not.

They were so damned close to success, even as the entire project balanced on a razor's edge of failure.

Shit. He hadn't allowed himself to consider failure. How could he, and still work toward such an impossible goal? What fool would even attempt the rescue of a small group of alien slaves imprisoned aboard a spaceship—held by another alien race preparing to plunder the earth of all its natural resources?

It sounded ridiculous no matter how he phrased it, so he did what he always tried to do when the fears surfaced. Mac pushed the negative thoughts out of his head. Refused to consider failure. Reminded himself failure was never an option.

Call it denial, call it what you will, but it was the only way he'd survived the past two decades. Focus on the desired outcome. Ignore the rest. Plan for everything that can possibly go wrong, and then put those plans aside and go with one that assured success.

Mac sucked in a deep breath, centered himself, and locked

his fear away. He consciously refocused his energy, squinting at the growing brilliance of the sun as it slanted across the huge array of satellite dishes. He studied them with pride, taking comfort in the fact they worked perfectly, that they had allowed his small team of young men and women to make telepathic contact with Zianne's people.

People of pure energy, enslaved eons ago aboard the Gar vessel and forced to power the huge star cruiser now hiding in orbit behind the moon. Unwilling accomplices in the Gar's plans to plunder Earth of all her riches. To take her mineral resources, her air and water—all that kept the planet alive.

The scope of the threat was beyond even Mac's wildest imagination, and his imagination had no limits. The satellite array was proof of that—the fact it had worked so well, that it had allowed his people to contact the Nyrians from the very first day gave him hope that their plan, what there was of it, would succeed. Somehow, they would rescue the captives.

Somehow, he would save Zianne's life.

Mac shifted his attention to the square cinder-block building they'd labeled the dream shack. The small building was the center of operations for the entire project, the place where his telepathic team members would hook themselves up to the massive antennae and, via the satellite array, focus their sexual energy on the Nyrians.

And the Nyrians had already proved they knew how to work with such a powerful and compelling source of power. Mac had learned their secret from Zianne over two decades earlier, that the Nyrians, a people without a physical form of their own, could take on corporeal bodies through the power of sexual fantasy.

Could take those bodies and hold on to them, and, once they were able to retrieve their soulstones, they would be free of the Gar and able to make a new home here, on Earth.

If everything went according to plan. "Damn but that's a big *if.*" Sighing, Mac rubbed his hand over his burning eyes. He'd not slept all night and today he would need to be sharp—on top of his game—if he was going to be any help at all. He stared at the dream shack, watching as the sunlight brushed the glass dome on top of the building. That had been an act of whimsy—installing a skylight so that the team members could watch the sky as they projected their thoughts through space. They didn't need to see the stars to know they were there, but from what feedback he'd gotten, all of them appreciated the view skyward.

He glanced at his wristwatch as the top half of the sun wavered above the dark edge of the plateau. It was barely six, which meant Finnegan O'Toole had a couple more hours to his shift.

Now there was a guy who'd proved first impressions weren't always correct. Finn had come across as a class A jerk—brilliant, but still a jerk. Then he'd shown more character than Mac or any of the others had suspected when he'd volunteered to go aboard the Gar star cruiser to help with the rescue.

A brave and foolish offer by a man who was no one's fool.

What kind of man would willingly step into danger like that? *Me?*

Yeah, Mac knew he'd do it in a heartbeat, except he was needed here. This was, after all, his quest, for want of a better word. The culmination of his twenty-year mission to find Zianne, to save her people, to destroy the Gar before they destroyed the world.

It sounded like a grade B movie when he spelled it out, except it was real. Terrifying, beyond belief, yet all too real.

Who in the hell, in their right mind, would think he had a prayer of success? Of course, no one had ever accused him of being in his right mind. Even Mac's strongest supporters figured he had more than a few screws loose.

In all fairness to himself, what genius didn't march to a different drummer? It was probably a very good thing that the world didn't know the truth—Mac Dugan didn't follow any drummer.

Hell no. He'd been following the directions of a beautiful alien who drew her physical form from his sexual fantasies. A woman who wouldn't even exist as other than pure energy without the drunken visual of a twenty-six-year-old postgrad student back in the early days of the computer age.

Only a handful of people knew the truth—that his whole career had been based on a four-month relationship with an inhuman creature he'd fallen in lust and then in love with. The same creature now trapped in the body of a little gray squirrel.

Shit. What a fucked-up mess. What chance in hell—

"Mac? I thought you came back to bed. How long have you been outside? Good lord, man, it's freezing out here."

Mac leaned his head against the back of his chair and stared upside down at the man shivering behind him. "G'morning to you, too, Dink. Couldn't sleep. Didn't want to disturb you guys." He straightened up and waved at the chair beside him. "Have a seat. You don't by any chance have coffee, do you?"

"You're kidding, right? Me? Make coffee?"

"One can only hope." He chuckled. He might be a world-famous investigative reporter, but Nils Dinkemann had never been known for his culinary skills. "I was afraid of that, but, yeah, I know. I lost contact with my toes a few hours ago." A thick down comforter settled over him, still warm from Dink's body heat.

"Okay. This works." Mac drew his feet up under the blanket and tucked all that soft warmth around him. "Damn that feels good. I think it's even better than coffee."

A moment later, Dink flopped down in the chair beside Mac's, wrapped head to foot in another blanket. "I heard some rattling and clanking downstairs," he said. "Sounds like your cook's putting some fresh coffee on. I'll get us some in a few minutes."

Mac grunted in assent. He turned and glanced toward the sliding glass door, but Dink had closed it. The glare of the growing sunlight reflected off the glass.

He couldn't see Zianne. "Is . . . ?"

"She's asleep. Still a squirrel. I left her wrapped in your jacket."

"Thanks." He sighed.

"You okay?"

Mac rolled his head to the right and stared at Dink. "You're kidding, right?"

Dink grunted.

Hell no, I'm not all right. "We'll know in approximately two more days, I guess."

Dink grunted again.

Two more days and Mac would know if all his efforts might actually pay off. And if they didn't?

He sucked in a deep breath. Exhaled. "Cameron was planning to meet the last two Nyrians during his shift last night, which means that by now all of them should have access to functioning human bodies. The first group will be coming to Earth tonight—once they have their soulstones—as soon as it turns dark."

"So what happens today?"

Mac glanced at Dink. There was none of the investigative reporter about him this morning. No, he just sounded like a very concerned friend. Right now, Mac figured he needed the friend more than the reporter, though if all went according to plan, he'd need the reporter even more once the Nyrians were all safe. "Today a couple of the stronger Nyrians are going to show Finn and Morgan how to disincorporate and move through space."

"Holy shit." Whispered softly, more a prayer than a curse.

Mac shrugged. "That's the only way to get them on the ship.

Breaking down to molecular particles and traveling with a host Nyrian through space. Sounds good in theory."

"I can't believe you actually got volunteers."

"Morgan Black and Finn O'Toole. Both good guys, physically strong, very sharp. The Gar shouldn't be expecting an attack, but they're always well armed. According to Nattoch, the Nyrian elder who's sort of their leader, the Gar carry weapons that can disrupt the Nyrians' energy field. Doesn't kill them, but can effectively immobilize them. It shouldn't affect humans, though. Once Finn and Morgan arrive on board the ship, they'll have to rematerialize and disarm the guards so the Nyrians can retrieve their soulstones."

And, Nyria help them, Zianne's soulstone as well. She was dying. Would die within the next few hours without an infusion of power from one of her fellow Nyrians, but even their generous gifts of power couldn't hold her here forever.

Not without her soulstone.

Mac sighed. So much could go wrong. So damned much.

Dink reached across the narrow gap that separated them, took hold of Mac's hand, and squeezed it tightly. "This is the one thing I hate most about being a reporter. Learning the plans, knowing the danger, and realizing there's not a fucking thing I can do to alter the outcome."

Mac squeezed back. "You're here, Dink. That matters more than you realize." He gazed into his friend's silvery eyes, but there was too much emotion, too much to consider right now.

Mac glanced away as the sun finally broke free of the horizon in a blinding blaze of orange and pink against a cerulean sky. It was easier to blame the tears in his eyes on the brilliant flash of sunlight shimmering off row after row of white satellite dishes, marching west across the array with inexorable certainty.

The sun would continue to rise, the days would pass, the world would go on.

But life? Not such a sure thing. Not anymore. This might be the last day for Zianne, but if things went wrong with their plan for rescuing her people, it could also be the end of more than the few remaining Nyrians.

If they couldn't stop the Gar, if the Nyrians were somehow compelled to continue powering their huge star cruiser, it could very well mark the end of everything, at least as far as Earth was concerned.

Zianne and Mac's love wasn't even a blip on the radar, not compared to the ultimate risks they faced.

It wasn't like humans had been such great stewards of their world, but they hadn't totally fucked things up yet. If the Gar had their way, once they moved on to other worlds, they'd leave nothing but a smoldering chunk of rock where civilizations had once risen and fallen. Where humans had grown and evolved.

Where Mac had met an impossible, improbable woman; where he'd fallen in love and followed a dream.

A dream that had all the signs of transforming into a fucking nightmare.

He didn't want to think about it. No, he had to believe in success. As Dink kept reminding him, it was the only acceptable outcome. He said it again, whispering the words to himself as he sat there on the deck, his hand tightly clasped in Dink's.

Failure is not an option.

Cameron Paisley's hand shook so bad he couldn't get the damned brush into the jar of paint thinner. This had never happened before. Not to this extent, not this total loss of self, of time and place and space while painting.

His fantastical landscapes of imaginary worlds had always come to him through dreams, but he'd generally been wide awake while he painted them. The amount of money they brought in certainly kept his eyes wide open, but this massive canvas was something else altogether.

He vaguely recalled finding the huge canvas in the closet with a bunch of smaller ones that were already stretched. He didn't recall getting it out. Didn't remember setting it up, pulling out his paints. Didn't remember a fucking thing.

It wasn't just big—measuring at least six feet wide and four feet high—but the art itself was haunting. Beautiful. Unbelievable.

Utterly terrifying.

Even more frightening? He couldn't remember painting a single stroke, yet he knew it was his work, done in his style. It was a world he'd never seen, and yet he knew exactly what it was. Where it was. And he knew, without a doubt, that it no longer existed as it once had. As he'd painted it.

He finally managed to drag his gaze away from the mass of dark and fearsome images, focus his attention on the jar of thinner, and jam his brush into the solvent.

As if someone physically forced him, Cam's eyes were drawn back to the painting. His hands were still shaking. Critics had asked over the years if his work was more than his imagination. He'd always said his paintings were the product of dreams.

This was no dream. This hadn't come to him during his shift in the dream shack. No, this had taken him over like a bad drug trip, had caught him up for . . . He glanced at the clock on the wall. Two hours?

Stunned, Cam stared at the canvas. He worked fast, but this painting was huge and filled with such detail that it should have taken him much, much longer.

Days, not hours.

It hurt to look. To realize what he saw in the bold strokes, the splashes of color, the finer details set within an unyielding maelstrom of shapes and images. He'd painted fear and death, abject loss and total destruction.

A world in the agonizing final spasms of existence.

Forcibly turning his back on the art, Cam grabbed a rag and wiped his hands clean. Somehow he had to clear his head; he needed to make sense of this.

Tossing the rag aside, he quickly slipped out of his clothes and left them in a pile on the floor in front of the easel. Naked and shivering in the morning chill, he walked quickly through the bedroom to the bathroom.

He caught a brief glance of himself in the mirror. As always, he averted his eyes and turned on the tap in the shower. So stupid, the way he always reacted to his own image.

Someday he'd probably wish he still looked like an overgrown teenager, but for now, it would be nice to look his age. It was hard enough getting the established art world to take a thirty-year-old man seriously. A guy who looked about seventeen got absolutely no respect.

Did it really matter? Shit, no. If he believed Mac—and there was no reason not to—if Mac's project failed, there wouldn't be a fucking art world to worry about.

Cam grabbed a washcloth off the rack beside the shower, stepped beneath the spray, and concentrated on emptying his mind of everything but the welcome heat of the water, the way tension slowly eased out of tired muscles beneath the pounding spray. A more welcome thought intruded, that he'd finally experienced what the other members of the dream team had known all along—sending sexual fantasies to Nyrians had one hell of a payback.

After two nights of fantasizing about his art and the pending rescue of the aliens, he'd finally gotten on track during last night's shift.

Had he ever. The thought had barely registered when a coil

of arousal shocked him into immediate awareness. His balls drew close to his body; his cock throbbed with new blood.

"Down, boy." At least this part of him looked and acted like a grown-up. Chuckling, he smoothed his hand over his taut shaft, paused a moment to slip his foreskin over the broad head and back again. A shiver raced along his spine. A shiver of pure carnal pleasure. He turned his dick loose and brushed his wet hair out of his eyes. Even without stroking himself, his arousal seemed to be growing, just from remembering his shift last night in the shack.

And to think he was getting paid for this! Being a member of Mac Dugan's dream team definitely had good bennies. Using his imagination to broadcast sexual fantasies to aliens who gained power from his wild thoughts might sound totally impossible, but when those fantasies were combined with Mac's powerful satellite array to boost their energy, the results were beyond amazing.

He thought of the two women who'd come to him during his shift, the last of the twenty-eight surviving Nyrians to make the journey to Earth for the combination of sexual power and visual images necessary to create their own corporeal bodies.

He'd certainly liked the bodies his two visitors had chosen, and he'd definitely loved what they did with them. Once the Nyrians had a solid form, they seemed to delight in the sensual pleasures their new human bodies allowed.

Granted, everything had happened in his head—or at least he thought it had—but it had felt like so much more.

Sort of like the painting. He wondered if Mac was awake, if maybe he ought to show it to him. Shit. He let out a huge breath. He could be wrong, but he was positive the damned thing was . . .

Oh. Fuck. The soft brush of something warm along his inner thigh jerked Cam out of his convoluted thoughts.

Out of his thoughts and right back here, to what could only be a dream. "Mir? Niah? What are you doing here?" He blinked furiously, clearing the water out of his eyes. Both women, his Nyrians from the night before, here? In his shower? He was awake, damn it. He wasn't fantasizing.

"Hello, Cam." Mir gazed up at him, all bright smile and gorgeous, naked body. She and Niah knelt at his feet, almost mirror images of one another except for coloring. Where Mir was all sultry and dark, with long black hair, dark coffee eyes, and skin the color of polished oak, Niah was her opposite. Platinum hair, eyes of molten silver, and skin so fair and fine as to make her look like a carefully constructed porcelain doll.

Yet her lips were red—deep red, slightly parted, and at this moment approaching . . . no. Oh, crap. They were sliding deliciously over the head of his wide-awake, please-play-with-me dick.

Groaning, he braced his hands against the slick walls of the shower and prayed his knees wouldn't buckle. There was no thought of stopping her—last night he'd quickly learned that Mir and Niah did exactly as they pleased.

Except, that had just been fantasy, right? Holy shit. What did it matter when they were here, now, in his shower? Mir stood. Rising gracefully as a sylph, she slipped around behind him, lightly tugged the wet washcloth from his nerveless fingers, and slowly swept it across his shoulders. She stroked his back, his buttocks, and the backs of his thighs while Niah slowly took him deeper and then deeper still, sucking his full length into her mouth, down her throat.

Oh. Fuck. He tightened everything—his buttocks, his thighs, the muscles across his stomach. Tightened and prayed for control, but he could feel it slipping, even as Mir dropped the washcloth and pressed against his back.

She was tall enough that her breasts hit just below his shoulder blades, her nipples beaded up so tight he felt them, twin little bullet points of sensation. Then she was sliding, sliding down, slowly dragging her breasts down his back, running her fingers over his flanks, dropping to her knees behind him.

This was so much more intense than last night when he'd slipped between fantasy and reality, and he'd wondered then if he'd survive their curious explorations. Now, Niah knelt in front, sucking his cock. Mir had gone to her knees behind him, pushing his legs apart, licking the sensitive curve of his butt and then wrapping long fingers around his sac.

He might have whimpered. Knew he was cursing steadily, though if he'd been asked exactly what words he used, Cam doubted he could have given an intelligent answer. Mir forced his legs farther apart, somehow twisting around so that she had her mouth on his balls and her tongue doing something that had to be illegal in most states.

Probably on the planet.

Did it matter? Hell no. Hell. No. No . . . shit.

He tried to stop it. Honestly, he'd never fought so hard for control in his life, but there was no way. Not any way at all to stop what these two women had so quickly set into motion.

Lips and tongues everywhere; fingers on his balls; a hot, tight mouth and throat taking control of his dick. A finger teasing his ass, pressing, entering, sliding deep, pressing . . .

He cried out. Cursed. Shouted.

Climaxed.

Cam struggled to stay upright, but gravity won and he slowly gave in. His knees buckled and his hands slipped along the wet tiles until he was half sitting, half lying on the floor of the shower with the water beating him in the face.

Mir and Niah giggled with utter delight.

He opened his eyes and stared at the women. "What are you doing here? I thought you were going back to finish your shift."

"Nattoch wanted us to gather more energy." Niah licked

her lips. "You weren't fantasizing enough to provide energy. We decided to help you along."

"You were sad," Mir said. She stood and offered him a hand. He wrapped his fingers around hers and she tugged him to his feet. "Your sadness distresses us. Come. Let's dry off and do it again. This time with laughter."

Cam thought of the painting in the other room. Thought of what it might be, what it meant. Then he looked at the women— two absolutely beautiful, wet, naked women—waiting impatiently for him to make up his mind.

He shut off the water, grabbed a towel off the rack, and ran it over Mir first, and then Niah. They preened like glossy, well-loved cats.

Cam dried himself. His legs had stopped trembling. His erection hadn't subsided a bit, and it was still awfully early in the morning. The painting could wait. He'd talk to Mac later. Tossing the wet towel over the shower door, he followed the women into the bedroom.

He glanced out the window as first Mir and then Niah crawled into the middle of his big bed. The sun was barely up. Mac was probably still asleep. Cam turned his attention to the bed.

To the women on his bed.

It was still made up from yesterday. He'd never gone to sleep at all last night. Not that he intended to sleep now.

At least, not for a while. Mir held out her hand. He took it, let her tug him close, but instead of her slim fingers and the look of pure devilment in her eyes, for some reason he thought of the painting in the other room.

The dark, angry red landscape with its familiar pattern of canals and lines, only he realized, now that he'd actually painted them, they weren't canals at all. Astronomers had been totally off base. Those Martian canals had been highways. He'd painted cities and farms, forests and parks and big factories, all in the midst of terrible upheaval. A once-living planet under attack.

Dead and desolate now, and the image of its change had come from someone aboard the Gar vessel. That had to be the source of this vision. He felt a terrible pain in his chest and thought again of waking Mac, of telling him what he'd seen.

Then he caught the scent of vanilla and honey, and the painting slipped from his mind, his thoughts filled now with the women he'd literally conjured out of fantasy. Gently, he pressed Mir back against the pillows and parted her thighs with both hands. Her skin was like silk, her smile filled with so many promises, so much hope. He sent a quick smile to Niah. "You next," he said. Then he winked as Niah settled beside them to watch.

He knelt between Mir's legs with his palms beneath her firm, round buttocks, lifted her for his pleasure, and discovered that, yes, she did taste exactly like vanilla and honey.

Morgan Black lay beside Rodie Bishop and watched the first rays of morning sun cut across the tumbled blankets. The bed seemed almost empty with just the two of them, but Bolt, their Nyrian lover, had returned to the ship at some point during the night. Morgan had slept through his departure.

Still so hard to believe that in the past few days he had not only interacted with aliens, he'd had some pretty mind-blowing sex with them. His thoughts drifted to the five Nyrian women he'd called with his fantasies—women who now had the human forms they'd need when the DEO-MAP team put their rescue into action.

Five Nyrian women, one Nyrian man.

And then there was Rodie.

She'd caught him by surprise, and yet it was as if she'd always been there, always a part of his life. The feelings he had for her, the woman herself . . . Hell, it still felt like a dream.

He'd never had a steady relationship with a woman before, and nothing all that serious with men. How could so much have changed? Now he had Rodie, though what he had with her was a mystery. How much was real and how much fantasy?

He didn't know for sure, but he was willing to find out.

He had Bolt and the other Nyrians, creatures he'd known for such a short time, and yet . . . they mattered. Mattered to him in a way that was almost impossible to describe. As if the forms they'd taken from his mind had left an indelible imprint on his soul.

Essentially, they had become family. His family. And not just the Nyrians—no, the entire dream team was closer than those few he could claim by blood. These were the ones who mattered.

Finn and Cam were the brothers he'd never had. Kiera and Liz were like little sisters. And Mac? How did he describe his feelings for Mac Dugan? Not just a friend, not even a brother. More a mentor, a trusted male, someone Morgan actually admired.

There were very few men he'd ever admired in his life.

And oddly enough, Finn O'Toole was one of them, which was almost laughable when he thought of his first impression of the irascible Irishman. He'd pegged O'Toole as a jokester without a serious thought in his head, a guy more concerned with bagging his next woman and adding another notch to his proverbial bedpost than with anything of substance.

He'd been wrong about Finn O'Toole. At least he hoped so, since he'd be trusting him with his life. Today, he and Finn would learn how to dematerialize, or disassemble, as the Nyrians called it. Essentially, he'd be reducing himself to the molecular level and hitchhiking within the energy mass of an alien creature in order to travel from Earth to the Gar ship that was currently in orbit behind the moon.

Yeah. Sure . . . and it was a good thing he didn't have a clue how this was going to happen or he'd probably be scared to death, but somehow, doing something that was so far beyond belief didn't register well enough to actually terrify him. Yet.

Rodie let out a soft snore and snuggled against his side. He tightened his arm around her shoulders. She was every bit as far beyond belief as dematerializing. Rodie Bishop was someone else he'd underestimated.

He'd thought she was interesting and kind of cute.

He'd had no idea she would totally rock his world.

Of course, when he'd signed on to this project, he really had no idea what he was getting into. Definitely a good thing, being so ignorant, or he'd never have agreed.

And then, just think what he'd be missing.

2

Kiera Pearce stretched, yawned, glanced at the clock by the bed—and did a double take. She shoved herself up on one elbow, squinted, and stared harder at the LED numbers.

"Oh, crap." She dragged her pillow over her eyes, flopped back on the mattress, and groaned. She'd read the numbers wrong and thought at first it was after ten. Damn it, not even close to seven, yet. She was so not a morning person, especially after a night like last night.

So why had she been waking up before seven every damned day she'd been here?

"Every day?" She giggled into the pillow. This was only her third morning. Why did it feel as if she'd been here for weeks? Months, even?

Maybe because I've never had so much good sex in my entire life? Well, there was that. If anybody had told her a week ago she'd not only be doing the deed with men—plural—she'd be doing it with aliens, she'd have thought they were nuts.

For a woman who thought she was wired primarily for sex

with other women—human women—Kiera had discovered a new appreciation for men.

At least these particular men.

Nyrians. Aliens capable of taking on perfect human bodies from sexual fantasies, which, as impossible as it sounded, totally confused her on a more practical level altogether.

She liked women. Loved women to the extent that women dominated her sexual fantasies. So how did she explain the fact she'd had seven different Nyrian visitors over the past two nights, each one conjured from her fantasies—and every single one of them a drop-dead gorgeous, testosterone-laden perfect male?

Not only were they men who'd left her sexually satisfied and smiling, each experience had led her to an entirely new level of self-awareness and self-confidence.

She still couldn't believe it. Not with the history she had with the male of the species.

Make that males of the human species.

What was so different about Nyrians that every one, every delicious, gorgeous, beautiful guy, had managed to give her absolutely mind-blowing orgasms while somehow avoiding the less pleasant traits of their human counterparts?

Like attitude. Like violence and the big *me, Tarzan, you Jane* dominance thing her ex had. Never again would she allow herself to be used as a punching bag. Not ever. Those days were over. Done. Finished forever.

The unwelcome face of her ex popped into her head. Kiera slammed her fist into her pillow.

Great. Now she was not only wide awake, but that lovely, sensual glow from last night was gone, her heart thudded in her chest, and she was totally pissed. Just great. Grumbling, Kiera rolled out of bed and stalked into the bathroom for a shower.

The sight of the wide-open, high desert sky and the slice of brilliant orange sun rising outside her window calmed her crappy mood. It looked like it was going to be another gorgeous day for all of them on the DEO-MAP project.

She stared out across the plateau at the satellite dishes lined up in neat rows. DEO-MAP actually stood for Discovering Extraterrestrial Organisms through Mental Acuity and Projection, something they'd accomplished almost immediately, but she really liked the name the protestors at the front gate had given it: the God Project. That sounded so wonderfully pretentious.

She smiled at the view, loving the open space and the big sky overhead, loving even more the way she felt about life in general—make that her life in general. Maybe she'd see if anyone was free to go on a hike around the plateau. Her shift in the dream shack didn't begin until noon.

She made it all the way to the bathroom before reality intruded. Today was the day. Today they'd start the rescue process, start bringing the first of the Nyrians to Earth.

Permanently.

If—and that was a big *if*—everything worked the way it was supposed to. She shivered and hoped like hell that wasn't any kind of evil premonition raising goose bumps across her arms. She wanted everyone safe, wanted the rescue to be a done deal, not something hanging out there, worrying her sick.

These past few days she'd vacillated between dream and nightmare, fantasy and horror.

Belief and disbelief. Fearing for the Nyrians, loving the ones she'd grown to know so well in such a short time, becoming so intimately involved in the lives of creatures not even close to human that she was already worrying herself sick over their rescue. Even being a part of the process didn't make it any easier or more believable, but there was no avoiding the truth.

In just a few short days, she'd learned to care about creatures she'd never even heard of a week ago. Creatures so far removed from humanity that it was difficult to realize they still shared the same feelings, the same fears, the same needs.

If only there weren't so damned many things that could go wrong. She slipped beneath the warm spray, thinking of the guys who'd shared her bed last night and the night before. Still hard to believe that such a major life change for her had started with an absolutely vivid fantasy in the dream shack in broad daylight.

She'd opened her fantasy with images of Liz and Rodie, doing her best to share the power from her imagination with aliens she really didn't believe in. Everything had started out simply enough, but she'd ended up with so much more than mere fantasy.

His name was Tor. She hadn't even thought to ask after the first encounter. No, she'd been too blindsided by the most amazing orgasmic experience she'd ever had in her life, but he'd said he would come back.

He did. But he hadn't come alone. He'd brought friends.

Oh, damn. Did he ever bring friends.

Smiling, she tilted her head beneath the spray and soaked her hair, added a bit of shampoo, and worked it through the tangles. Rinsed and used some conditioner. The air was dry up here in the mountains, and she'd noticed her hair was drier than usual. She didn't mind curls, but the frizz had to go.

Blame it on the elevation. Mac said they were at seven thousand feet, which was a long way from the San Francisco Bay Area.

Seven thousand feet high in the farthest, most northeastern part of California in the Warner Mountains. High desert country, Mac called it. Lots of stunted-looking pine trees and weird, stinky plants—and fifty huge satellite dishes that were their link to the Nyrians.

Kiera's mind wandered as she washed herself, running the soft cloth over her breasts and belly, between her legs. She was tender there, but that was to be expected. So far she'd not been with a single Nyrian who was less than well endowed.

She was almost positive they hadn't gotten that from her imagination, and the original plan Mac had, of sharing their sexual energy via explicit sexual fantasy, had quickly morphed into actually having mind-blowing sex with Nyrians taking on corporeal bodies.

It hadn't taken the Nyrians long to discover that, while sexual fantasy was powerful energy for their kind, actually taking on a human body and having sex, experiencing it with a human, was like the difference between a D-cell battery and an atomic reactor.

Even the power they drew from the sun wasn't as strong as what they took from sex, something Kiera found a bit hard to believe, but who was she to disagree? Especially considering what they gave back.

A sexual experience unlike anything she'd ever known. More than physical, more than merely two bodies rubbing together. No, there'd been a mind-blowing emotional connection that was every bit as powerful as the physical. She'd tried to describe it to Mac the first time Tor had come to her, how she'd felt as if he knew things about her she'd never figured out on her own.

How he'd made love to her, made her lose control, lose her inhibitions and her fears.

It was amazing and wonderful, scary and thrilling and all of those feelings together, and they'd continued to grow stronger when he'd come to her again that night. Only he'd brought friends with him. Aza and Jesat. Weird names, gorgeous bodies, really wonderful men.

She never would have pictured herself referring to any man as wonderful, but now she knew a whole pack of them! And she'd have to count the guys here—Mac Dugan, their leader, and Finn, Cameron, and Morgan.

Her list of acceptable males was definitely growing. She'd added four more last night, men Tor had brought to her during her daytime shift so that they could get visuals for their human shapes. Then they'd all returned after dark, when it was easier for them to stay.

That would change, once they had their soulstones. She wasn't quite sure how that worked, only that the Gar controlled the Nyrians by keeping them apart from their soulstones. They could survive for short periods of time without them, but then they needed to return to the ship, to captivity, to recharge with the stones.

They said that once they had their stones and came to Earth, they'd be able to stay here forever, holding on to their human bodies, living free for the first time in eons.

Living as human beings on Earth, rather than being instruments of Earth's destruction. If everything worked according to plan. She refused to imagine anything else. She couldn't think of failure, because she didn't want harm to come to any of the guys she'd gotten to know so intimately.

Kiera chuckled, rinsing the conditioner out of her hair as she pulled up the memory of each one. Tor, of course, because he was her first and he was special, but she hadn't found any fault in Dake, Teev, Sakel, or Bane.

Never in her wildest dreams would she have pictured herself naked with five men at once, but thinking of them now made her womb clench and her sex ripple with pleasure. Before joining DEO-MAP and coming up here to the site, she'd have been fighting a panic attack if five men had appeared in her bedroom.

Instead, she'd behaved like an absolute slut.

A totally well-satisfied slut. Damn. What a night. Chuckling, she reached for the towel and wiped the water and conditioner out of her eyes.

Blinked. And shrieked. She almost slipped on the slick tile, but a strong hand steadied her. Strong arms kept her safe.

"Tor! Good lord, man." She flattened her palm against her chest and felt her heart pounding. "You scared me to death. Where did you come from?"

Leaning against the tile wall of the shower, he merely grinned and glanced up. She rolled her eyes, but her heart was still thudding like crazy and she had to take a couple of deep, steady breaths before it started to slow down.

She reached out and touched his chest, needing to stroke that dark, chocolaty skin to prove he was really here. Naked. In her shower. "How can you be here now? Isn't your shift over?"

He sighed, leaned close, and brushed the hair back from her eyes as the water beat against both of them. "I missed you. I have a little more time before I must return, but I wanted a moment alone with you." He cocked his head to one side, studying her. "I had to share you last night."

She grinned. "You did, and I thank you for your generosity."

His laughter was deep and rumbled up out of his chest. "You're more than welcome. Aza and Jesat couldn't stop talking about their night with you, and now I have to listen to the other four." He sighed as if the weight of the world rested on his shoulders. "All they can talk of is the rescue, not because we will finally be free, but only so they can come back to you."

His words drifted over her like a gentle caress. "That's actually very sweet. I figured they only came back last night to strengthen the visuals for their human forms. I didn't really think of how they felt about, well . . ." She shrugged. It still wasn't easy, this standing here naked with a man she hardly knew. Yet he knew her more intimately than any other man she'd ever known, including her ex-husband.

Tor rested his palms on her shoulders. "They . . . we, all feel more than you realize when we are with you. Our lives have been barren for so long." He leaned close and kissed her. The smooth glide of his full lips over hers left her breathless. Needy.

Slowly he broke the kiss. "I must return, but I had to speak with you, Kiera Pearce. I have to tell you that even if this plan of yours does not succeed, if none of us or only a few of us are saved, I will never forget you. I will treasure the time we have spent together as the most memorable hours of my life."

He leaned close and kissed her again, and there was so much feeling behind his kiss, such a sweet desire to claim her without any hint of trying to subdue her. Tears gathered behind her lashes. She felt a tightening in her chest, in her throat.

He ended the kiss and rested his forehead against hers. "I've lived a very long life, Kiera. This time with you has been but a tiny fraction of all my years, and yet the hours spent with you in my arms mean more to me than anything. I've known you such a short time, but don't ever doubt my feelings for you. I've been inside your heart and mind, and you are pure and good."

She stared at him, her heart and mind spinning in separate directions, yet both reached the same place at once, still confused, but certain that something existed between her and this man from another world. "I wish I understood this better, Tor. My feelings for you are so intense they're a little scary. You matter to me in a way no one has before."

Her life would never be the same, no matter what the outcome of Mac Dugan's plan. Her emotions were so tangled up in this man, so connected that it didn't make sense. Not after knowing him for only a couple of days.

Even knowing he wasn't human changed nothing.

She clutched his broad shoulders with both hands, digging into solid flesh that would disappear when he took his natural energy form and returned to the ship. "Be safe. I want time to explore what we're building together, okay? Don't take unnecessary risks. Promise you'll come back to me."

He nodded. "I promise I will do my best." Then he kissed her quickly and disappeared in a swirl of blue and gold sparks. Kiera stared at the empty spot in the shower, at the water beating against the tile. Everything felt desolate, empty beyond belief without him.

How could that be? It made no sense, but at the same time, she couldn't deny the feelings welling up from deep inside. Maybe it was the fact he'd been inside her mind, a part of her thoughts as much as he'd connected with her body. Maybe it was just that he was everything she'd dreamed of in a man, and yet, until now, had never expected to find. For whatever reason, Tor filled a need she'd not known she had. He made her whole. Complete in a way she'd not imagined.

And there was the terrible, frightening possibility that she could lose him, long before she'd really had a chance to know him. Sighing, Kiera turned and shut off the tap. Reaching blindly for the towel, she methodically began to dry her arms and legs. Sponged the water out of her hair, rubbed the towel across her eyes. A sob caught in her throat. Another and then another, and she knew there was no hope of regaining what little control she'd struggled to hold close.

Giving in to all the fears she'd tried so hard to block, Kiera buried her face in the soft folds of her towel and wept.

It wasn't only because her heart was breaking. Analytical as ever, her thoughts seemed to twist around a single thought, that now, after she'd finally discovered a man she could trust, one she could possibly love, she might truly learn the meaning of loss.

Liz shivered in the morning chill as she crossed the open area between her cabin and the main lodge. This was quickly becoming her morning routine, to get up a little after six, work out in her cabin for a bit, take a quick shower, and then head to the lodge for some of Meg's delicious coffee and a couple of rolls. It gave her plenty of time to walk over to the dream shack and relieve Finn in time for her eight o'clock shift.

That was a favorite part of her day, too. Seeing Finn. Go figure. Opening the door, she stepped inside, inhaling the rich aroma of fresh coffee and the sweet smell of hot cinnamon rolls.

"G'morning, Lizzie."

"Hey, Mac. I didn't see you. Hello, Mr. Dinkemann." She didn't break stride on her way to the counter with the coffee, but after she got a cup and a plate with a couple of warm rolls, she walked over to the comfortable chairs by the front window.

It was weird enough, being on a first-name basis with a guy as rich and brilliant as Mac Dugan, but Nils Dinkemann, too? She knew she must be grinning like an idiot when the famous newsman stood to greet her.

"Don't get up." She took a seat beside him on the big couch and set her plate on the coffee table.

"Then don't call me Mr. Dinkemann." The emphasis was definitely on the *mister,* but he was laughing as he flopped back down on the couch, and damn but his teeth were as perfect as they looked on television, his smile just as sexy. Of course, so was the rest of him.

She raised her eyebrows. "Nils?"

"Dink. That's what Mac's called me for years. At least the only name acceptable in polite company." He glanced at Mac with enough affection in his eyes that Liz didn't have any doubt at all where he'd spent last night. Then she noticed the twinkle in Mac's blue eyes and hoped like hell she'd been blocking her thoughts.

This telepathy thing was really cool, but it could sure get a girl into trouble. "Okay. Dink it is," she said, shoving all inappropriate thoughts out of her head. *Coffee. Think coffee. Coffee's safe.*

"Mac tells me you've been part of the Mars project. I'm hoping to do a story on that when it's ready for launch."

She sipped her coffee and nodded. "I was, before signing on for this. It was my first NASA job and I really learned a lot."

She laughed. "Nothing like what I've learned here." She rolled her eyes. "Wow."

"And you're like, what? Twelve?"

She glared at him, but it was hard with a mouth full of cinnamon roll. Even harder not to laugh when she growled, "Try twenty-five, *Mr.* Dinkemann."

"Ouch. I take it age is a touchy subject?" He flashed her that perfect grin that women all over American had fallen in love with on the nightly news.

"Just a bit. At least the Nyrians don't seem to mind my rather youthful appearance."

Mac shot a quick glance at Dink before turning the full wattage of his sexy smile on Liz. What was it with the men here? "I take it you had visitors last night."

"Oh, yeah." She giggled, as much at herself for blushing as the fact she was even having this conversation with two gorgeous men older than her father. "You never explained the terrific benefits with this job, Mac. I mean, we're talking way beyond your standard health plan." She shot a quick glance at Dink, who was obviously trying as hard as she was not to laugh.

Mac grinned as he nodded. "Yeah, I imagine there aren't too many companies that can promise employees will get to experience exquisite alien sex with multiple partners." He glanced at Dink. Both of them cracked up.

"You must be reading my mind." Lizzie took another bite of her warm cinnamon roll. "Seriously, I've spent quality time—emphasis on quality—with a total of two women and four men over the past couple of nights." She sighed dramatically. "And not necessarily one at a time." She fluttered her fingers in front of her face while the guys chuckled.

"I just hope all the Nyrians have connected well enough to you guys to have a body when it's time to escape." Mac shot a worried glance at Dink.

Liz nodded. "Actually, I think Morgan and Rodie were hoping to get most of the remaining Nyrians last night, and Cam was going to catch any who were left, so they should all have their human forms by now."

Mac glanced up and grinned. "We can find out how Morgan did. G'morning, Morgan."

Liz glanced over her shoulder as Morgan headed straight for the morning buffet. "Hey, Morgan. Where's Rodie?"

"Still asleep." He glanced her way as he poured himself some coffee. "We were up more than we'd planned last night."

Liz flopped back on the couch, laughing. "I hear ya on that."

Morgan took a seat beside her and raised his cup in a toast to Dink and Mac. "What'd you want to ask me, Mac?"

"If you and Rodie managed to get everyone covered last night. Did you?"

"All but two." He sipped his coffee. "We figured we'd better leave someone for Cam. The rescue plan was his idea after all, and when he relieved Rodie after her shift, he said he was looking forward to his first actual sexual fantasy."

Dink chuckled. "You guys must realize that you're driving me nuts. As an investigative reporter, all these fascinating tidbits and no details I can actually report are killing me." He took a swallow of coffee. "Though I have to admit, if I were to take the story public right now, no one would believe a word of it."

Liz glanced from Morgan to Mac and then smiled at Dink. "I'm right in the middle of it, Dink, having killer sex with guys who turn into flashes of light and disappear, and I still hardly believe it." She shook her head and glanced at Mac. "I'm not complaining, though. Honest."

Then she saw the somber expression on Mac's face and her heart fell. "Mac? Is Zianne okay? Where is she?"

"At the dream shack with Finn. We took her over in the

hope that any Nyrians who might show up today could share energy with her."

"You're not expecting many?"

"Not really, though we want you at the shack, keeping a steady stream of fantasies going through the array. I have a feeling most of the Nyrians will be preparing for tonight's first shift change when they start their escape."

"It's getting close, isn't it?" She thought of the men she'd been with last night, so excited they were finally breaking free of the Gar. How afraid they were of failure, but accepting, too. "The guys with me last night, Ian and Darc, are more than ready. They didn't stay long, but they wanted me to know how much this means to all of them."

Morgan nodded. "Bolt said the same. In fact, I had hoped he'd be the one to teach me how to dissemble, but it seems their shift schedule won't work for that. He was with us last night."

Lizzie wrapped her fingers around Morgan's and squeezed. "Are you okay with that? With turning into nothing but particles and actually going on board the ship? I'd be scared to death."

He chuckled softly and patted her hand. "Lizzie, I'm so terrified we don't even want to go there, but I have to do this. I want to, and so does Finn. We talked about it, about taking a risk like this, and we both realize this is bigger than anything either of us has ever been involved in. It's huge. To be part of it, to do something no human being has ever done before . . ." He raised his head and glanced at Mac. "Something else we discussed. If this doesn't work, Mac, if we don't make it, Finn and I don't want you to feel guilty. You're giving us an opportunity that's unique, that's impossible to explain. We don't want you having any second thoughts, because we sure as hell aren't."

*　*　*

Morgan's comment slammed into Mac. His dark eyes glittered with the passion of his beliefs, yet his words were softly stated, given power by their seemingly offhand manner.

The power of what he offered, the amazing generosity of his words, threw Mac's brain into almost immediate turmoil. He blinked, trying to process what Morgan had said. It was amazing, that men he hardly knew would be willing to die for a goal Mac had worked toward for two decades. Mac's goal, not theirs, and yet Morgan spoke as if the danger was of no consequence, as if the attempt was what mattered most.

Who could expect such a thing? What kind of men were willing to give everything for someone they hardly knew, for creatures not of their world?

And yet . . . as Mac's thoughts went from logical and organized into an emotional free fall spinning out of control, the shift into chaos sent his mind into a rhythm that had been lacking. He discovered a pattern to the myriad twists and turns, the thoughts and ideas that for so long had felt like a convoluted mass of pointless incoherency. Morgan's softly yet powerfully spoken words forced an amazing clarity to Mac's mental process, until the convoluted threads of consciousness once tangled and knotted suddenly shimmered with logic and form.

Opening up in his mind's eye was a perfect tapestry of his life now and to come, woven in all the colors of the rainbow. Instead of a mass of twisted knots, each thread was finding its place within the pattern, forming the image of what was to come.

In that image, he saw Morgan and Finn. He recognized Liz and Cameron, Rodie and Kiera. Zianne was there, and Dink, all of them together, connected by those amazing threads of fate, surrounded in brilliant flashes of energy, a powerful wall of Nyrian souls, free from captivity at last.

Morgan was right. This was so much bigger than any single

one of them. It wasn't all about Zianne, or all about Mac and his twenty-year crusade to save his lost love. It wasn't about the innovations or the inventions or even the money. This was about something bigger than all of them. It was stopping the Gar from their marauding journey through space. It was saving the remnants of a once thriving society, giving the Nyrians the chance to live out their days on a world that would hopefully welcome them as the intelligent, sentient beings they'd shown themselves to be.

And on a smaller scale, it was about each of them finding more within themselves. More strength, more understanding, maybe even more love.

Mac glanced at Dink and then smiled at Morgan. "You and Finn . . ." He shook his head. "The two of you honor me with your bravery. You honor all of us. This is not something I ever intended to ask of any of you. I hope you realize I would give anything to go in your place, but I know I have to be here. My head knows that, my gut agrees, but my heart's having a problem with staying behind."

He glanced at his watch. "Last night we spoke with Nattoch. He said we should have the first group arriving just after dark this evening. I expect they'll send the weaker members first, so we'll need to be ready for them."

He glanced at the others, his eyes open to visual clues, his mind open to their thoughts. Amazing. There was absolutely no fear, no sense of nervousness beyond the flutter of excitement he sensed in Liz. Morgan's mind was steady as a rock, his thoughts turned toward the next few hours when he and Finn should be learning to disassemble, to turn their corporeal bodies into nothing more than mist and energy.

Just the thought of attempting something like that sent a chill up Mac's spine, and yet all he could feel in Morgan was anticipation. The guy was amazing, so brave it was scary.

Either that or just plain nuts.

Lizzie downed the last of her coffee and grabbed a paper napkin to wrap her second cinnamon roll. "Time for my shift." She leaned over and gave Morgan a quick kiss. "For luck, Morgan. I'll be thinking of you."

He grinned. "Thanks. I'm not sure who's going to be teaching us, but now that Finn's getting off duty, I expect someone to show up before too long."

Liz waved and headed for the door. Rodie opened it just as Liz reached for the handle. "G'morning, Rodie."

"Hey." Rodie held the door for Liz and shut it quietly behind her. Then she headed straight for the coffee.

Mac watched Morgan watch Rodie and had to bite back a grin. This was a match he never would have suspected, but the two of them had clicked almost from the beginning. He wondered how Rodie felt about the risks Morgan had chosen to take. She didn't seem to be the least bit upset.

He glanced at Dink and caught his buddy staring at him. Mac frowned, but as much as he wished he could read Dink's thoughts, the man didn't have a bit of telepathic ability. His reporter's instincts were just that—pure instinct. His mind, however, was nothing but a solid wall to Mac's subtle search.

What could Dink possibly be thinking right now? After a night of lovemaking—Dink, Mac, and Zianne, the three of them falling so easily into the sexual roles they'd taken so many years ago—what were Dink's thoughts this morning? To come so close to the perfection they'd shared when they were young and still wide open to new experiences, now to be standing here on the precipice, so close to either success or absolute failure?

Was Dink afraid? Excited? Frustrated by his inability to report on such a huge event? There was no way Mac could tell—not from the enigmatic expression on his friend's face.

The door opened, tugging Mac away from his meandering thoughts. He glanced up as Finn sauntered into the dining hall. "How'd it go, Finn?"

"Quiet." Talking over his shoulder, he went straight to the coffee. "Tara and Duran were with me last night before I took my shift, but no one showed up at all while I was in the shack. It was actually more spooky than lonely."

Mac straightened and caught Morgan's sharp glance. "No one at all? No contact?"

Finn shook his head. "Not a thing. I figure they're taking the time to build up energy for when the exodus starts tonight."

"Could be, but I expected some contact. Did Cameron say anything about visitors?" It wasn't easy to keep the tension out of his voice. They were so close, but so many things could go wrong.

Finn sat down with a bagel between his teeth, his cup of coffee in one hand and a cinnamon roll in the other. He set the coffee down. Placed the bagel on top of the roll. "Yep. Said he had two women show up and finally figured out what all the fuss was about. I think he's sorry he spent so much time with Nattoch." He laughed, took a swallow of coffee and a bite of the bagel. "Last night was his first night with any of the Nyrians. I imagine he's hoping it won't be his last."

Mac chuckled. Cameron fascinated him. Brilliant with an amazingly creative mind and a grasp of concepts, logistics, and planning that rivaled any of the other unbelievably intelligent members of the dream team, and yet he looked—and sometimes acted—about fifteen. It was hard to imagine the kid with two seductive Nyrian females, but it explained why he hadn't shown up for breakfast this morning.

A funny little chill raced across his shoulders. Lizzie popped into his head, but the thought was faint, and he hated to intrude on the girl's fantasies. Then the overhead lights in the dining hall dimmed. Flickered for a moment or two before returning to full strength.

An unexpected drain on their energy? What would cause

that? Their power supply was damned good, unless something was interfering with the operation. He thought of the protestors at the front gate, the fire that had been intentionally set, and wondered if they were up to more trouble.

No. Ralph was keeping an eye on the bastards. Mac pushed the thought aside, but just as he reached for his coffee, the door to the dining area shot open. Kiera hung on to the handle, eyes wide and hair streaming behind in an unruly mass of curls.

She stood for a moment in the open doorway, chest heaving as she gasped for breath. "You've got to come to the dream shack. Lizzie's got her hands full."

Mac was on his feet and heading for the door before the others had even reacted. "What's happened?"

"Nyrians." Kiera sucked in a deep breath. "A whole shitload of 'em just showed up. Lizzie thinks they have their soulstones but they're way ahead of schedule and scared to death. All I know is what Liz 'pathed to me. I was on my way here, closer to the lodge, so I didn't take time to go check." She spun about and headed back to the shack with Mac on her heels. Morgan, Finn, and Dink were right behind them.

Cameron must have heard the commotion, because he raced across the open area and caught up to them as they reached the dream shack. Mac threw open the door. The small building was absolutely packed with people, all dressed alike in either loose pants or tunics. Lizzie was on her knees beside the tote bag holding Zianne in her arms. Two Nyrian women appeared to be sharing energy with the tiny squirrel.

"Hey, Mac. Guys." Lizzie looked up with a rather shell-shocked expression on her face.

"What happened?" Mac glanced at the silent group and then at Lizzie.

She gestured helplessly at the Nyrians crowded into the small space behind her. Mostly women, a few men, they huddled close to one another and stared anxiously at Mac and the others. Liz carefully placed the squirrel back into the tote bag and stood, folding her arms almost defensively across her chest.

She focused on Mac, her expression grim. "It appears we're going to have to move the rescue up a bit. According to these guys, the Gar are already on their way to destroy Earth."

Well, thought Mac as, just a bit stunned, he gazed at the small crowd. At least now he knew what had stressed the power supply. He glanced over his shoulder at Dink, who stood by the door with a huge smile on his face.

"What's so funny?"

"I'm just thinking about the story I get to tell. You know how I love a good story."

"Yeah. Right." Mac shoved his fingers through his hair. "Let's just hope there's a world left to tell it to."

3

"Mir? Niah? But you just left my room!" Cameron shoved past Mac and reached for two absolutely gorgeous women—one with flowing dark hair, deeply tanned skin, and eyes like the night, the other as fair and light as her partner was dark. "What's going on?"

They each clutched a hand and snuggled close against Cam. He shot a quick glance at Mac and shrugged, then pulled both women even closer. He dipped his head close and kissed each one quickly, then whispered, "Tell me what happened."

The dark-haired beauty glanced at her fairer companion and, instead of answering Cam, slowly turned and focused on Mac. She took a deep breath. "I am Mir," she said, bowing her head slightly. "This is Niah. You are Mac. We know of you from Zianne. We had just returned to the ship and retrieved our soulstones when Nattoch instructed all of us to flee immediately for Earth. We were so surprised by his request as we had just returned. All he said was that we had to hurry because the Gar had begun the process of preparing the ship for travel. We have to assume they are planning to attack Earth sooner than expected."

Her eyes were wide and filled with apprehension, though he didn't sense overwhelming fear. Mac could feel her resolve as well as the trust she had placed not only in Cameron, but in the entire team. She had no doubt they would be able to help her people.

He wished he felt as confident.

"Okay." Shit. What now? Mac shot a quick look at Morgan, who was practically buried in frightened women. Was one of these terrified souls planning to teach him to disassemble? "Let's get everyone moved to the lodge where we have more room to talk. But first, are any of you here to help Morgan and Finn with training?"

The Nyrians all glanced at one another, but only one woman spoke up. "None of us, but . . ."

"Tara?" Finn stepped past Mac and grabbed the redhead in both arms, hugging her tightly. "Where's Duran?"

"I don't know." A sob broke through her words and she blinked rapidly. Did Nyrians cry? Mac wondered if she had any idea what tears were, if she was at all familiar with the emotions this human body was capable of, because she looked utterly confused by the moisture overflowing her eyes and running down her cheeks.

With one more deep breath, she appeared to get herself under control. Clutching Finn's arms, she said, "Nattoch told me to leave as soon as I retrieved my stone. I did not question him."

"Are you all right?"

She nodded, but Mac watched the shimmer of tears that continued to spill from her brilliant green eyes. "I'm okay, Finn. I am, but Duran . . . he's still on the ship. I was late for my shift and he had already turned over his stone and gone to the engine room. Nattoch told me to keep my stone, to leave. I did as he asked."

She bowed her head, sobbing openly against Finn's chest. He kissed the crown of her head, gently nuzzling her thick, red hair, and it was a gesture so tender, so at odds with Mac's original view of Finn O'Toole that it twisted something in Mac's heart.

What was it about these Nyrians that they could change even the most cynical among them? But holy crap, their rescue plans were totally shredded. Now what? "Morgan, Finn, I don't know what we do now, other than get everyone comfortable until we receive further word."

"I think that's the best idea. At least it works for me. You okay with that, Finn?" Morgan stepped aside, speaking softly to the women who'd claimed him so quickly, sending them with the others.

Four men who seemed to be with Kiera helped her and Cameron organize the rest of the Nyrians, quickly moving them out of the dream shack. Finn kissed Tara once again and pressed his forehead to hers. "Go with Cam and Kiera. We'll figure out a way to get Duran and the others. Please try not to worry."

"Oh, Finn." She pressed her fingers to her lips to stifle her sobs and took a deep, shuddering breath. "I think not worrying is impossible, but I trust you to do whatever you can." She stretched up on her toes and kissed him. Mac felt the spinning emotions swirling between the two of them, emotions so deep and powerful they left him aching. He averted his gaze as Tara finally pulled away from Finn and followed the others.

Rodie stood at the open door and hugged two slender women. Mac noticed that all three of them had tears in their eyes and he had to consciously drag air into his lungs. The small, crowded room was closing in around him, the emotions in the dream shack throwing Mac into sensory overload.

Each of the Nyrians here owed their physical form, their human body, to one of his team members. All of them already had a powerful connection, yet none of them had learned to shield their emotions in this form. Now their fear was shared. Their need, all of their fears and hopes, swirling in a telepathic maelstrom that buffeted his mind and tore at his heart.

Cam paused at the open door and caught Mac's attention. His calm, pragmatic manner gave Mac something to focus on.

"We'll get them something to eat and wait for you in the lodge," Cam said. "Is that okay?"

It had to be. For the moment, Mac was lost—stunned by the sudden change in all their plans, the onslaught of emotions, his own inability to block and break free. "Thanks," he said, scrambling to organize his thoughts. People counted on him to make the right decision. This was his project. He had to remind himself he was their leader, the one they'd all look to for answers.

So why in the hell was his mind totally blank right now?

Because you've dropped your shields, Mac. You need to protect yourself. Raise your barriers so you can think without everyone tangling your thoughts.

Zianne! Thank you. Are you okay?

Tired, Mac. Very tired. I'm going to rest. Don't worry about me. We have greater worries now. Block. You have to block. I can still get through if I need to.

I love you.

I love you, too, Mac. It will work. It has to work.

Zianne's thoughts slipped away. The door closed and loneliness washed over Mac, a sense of loss that, in spite of his logical mind, made him feel as if Zianne had unfairly closed him out. But she was right. He was drowning in everyone's emotions, feeding on them to the point they were immobilizing him.

Mac took a deep breath, raised the shields he'd totally ignored, and focused on the people who remained. Dink, Morgan, Rodie, Finn, Lizzie. And Zianne. Dear gods, how he loved her.

"Mac?"

Still not thinking as clearly as he should, Mac turned to Lizzie.

"We've got more company."

Energy sparkled and swirled in the air around Liz, then slowly settled into two distinct pillars of blue and gold. A tall, beautiful, bronze-skinned man stepped out of the closest column. Like the other men, he wore loose-fitting pants and nothing else.

"Bolt!" Morgan slipped past Mac and took the guy's hand as Rodie threw herself against Bolt's chest, practically toppling the Nyrian. "What's going on?"

The second column wavered a moment before forming into an equally beautiful, dark-haired, fair-skinned man with brilliant blue eyes. "Duran?" Finn pushed past Morgan and Bolt and grabbed the Nyrian in a powerful hug. "Thank the gods you're safe. Tara's worried sick. Me, too." He stepped back, still holding on to Duran's arm as he looked the man up and down. Finally reassured his Nyrian was unharmed, Finn turned to Bolt. "What the hell happened?"

Bolt gazed at Morgan and Rodie, sighed, and shook his head. Still holding Morgan's hand with his free arm wrapped around Rodie, he acknowledged Finn with a quick glance but addressed Mac. "It's not good. The Gar appear to be moving against Earth ahead of schedule. I think they realize that humans have spaceflight capability, and they're afraid you'll be able to mount a defense of your world. The Gar are and always have been a cowardly race. They want what your planet has to offer, but they're not willing to face risks to take it."

Mac glanced at Dink. He stood to one side, studying Bolt, obviously fascinated. Always the newsman. "When do they plan to attack?"

"Soon," Bolt said. "It's already begun. Approximately two of your hours ago, they left their orbit behind the moon. Nattoch thinks it will take them about three of your days to get into position where they can begin to siphon off your atmosphere, unless they decide to hunt first. If inhabitants aren't edible, they generally steal atmosphere first, which kills off the living creatures. Then they'll go for minerals, water, even fossil fuels, but that's not going to happen here."

He folded his arms across his broad chest. "We've made the decision to stop them. We're taking a stand here, with your world, whether the rest of our people survive or not. Our hope is to save as many of us as we can before this ends. There are already too few Nyrians on board to power the vessel for more than a few hours, but we need to kill the ship before it gets too close to Earth. In less than twenty-four hours, they'll cross that line and it will be unsafe for us to destroy the vessel."

Mac nodded. "We'd become collateral damage from the size of the explosion?"

Bolt nodded. "Exactly. Nattoch made the decision to send the first group now. Duran and I are the only ones without our soulstones. The others . . ." He turned and smiled in the direction they'd gone. "All of them are whole and free. Xinot, Ian, and Darc are running the entire ship on their own. We stayed long enough to make sure they could handle the power needs without giving our escape away. We've never attempted it with only three of us, but they were doing well when Duran and I left."

"I didn't do a head count." Mac glanced toward the door and then focused on the two Nyrians. "How many of you are left, and what's our time frame for getting all of you off the ship with stones intact?"

He couldn't keep from glancing at Zianne. The tiny squirrel slept soundly in spite of the infusion of energy. This wasn't looking good for her at all. How the hell were they going to rescue the others and find her soulstone in time?

Bolt glanced at Duran before answering Mac, almost as if requesting permission to speak. Mac wondered at the Nyrian hierarchy. Nattoch was obviously in charge as their elder, but what of these two?

Did it matter who called the shots?

No, he realized. In the long run, all the Nyrians mattered equally. Somehow, they had to save all of them.

"We do shifts that last approximately ten of your hours," Bolt said. "The last shift started about two hours ago. In approximately eight more hours, the shift will change again."

Mac glanced at his watch, surprised to see it was almost nine. The morning had flown by. "That's just before five o'clock, our time. Still light out. Nattoch said it was easier for you guys in darkness. Did you have any problem coming now, in daylight?"

This time Duran took the lead. He and Finn were still hanging on to each other, but his voice was strong and he carried himself like a leader. "Not as much as we expected." He glanced at Bolt. "I don't think it's the issue we've had on other worlds, where their suns had an adverse effect on our ability to hold corporeal form. The frequency spectrum of electromagnetic radiation from your sun isn't as destructive as many others. It takes a bit more of our energy when we don't have our soulstones, but essentially we were being cautious."

Sighing, he slowly shook his head. "The time for caution is past. If we want to save ourselves, we have to act now, but if we must, Bolt and I will return on our own to help the remaining members escape. As soon as Xinot, Ian, and Darc retrieve their soulstones at the end of their shift, they're coming to Earth, along with Teev and Sakel. Nattoch, Tor, and Arnec will be the only ones left on the ship when we return for Zianne's soulstone as well as our own. I promise you, we will do our best to retrieve hers, but even if we fail, we'll be able to stop the Gar and ensure the rescue of at least a few more Nyrian lives."

"Screw that," Finn said. He shot a quick look at Morgan. "I say we figure out this disassembling shit and get ourselves ready on time."

"Agreed." Morgan kissed Rodie. "Hon? Can you go tell Tara that we've got Duran here safe and sound? I know she's worried. No need to tell her he doesn't have his soulstone, because we're going to get that for him in a few more hours."

"Gotcha." Rodie gave Morgan a quick kiss, planted a bigger one on Bolt, and then stood on her toes to kiss Duran as well. "I'll make sure Tara's okay. And I sure as hell hope you're a good teacher."

Spinning out of his reach before he replied, she slipped out of the dream shack. Mac looked at the closed door a moment and then found himself staring at the sleeping squirrel. After twenty years—a lifetime of hopes and dreams—it was all coming down to the next few hours. He hoped that painful ache in his gut wasn't a premonition of failure.

Bolt interrupted his thoughts. "Finn? May we use your cabin? Or Morgan's. We need a quiet place without chance of interruption where we can work on this. It's really not that complicated, even for corporeal beings such as yourselves, but you'll need somewhere to practice where we're not disturbed."

"You're welcome to mine. That okay with you, Morgan?"

"Definitely. Let's go. Mac? We'll keep in touch, let you know how we're doing."

He nodded and watched them leave. Soft fingers wrapped around his wrist. Comforting him with her touch, Lizzie stared up at him with tears in her eyes. "Mac? They'll be okay. I really believe that. And Zianne does, too. She's resting. That's all. She wants to save all the energy she can for tonight, in case she's needed."

"Thanks, Liz." He let out a deep breath, checked briefly to see that Zianne still slept, and covered Lizzie's hand with his. "You gonna be okay in here on your own? Can you finish out your shift, just in case someone needs the energy?" She nodded, blinking back tears. Mac glanced at Dink, who stood quietly beside him. "Well, Dink? How would you like to go interview a few Nyrians?"

Dink's grin spread slowly across his face. "You mean that? Shit, man. Why are we hanging out here?" He leaned over and kissed Lizzie full on the lips. "Sorry, Liz. You just got beat out by a whole passel of aliens."

She sighed dramatically with one hand over her heart. "Mac. You never said he was so fickle!"

He shouldn't feel like smiling, but he did. For some damned reason, in spite of the danger, he had the weirdest feeling things were going to be just fine. "Sorry, Liz. He is. I should have warned you." Then, sobering for a moment, he brushed his hand over her smooth hair, feeling the narrow threads of the mesh cap hooking her to the array. "Anything happens, you need us for anything at all, don't hesitate to call."

"Gotcha."

Mac leaned over and kissed her. Not to be outdone, Dink planted another big kiss on her as well, one she appeared to return with a bit more enthusiasm than she'd shown Mac. Still, when Mac matched her thumbs-up as he and Dink left the dream shack, she was smiling at both of them.

Finn opened the door to his cabin. It actually looked pretty clean, with the crap off the floor and the blankets pulled up on the bed to cover the pillows. He hadn't actually made the thing, but considering how it had looked by the time Duran and Tara had left after their last visit, he was just glad the bedding wasn't in piles on the floor.

"Coffee?" He glanced at the others. "Stiff drink, maybe?"

Morgan laughed. "That might help, but then I wouldn't be worth shit later." He flopped down on the couch. "I'll pass."

"Gotcha." Finn glanced at Duran and Bolt and swept a hand out. "Take a seat and tell us what we need to do."

Bolt hitched one hip against the back of the couch while Duran sat in the chair beside it. They gazed briefly at one another. Finn was sure there was a hell of a lot of communication in that brief connection. Duran leaned forward, looping his big hands over his knees.

"You've watched how we give up our corporeal bodies and return to the molecular level, which is our true energy form, before we depart, and you've seen the same thing in reverse when we arrive. You have this ability, just as we do, though your form is not pure energy like ours. But, it's close enough. It's also something that we didn't realize at first was possible. It was Nattoch who first discovered that your brains are capable of giving the same instructions to your cells that ours do. It was when he met Cameron. Since then, all of us have looked for the ability as we've met each of you. We know now that not all humans can disassemble. We've checked out others here—the security people, the one who cooks, her mate—none of them have the ability. But for whatever reason, all of you on Mac's team do. We think it is somehow tied to your telepathic ability. We're not really sure, but it's merely a matter of your learning how to access that part of your mind and essentially flipping on the switch."

Bolt interrupted. "Duran and I have tried to figure out the easiest and safest method of doing this. If you can disassemble and then meld with our energy forms, we believe we can carry you locked within our individual energy fields to the Gar ship."

"Our minds are locked on to the ship as our home, just as we've learned to lock on to your minds through the array to find our way here." Duran glanced at Bolt again and shrugged. "It seems complicated, but it's really quite simple once we access that part of your brain."

"Okay." Morgan looked at Finn with one eyebrow almost comically raised. "So how do you plan to go about finding that switch?"

Duran and Bolt exchanged glances once again. Both of them burst out laughing. "Sex," Duran said. "How else?"

"Duh." Finn rolled his eyes. "What was I thinking?" It made sense, though. Sexual energy empowered Nyrians. It was how they'd connected in the first place.

Duran stood and slipped out of his loose pants. He kicked them aside with one foot, perfectly comfortable with nudity in his human form. He was already hard, his cock rising high and proud against his flat belly. He lightly stroked his erection, as if the touch was an afterthought.

"Finn? Do you want to go first?"

"Not a problem." And if there was, it was probably too late to complain.

Duran nodded. "Okay. I'm going to take you in the superior position. I want you to link minds with me. Dampen all your defenses so that I have full access to who you are, how you think. Everything that makes you the man you are must be open to me. Total subjugation of self. Can you do that?"

Finn looked at the tall, strong male he'd known for only a couple of days, and wondered if he could give up that much of himself. He was just getting used to the whole guy-on-guy thing, but his answer came in less than a heartbeat. Of course he could. He could do anything if it meant saving Duran and Tara and all the others. Wasn't that what this was all about? With nothing more than a shrug of his shoulders, he unsnapped his jeans. The zipper sounded uncomfortably loud, and he wondered if Morgan and Bolt were going to be screwing while he and Duran were doing the same thing, but Morgan just sat there on the couch waiting, with his steady gaze fastened on every move Finn made.

He should have felt embarrassed with such close scrutiny from a guy he was only beginning to think of as a friend, but arousal spiked hard and fast as he kicked off his moccasins, slid the denim pants down his legs, and then dropped his shirt on the floor beside his pants.

Without thinking beyond the immediate act of undressing, he shoved his knit boxers off and stepped out of them. His hand automatically went to his dick and he stroked the hard shaft. Only vaguely aware of Morgan and Bolt's avid attention, Finn slicked his hand up and down the full length of his cock, rolling the foreskin over the sensitive tip, reveling in the pulse of blood through heavy veins and the tender ache in his balls as they tightened and pulled up close between his legs.

He studied Duran's thick penis, the way it thrust up against the man's belly, and he thought of that first night, when Duran and Tara had come to Finn's cabin and told him they'd chosen him. Of all the people here, they'd connected with his mind and wanted him as their conduit.

Duran had been more reticent then and Tara had taken the lead, but it appeared the Nyrian was stronger than Finn had first realized, or maybe it was just that he felt more confident in this role. He was the leader, the one teaching Finn, but there was something about the obvious power in Duran's body language now that Finn found extremely arousing. He'd never thought of himself as a submissive type, but he realized he didn't mind submitting to his Nyrian lover.

As the thought crossed his mind, his dick seemed to stretch and swell within his grasp. For Duran. For the one who had chosen him. Emotion washed over him in a powerful wave. The idea still choked him up, the fact someone had chosen him specifically for the man he was. It reminded him just how needy he'd been. How much he still needed.

Duran stepped close and rested his hand on Finn's shoulder. Forced him to make eye contact with the power of his own steady gaze. "We need each other, Finn. All of us need each other. Not just for the survival of my people, but for you and your people here as well. Each of us has a need to be loved, to be wanted for no other reason than who we are. What we are. Look how much we've learned already, that our differences are not nearly as great as those things that make us the same."

Finn could only nod in agreement. He didn't try to speak, afraid his voice would crack, that his nerve would fail. He'd never been good at emotions, never been successful with any relationships because he flat-out hadn't wanted them.

He wanted this. Wanted Duran and Tara, wanted the connection with the rest of Mac's dream team. And most of all, he wanted everything to turn out the way they hoped.

Damn but he didn't want to screw up. That possibility scared the crap out of him. He'd not been all that good at following through on things, but . . .

"It's okay." Duran stepped even closer. He placed both his hands on Finn's shoulders and stared at him. Duran's brilliant blue eyes bored into his. Took charge of Finn's fears. "When we make love—and that is what we'll be doing. Not sex to find mere gratification, but lovemaking to reach a connection only lovers can find, one so deep, so intensely personal, that we will meld as one. You and me, Finn. Just the two of us. Let me in. I want to fill your body, your mind, and your heart. Can you do that?"

Finn nodded, caught in the deep, hypnotic blue of Duran's eyes, the perfect curve of his lips, the warmth of his hands. Morgan and Bolt might still be in the room, but they didn't matter. Nothing mattered but the connection to Duran.

"Where do you want me?"

"Here." Duran ran his fingers over the high back of the leather chair. "Spread your legs, lean over the top. Place your hands on the arms of the chair, your chest close against the cushion. I want you comfortable and yet you must feel totally submissive to me, something that is not in your nature."

Wondering how Duran had picked up on that little personality trait so quickly, Finn nodded, leaned over the back of the chair and flattened his palms against the thick arms. The soft leather felt warm against his belly. The tip of his erection gently brushed the sleek leather back. Duran knelt behind him and spread Finn's legs farther apart until his toes barely connected with the floor. He felt vulnerable. Helpless, and so damned horny he could barely breathe. Cool air wafted across his hot testicles and his arousal spiked another notch.

Self-consciously, he raised his head and realized he looked directly at Morgan and Bolt. At some point, Bolt had moved from his seat on the arm of the couch and now sat beside Morgan. Both of them were naked. Both highly aroused.

Finn hadn't noticed when they'd undressed, but their clothes lay in a pile on the floor. Now they sat close, each one stroking the other's cock, both of them watching Finn.

He groaned softly, his own desperate need growing on the need of the others.

"Hold that position."

Finn glanced over his shoulder as Duran walked into the bedroom and quickly returned with the tube of lubricant Finn had taken from the supply room. Amazing what a guy could find in that big pantry, but leave it to Mac to prepare for everything, though one thing Finn certainly hadn't counted on when he took this job was the fact he'd be getting fucked in the ass. That definitely hadn't been on this het-boy's radar.

What an idiot he'd been. He rested his cheek against the leather cushion, almost bent double over the chair's back, and let his thoughts wander over the last couple of days while Duran spent some quality time working lubricant in and around his butt. He'd never had a clue how sensitive that area was. Not once had he imagined he'd ever have sex with a man.

Now he welcomed it. Dreamed of Duran taking him as much as he loved fantasizing about dominating Duran, though he'd definitely want to talk about this with Duran later. He knew that it wasn't really about domination or submission, at least not what passed between the two of them. It was about sharing, about connecting. About feeling so close to another man that their deepest emotions were shared.

The tube clattered to the table beside his chair and Duran ran his big hands over Finn's flanks, up his sides, along his ribs to his underarms. Down his back, trailing fingers along his spine, and back again, where he grasped his shoulders and gently dug thick fingers into taut muscles.

He repeated the same words, over and over again. "You are mine, Finn. Relax your body. Open your body to me. Open your mind." His voice maintained a soft and soothing, hypnotic cadence. "Open your body to me. Open your mind. You are mine, Finn. Your heart is mine, your body is mine. You are mine."

He leaned even closer and his warm breath tickled Finn's shoulder. A chill ran over his spine as he felt the broad head of Duran's penis brush lightly against his thigh. Just a touch. Nothing more, but Duran's hands continued retracing the same pathway, his breath warm against Finn's shoulder, his voice uttering the same soothing words.

"You are mine, Finn. Open to me. Let me in."

He spread his fingers across Finn's lower back, gently stroking down over his buttocks, up again, pausing at the dip in Finn's spine just below his waist, trailing along the crease between his cheeks and on to stroke the insides of his thighs. Finn groaned and spread his legs farther apart. He felt Duran kneeling between his thighs, the broad shoulders pushing them apart even more.

Duran's hot tongue swept over his balls, circled around the wrinkled sac. Blood surged, hot and heavy, into Finn's already erect dick. Finn clenched his buttocks and moaned. "Shit, Duran. I can't take much of that."

Duran chuckled and licked him again.

"Damn." Finn gasped as the muscles in his butt clenched again. He dug his fingers into the leather arms of the chair.

"I want you desperate for me, Finn." Duran blew a soft breath of air against his hot sac.

"I'm there. Trust me on this, okay?" Shuddering, Finn struggled for control as he fought the beginning tremors of orgasm. "Damn it, Duran. For a guy who's new at sex, you learn way too fast."

Again that hot tongue stroked his balls, but Duran wrapped his fingers tightly around the base of Finn's erection. No way could he come with pressure like that.

His balls ached and pressure built.

Duran's soft chuckle sent a warm breath of air over Finn's sac. He cursed softly.

"Nyrians are entirely telepathic," Duran said.

Gods but those warm puffs of breath on his nuts were going to kill him.

"We tend to share our experiences, Finn. You are the recipient of all any of us have learned from your kind over the past few days. All Zianne has learned from Mac."

Morgan laughed. Finn raised his head and glared at him, but Morgan suddenly cursed and pressed his head against the back of the couch. His eyes closed, his lips twisted in a grimace as Bolt bent over his lap and sucked his cock deep.

The cords stood out on Morgan's neck. His entire body went rigid. Finn almost laughed out loud. *Serves you right,* he 'pathed.

Morgan responded, but even his mental voice sounded breathless. *Crap, Finn. How do they do this? I've never been so turned on in my life. Oh . . . shit. Bolt!*

Finn slipped out of Morgan's thoughts when he realized Duran was standing behind him again. The Nyrian's thick cock pressed against his ass, slipped along the crease, and stopped against his tightly clenched sphincter. Duran pressed forward until Finn felt the burn, the steady pressure as his body automatically tightened to fight the intrusion.

He took a couple of deep breaths, fighting for control. Slowly exhaling, Finn pressed back against Duran. He felt the slightest give, as that small, taut muscle released. Finn pushed a bit harder and Duran's cock slipped through, steadily filling him while Duran kept that ferocious grasp around the base of Finn's cock.

Let me in, Finn. Let me all the way in.

Duran's hips thrust forward. Finn grunted and held tight to the arms of the chair. *Shit, Duran. Poetry at a time like this?*

The soft chuckle that was all in Finn's head sounded moderately threatening. Duran managed a hard twist with his cock on the next thrust, rubbing in a most effective manner across Finn's prostate. He groaned.

Would you prefer a novel, Finn? Maybe a ballad in three parts. Or something more esoteric? I see it now, a large tome titled The Effect of Nyrian Sexual Domination on Hardheaded Irish Humans. *Yes, I think that one works.*

The only warning Finn got was the tightening of Duran's fingers around his cock before the Nyrian slammed into him. Finn grunted as Duran buried himself deep. Their balls pressed together and Duran's hand squeezed tighter around the base of Finn's dick.

Finn struggled to catch his breath. *For a guy new to the language and the body, you're sounding awfully cocky.*

Duran picked up the pace, rocking fast and hard against

Finn until the *slap, slap, slap* of thighs meeting thighs, of groin against butt, echoed in Finn's head. Duran growled, a primal, sexual, sensual sound that wrapped around Finn both inside and out. He pressed his lips against Finn's ear, but the words weren't actually spoken.

Finn felt them deep inside. Felt Duran's mind driving deep into his, as deep as his cock filled Finn's ass. *You can say that to me, Finnegan? You, a human who plans to invade an alien spaceship before it destroys your planet? Invade and kidnap the slaves they hold? A human who thinks he can disassemble his very molecules, travel through space, fight a powerful alien race, and return victorious? And you think I'm cocky?*

He slammed deeper and harder until Finn saw stars. With his lips still against Finn's ear, Duran whispered, "I think you're the cocky bastard who deserves that title."

Yes, you son of a bitch. You're damned right I'm cocky. Now fuck me, and do it right. Get into my head and scramble whatever you have to, because we only get one shot at the bastards.

Duran's soft chuckle came with a velvety stroke of fingers along Finn's shaft and a deep, long thrust into his bowel. And Duran's voice in his mind, this time a subtle caress filled with love and hope. *You are so right, Finnegan O'Toole. You are one cocky bastard, and I thank Nyria we've got you on our side.*

Finn shivered. His climax was building, but he didn't feel anything different, couldn't see that they'd accomplished anything beyond what was probably the most amazing fuck of his life.

Then Duran's mental voice seemed to pause within his mind. There was a subtle shift, almost as if the two of them had stepped from one room into another. The pressure built in Finn's cock; his balls tightened within his sac and the pain was so sweet, so all-consuming that he whimpered. Not a moan or a manly groan, but a soft and needy whimper.

Finn shuddered at the changing sensation. Duran covered

him like a warm blanket, steadily pumping deep inside his ass. Steady, strong, and so perfect, until the sensation shifted yet again. So subtle. So absolutely perfect.

And something . . . something unfamiliar in Finn's mind opened. A thought process he'd never noticed, a part of his mind forever closed away, suddenly unlocked. He sensed it, open and waiting for him to find the switch, to reach for it, and then, without a moment's hesitation, to flip it from one side to the next.

Climax welled up from deep inside. A shattering burst of power from brain to spine, from balls to cock—a shimmering flash of painful pleasure and perfect energy. Finn's back arched, his muscles clenched and he cried out. Duran's final thrust seemed to go clear through his gut.

The sharp, sweet pain of release overwhelmed his senses until Finn's focus narrowed itself to the rhythmic pulse of pleasure. His cock, Duran's, both of them pulsing in metered time with their thundering hearts.

Nothing was as it seemed, and yet all felt refreshed. Renewed. Forever changed as Finn realized he was somehow floating freely in the small front room of his cabin, surrounded by the sparkling blue and gold energy that was Duran. He felt whole, and yet knew he was not. Knew he was little more than mist and molecules, a part of the Nyrian who held his disassembled essence within his own sparkling energy.

Morgan was still on the couch beside Bolt, staring at the spot where Finn and Duran had been fucking, but he didn't move, as if his body had been caught in stasis.

No, Finn. He is moving, but we are moving at a much faster speed, our very atoms spinning beyond what Morgan can see with human eyes. Give yourself over to me.

How?

Relax. Let me hold you. I want to see how well we can travel together in this form.

Okay. Where?

Out.

Before he could question that enigmatic statement, Duran had wrapped his colorful energy around Finn and they flashed through the walls of the cabin, out beneath the midmorning sun, across the vast plateau with the satellite dishes shimmering beneath them. The world beneath was a motionless tableau as they moved over the edge of the property, the two of them nothing more than a burst of sparkling light.

Wait! Duran. What's that? Slow down. We need to see what they're doing.

Duran retraced their path and Finn caught the image of at least a dozen bodies in the brush below, appearing immobile as statues to him in this disassembled form. Still, he knew they were climbing up the side of the hill, saw they were armed with heavy bolt cutters and other tools and equipment, all of them heading toward the chain link fence at the edge of the property.

We have to warn Mac!

We will. We're returning now.

And within a mere fraction of a second, they were back in the cabin and Finn was back in his body, leaning over the edge of the chair, his cock pumping thick streams of semen over Duran's fist.

"Where'd you go?" Morgan leapt to his feet, his cock still high and hard against his belly. "What happened?"

Finn gasped for air, sucked in another lungful and then drew in more as he came down from an unbelievable orgasm. His body tingled and he broke out in goose bumps when Duran pulled free and, with a self-satisfied smirk, headed to the bathroom to clean up.

It took Finn a moment to find his voice. "First of all, it worked. I found the switch, and Morgan, that's what it is. A switch in the brain that lets you disassemble. I turned into energy, just like Duran, but we were moving at a rate that's so much faster than humans that you and Bolt looked like you were sitting still."

"Crap. That's awesome." He turned to Bolt, but Finn caught his shoulder.

"You're right. It's fucking awesome, but Duran took me on a bit of a ride around the plateau. There's about a dozen guys climbing the hill on the backside, armed with bolt cutters and shit. I need to warn Mac. You need to find your fucking switch."

"Got it. Go."

Finn grabbed his jeans and dragged them on without hunting for his boxers. He slipped his feet into his worn moccasins. "Tell Duran I'll be right back. I need to tell Mac we're under attack."

4

The door slammed behind Finn. Morgan glanced over his shoulder at Bolt, who was still sitting quietly on the couch. "I need to find that fucking switch, Bolt. Now."

Bolt nodded. "I agree, but I would like Duran's help. Now that he's shown Finn the way, it will be even easier to teach you with Duran's guidance."

"Whatever." Morgan tried to play it cool, but energy practically screamed across his nerve endings. Finn did it! He'd watched the guy disappear. Flat-out disappear. He just blinked out, right in front of them. Shit. One minute he was there, getting his ass reamed by Duran, and then *poof!* He was gone. Seconds—just a couple of seconds and then they were back, Duran still fucking Finn's ass, and Finn saying they'd flown around the entire site.

This was just too fucking cool for words.

"Morgan?"

He jerked, startled when Duran appeared next to him. He hadn't even heard the guy come back into the room. He really needed to get his head back in the game. "Yeah." He nodded. "Bolt says he wants you to help. Is that okay?"

"Of course." Duran shrugged like it was no big deal.

Such human gestures, and yet these guys were all aliens. The thought crossed Morgan's mind that they'd all accepted the goodness of these people on faith alone. Well, faith and some damned good sex. Then he glanced at Bolt and realized he had no doubts about him at all. That the only reason Morgan felt a bit uneasy with Duran was that he'd just watched the guy fuck the ever-lovin' hell out of Finn.

Watching the two of them had been one of the hottest things Morgan had ever seen in his life and he was still strung tight as a rubber band. He wanted Duran fucking his ass, wanted Bolt sucking his cock, wanted both guys banging him hard, making him so hot that he'd forget how scary all of this was. Forget that he was preparing to travel through space within the formless energy of an alien, board a spaceship, and attempt to rescue the last members of the Nyrian race.

Shit, yeah. He took a deep breath. Let it out in a loud huff and felt a bit calmer. "We'd better get started, then. If you saw the group coming up the back side of the mountain, we need to be ready to stop them. Tonight, of all nights, we have to have everything under control."

Duran nodded. "I agree." Then he laughed. "But I have to admit, this is one of the more pleasurable methods of teaching I've ever experienced." He grinned at Bolt. "Ask Bolt. I was a teacher on Nyria, before the Gar came. There I dealt with young Nyrians who were more interested in mischief than in learning."

Bolt stood beside Morgan. "You realize that's probably because we didn't use sex as a teaching tool." He wrapped his hands around his erect cock. "Obviously inappropriate with the young, but I could get used to this method of teaching adult humans."

Duran grinned at Bolt, and it was like watching a couple of guys in the gym joking back and forth. Impossible to see them as anything but human. Then Duran turned to Morgan, and all sense of humor fled. He folded his arms across his broad chest and took a more serious stance. "Morgan, are you okay with both of us having sex with you? Both of us taking a dominant role? Our dominance and your submission is important to the learning process, though we should only need to do it this way once."

He thought about that, about submitting to two men. He was used to being the top, but that had changed dramatically over the last couple of days. In fact, everything he'd ever thought about himself seemed to be undergoing a dramatic shift. "I'm willing to give it a try," he said. "I haven't done anything like this before, so I don't know how I'll react, but I'm open to trying whatever works."

"Good." Duran seemed to relax a bit. "We realize we're thinking with our Nyrian minds. Our thoughts tell us you'll be more comfortable with Bolt, a man you're familiar with, and that should make it easier for you to accept me as well. I've learned the human pathways for finding the switch in Finn's mind, which should make it easier to find yours." He shrugged and Morgan got the feeling Duran was uncomfortable trying to explain himself to a mere human, but at least he was trying.

Morgan almost laughed. He really needed to let the poor guy off the hook. It was bad enough that the three of them were standing here bare-assed naked, having this discussion. "So all you're saying is that it'll help if we all work on this together. I'm okay with that. Where do you want me?"

Duran's sigh of relief was almost audible. Almost. "With three of us, the bedroom would probably work best." He led the way into Finn's room. "On the bed, on your hands and knees."

"Okay." Morgan took the position in the center of the bed.

Bolt crawled up beside him, then rolled over and slipped beneath Morgan's belly. His erect cock was right in front of Morgan's face, the broad tip practically brushing his lips.

He was leaning forward to take it in his mouth when Duran stopped him. "Not yet. Hold perfectly still." He turned and walked back into the front room.

Morgan dipped his head and stared at Bolt lying between his thighs. "He can say that because he just came. I'm hard as a post."

Bolt laughed. "I was thinking the same thing. You have no idea how much I want you to suck on me now."

Morgan's laughter was a little tense. "Oh, I think I can imagine."

Duran returned with the lube in his hand. "Now," he said. "Touch each other, but only with your fingertips."

Bolt's fingers softly stroking over his sac rather than his erection caught Morgan by surprise. He gasped and his buttocks clenched. He heard Duran's soft chuckle.

"Did I mention I love control?"

"I kinda figured that much. You know that's a very human desire, don't you? You remind me of my seventh grade math teacher." Gritting his teeth, thinking of anything but what Bolt was doing to his already sensitive genitals, Morgan first ran his fingertips up and then down Bolt's shaft, swirled one finger around his perineum and then rubbed gently against his anus. Bolt groaned. His fingers kept up their tickling exploration of Morgan's balls and then slowly trailed the length of his dick.

As if this wasn't enough to have him crossing his eyes, Morgan felt Duran settling between his calves, kneeling directly behind him. He imagined the guy stroking that huge cock of his, and the visual made him tense every muscle in his body.

Warm hands caressed his buttocks, thumbs traced a line along the cleft between his cheeks. He waited for the cool wash of lube.

Instead, he got a warm, very mobile tongue. "Shit!" He gasped and sucked in a deep breath. "What the fuck are you doing?"

"You don't like this?" Duran's tongue circled the sensitive ring of his anal sphincter, pressing gently as if for emphasis.

Morgan mumbled a reply as Duran's tongue worked at the tiny opening, licking, stroking, and then pressing harder. *Screw Duran's orders.* Morgan leaned over and sucked Bolt's cock deep between his lips. He had to concentrate on something else, something that wasn't his ass being licked and rimmed by Duran's tongue or he was going to lose it right here and now.

Nothing had ever felt like that. So intimate and yet not nearly enough of what he wanted. What he needed. Hell, they didn't have time to screw around. He needed to learn to disassemble, needed to have time to practice forming and reforming, coming out of that state the way Finn had—body and mind sharp and ready for action. He sucked harder, felt Bolt's answering groans and the hot suction of his mouth as he took Morgan deep.

Felt Duran's sigh against his ass. "I see you're both ignoring me. Why am I not surprised?" Then he was slapping lube against Morgan's butt and, from the squishy sounds, apparently covering his cock as well.

There was no warning, no easy teasing foreplay. No, he just pressed the broad head of his cock against Morgan's small, tight sphincter and pressed forward. Hard.

Let me in, Morgan. Into your body. Into your mind.

Morgan grunted, but he forced himself to relax, to push back against Duran's thrust. He felt the muscle relax, then give just enough to allow Duran to breach his anus without too much pain. The burn was sharp, the pleasure even sharper.

Let me in, Morgan. Let me into your body, let me drive deep and hard. Let me in. Relax. Don't fight me. Let me in.

Duran went deep and then paused, giving Morgan time to adjust to his size and the depth of his initial thrust. He'd gone as far as he could, balls deep, and the soft cadence of his words filled Morgan's mind just as that long, thick cock filled his body. Bolt held still as well, holding Morgan's cock between his lips, his tongue probing gently at the tiny slit.

Morgan felt the layers of sensation building as he drew Bolt's cock inside his mouth, working the broad head with his tongue, frantically reaching for that final push that would take him over. He needed to overload with sensation, enough to open his mind, his body, and his heart to these two men.

Duran's voice was a steady song in his head, a rhythmic poem with a hypnotic effect, tied to their hearts, their lungs, their very thoughts. *Let me in, let me see you, feel you, let me touch you. Open to me, Morgan. Open to sensation. To life and love and all that your body, your heart, and mind can take.*

He fell into the words, the rhythm, the steady thrust and release as Duran drove deep and then pulled back, in and then out, harder, deeper until Morgan was caught in the maelstrom of mouths and cocks, hands stroking and minds linking. He felt Bolt inside his mind as his mouth engulfed Morgan's full length, but it wasn't enough. Not nearly enough.

Something was missing. Some*one* was missing. Rodie? This wasn't right without Rodie, but how could that be? They were too new, too fresh together for him to feel this deep yearning for her touch, for her mental connection.

But merely thinking of Rodie took him beyond control. He trembled, struggling to hold on, but Duran thrust hard and Bolt's cock jerked between his lips. Morgan felt his own climax racing from spine to balls to burning release, the three of them coming together, their bodies shuddering as one, hearts thudding, cocks spilling seed, lungs filling with air, in and out and in again.

They collapsed, the three of them together on the bed, bodies sticky with semen and sweat, mouths gasping for air, the sense of failure riding Morgan hardest of all.

It hadn't worked. Morgan sucked air and wondered what had gone wrong. "What happened?" He rolled his head to the side and frowned at Duran's shocked face. "No switch, obviously. How come?"

Duran shook his head. "I'm not sure. There was a wall. A solid wall keeping me away. You didn't open to me, even at the point of climax. I don't understand."

Bolt raised his head, his entire focus on Morgan though he spoke to Duran. "I do. I should have guessed. Morgan is bound to Rodie. I felt her in his heart as well as his mind. She needs to be part of this if you're to pass through that wall. He's holding himself back, protecting what belongs to her."

Rodie? No way. "Where the hell did that come from?" Morgan pushed himself upright and glared at Bolt. Bound to Rodie? Hell no. He might have been thinking of her but he wasn't bound to anyone. Not Morgan Black. The most commitment he'd ever made was to this project and Mac. When it ended . . . hell. He didn't know if he and Rodie would even keep in touch when it was over.

So why did that thought make him so uneasy? He shook it off and focused on the problem at hand. How the hell could these guys think his feelings for her were keeping him from linking to Duran? That was a bunch of crap. "I don't belong to anyone." He shook his head and glared on Duran. "I mean, yeah, I like Rodie. She's great. She's smart and funny, but we're not married. Not committed to each other in any way. We're . . . we're fuck buddies. You know? Friends with benefits. I'm bi, anyway. If I ever commit to anyone, it's probably not going to be a woman."

And why did the thought tease the edges of his mind that he was denying much too vehemently, that he was trying to prove something to himself, not necessarily to Bolt and Duran?

"You admit that the sex with Rodie is good, right?" Bolt

shoved himself back and leaned against the headboard. His chest was covered in sweat, the muscles glistening, and his hair hung in tangles around his face. The guy was so fucking gorgeous that Morgan wanted to crawl across him, wanted to lick the sweat off his pecs, let their bodies slide together.

But that wasn't going to solve the problem. "Yeah," he said. "Sex with Rodie is fantastic. You know it is—you've been with us."

Bolt laughed. "I just wanted to hear you say it. I'm going to go get her. Bring her back here to join us. I think Rodie's presence will help us get inside your head."

Before Morgan could come up with a fitting response, Bolt had turned into energy and disappeared. Just the way Morgan should be able to do, if he'd only gotten it right. Shit.

He turned and caught Duran staring at him with a bemused expression. "I don't understand. Why do you not acknowledge your feelings for your mate?"

"She's not my fucking mate!"

Duran slowly nodded his head. "If you say so."

Morgan sucked in a deep breath. Why did it feel wrong to say she wasn't his? What if she was? What if the feelings he had for Rodie were more than just the way a guy felt about a good friend who was also a hot lay? He liked her a lot. He wanted to be with her, liked waking up beside her, but hell, they'd only known each other a couple of days. He couldn't be bound to her. Not in any way. What were these guys thinking?

More importantly, what was he thinking?

A couple of minutes later, he heard footsteps out in front. The sound of the door opening. "Morgan? Are you in here?"

"Hey, Rodie. I'm in the bedroom." He shot a quick look at Duran. "Not a word, you son of a bitch."

Grinning, Duran shook his head.

"Bolt said you needed me. Is anything wrong?"

He glanced up. She was standing beside the bed smiling at him, and everything sort of settled into place. What was it about Rodie that made his life feel so balanced?

Morgan chuckled and pulled her into the circle of his arms. "It appears I need some really good, mind-blowing sex if they're going to get into the part of my brain that lets humans disassemble. Unfortunately, what I'm getting from these two jerks isn't good enough. We decided to call in the reinforcements, and that would be you."

"Me?" She laughed and threw her arms around his neck. "You're kidding, right?"

"Nope. Not kidding at all. Think you're up to it?" He glanced up and saw Bolt leaning against the doorframe, his arms folded across his chest. "And you, Bolt? You up to whatever Rodie throws your way?"

"I think I can handle it." He winked at Duran. "This poor guy might not be able to."

"We shall see." Duran turned those sapphire blue eyes on Morgan. "This time, you direct. What would we need to do to take you beyond your sexual limits? Into . . ." He frowned and glanced at Bolt. "What did you call it?"

"Into the zone. Out of reality and into a place where all your defenses are down, where you feel totally free to open your heart and mind. To be the man you are, not the one your society dictates, or the man you think others want you to be."

Bolt directed his comment to Morgan, whose first reaction was to laugh them off. But Bolt's somber voice and serious expression made him stop and think. Had he ever felt totally free? He glanced at Rodie and realized that, yes, he had. Ever since she'd come into his life.

So why had he been so afraid to admit how he felt?

Because he was concerned with his image. With what, as Bolt phrased it, society dictated. He'd always played the loner, the tough guy, the one who didn't need anyone else, but why?

Such a simple, uncomplicated answer for what felt like a terribly complicated set of emotions. When you needed people, you made yourself vulnerable. When you trusted people and they didn't come through, you got hurt. But Rodie? Rodie hadn't made any promises, but she was someone he knew he could count on. He'd known her only a few days, but he'd been inside her head—he trusted what he saw.

How he felt. Even more important, he trusted how Rodie felt. And just like that, he knew what he wanted. What he needed to make himself open up to possibilities. He reached for Rodie's hands, and the first thought that entered his mind was this was how a couple stood during a wedding when they made their vows.

It should have scared the crap out of him. Instead, it made him smile when he looked into those beautiful eyes that were so much more than merely brown. He had to clear his throat to get the words out, but his voice sounded just as true as he felt.

"I want to make love to Rodie. Just to her, actually, but it sounds as if you two need to be part of this if you're going to unlock my brain." Morgan stared at Rodie, at the wild mane of curls tumbling down her back, the full, red lips, and the decidedly naughty twinkle in her eyes. "I want to bury myself balls deep in Rodie. Duran's already made it clear he's an ass man, so I guess he gets me from behind. And Rodie?" He grinned at her. "Rodie takes Bolt any way she wants."

The actual logistics proved to be a bit more complicated than Morgan had figured, but he decided before too long that laughter with sex when you were planning something that could get you killed wasn't such a bad thing. They ended up with Duran on his back and Morgan facing away, kneeling over him, tightly impaled on the Nyrian's huge cock. Rodie straddled Morgan's hips and after a couple of misses, he planted his dick perfectly between her slick folds, sliding into her hot, slick sheath.

She sighed as she lowered herself fully over him and wrapped her arms around Morgan's waist. Bolt knelt between Duran's legs, behind Rodie. He used the lubricant generously, playing with her, touching and rubbing and teasing until she was close to climax merely from his touch. When she was ready, he carefully entered her from behind, slipping gently into her.

Morgan recognized her groan as one of pleasure not pain. It was such a weird and wonderful feeling, that big cock of Bolt's sliding into Rodie's slick channel, riding along Morgan's shaft with nothing more than the thin barrier between Rodie's two passages separating the two men.

It was absolutely amazing, beyond anything Morgan had ever experienced in his life, and he knew they'd gone so far beyond Rodie's comfort zone that outer space was no longer such a big deal. He also knew she went along with it only because it was exactly what Morgan needed.

It was that point that made him realize a basic truth—Rodie would do anything for him.

Just as he would do anything for her.

It appeared Bolt and Duran weren't so far off base. There was more to this relationship he and Rodie were building than he'd allowed himself to admit.

Now he just had to hope he didn't go and get himself killed.

When the time came, when orgasm overwhelmed Morgan and his mind opened wide to the unbelievable torrent of sensation, Duran slipped through whatever defenses Morgan might have once had. It was such a simple thing to feel the presence of that switch he'd mentioned. Even easier to flip it from one side to another, to suddenly find himself nothing more than molecules of energy, caught up in Duran's blue and gold brilliance, watching Rodie and Bolt as if they weren't moving at all.

Duran spun him around the room, through the wall and out into the brilliant sunlight. They took a quick pass over the plateau, saw the security forces patrolling the fence line where Finn had

"Yeah." And just like that, he found the switch. Flipped it, and for all intents and purposes, disappeared. Somehow, he re-formed beside Duran, laughing at Rodie's startled expression.

Will you show me how?

I will. Later, when we're not trying to save the world. And when I figure out just what the fuck I'm actually doing.

She laughed. *Promise me?*

He gazed at her a moment and thought of what Duran and Bolt had forced him to face. It really wasn't that difficult at all to admit how much Rodie meant to him.

I promise, he said. Well aware he would promise her any-thing—and always do everything in his power to deliver.

Kiera set a glass of ice tea in front of Mac, but he was so caught up in his phone conversation she doubted if he even no-ticed. She walked across the room and sat with the four of her guys who'd escaped so far, and another Nyrian, Ankar, who had originally come during Lizzie's shift to share energy with Zianne.

It was so weird. She hardly knew any of them, and yet she'd been intimate with all but Ankar, and damn it all, but they all mattered to her.

Ankar, Aza, Jesat, Dake, and Bane were safe. The five of them had their soulstones, they were firmly in control of their human bodies and she wished she could just relax and enjoy the fact they weren't slaves anymore, but until the others were free, none of them could relax. And she still needed to get Teev, Sakel, and Tor off the Gar ship, and Tor was going to be one of the very last. He'd actually be fighting the Gar if it came down to a battle.

"They will be all right, Kiera."

Bane's big hand covered hers. "I hope so. There's so much that could go wrong."

"Like the ones climbing up the back of the mountain?"

seen the men with bolt cutters advancing up the side (
mountain.

And then they were back and he was himself again, re
ing around Rodie, with Duran beneath him once mor
rhythm hardly broken at all.

But Rodie's eyes flashed with excitement and she clu
his arms. "You disappeared! It was only a couple of sec
but you were gone. I saw the sparkles and then you just fri
disappeared!"

He felt like a kid with a new toy. He'd done it. They'd
it together—Bolt and Duran providing the experience, b
had taken Rodie's presence to free him. He thrust deep as
did the same, the two of them filling Rodie's body as
oughly as Duran filled his. Morgan wrapped his arms arc
Rodie as she shuddered against him, her body caught in
midst of her climax. He felt Bolt's release deep inside her c
nel, and Duran's cock jerked inside Morgan.

This time, with their goal accomplished, Morgan set hin
free, felt the coil of heat, the pleasure that was so close to
they were impossible to separate as his orgasm took control
muscles clenched, and the thick stream of his ejaculate foun
way from his balls to freedom deep within Rodie.

Morgan cried out, a curse backed with laughter as the
of them climaxed together, bodies clenching, muscles tigh
ing and then losing all tension, all of them going entirely li
Morgan lay backward, collapsing against Duran's chest. Rc
fell forward on top of Morgan, and Bolt, still buried deep in:
Rodie, ended up lying over all of them.

Laughing. All of them laughing except Duran, who quic
disassembled and reformed across the room where he could
tually draw a breath without the weight of three adults press
him into the bed.

Long minutes later, Bolt raised his head and smiled at M
gan. "You did it. Now, can you remember how?"

"Exactly." She listened in on the phone conversation Mac was having with the sheriff.

"Damn it, Ted, I know he's on his own property, but they're just down the hill from my property line, which is defined by a chain link fence. Every last one of the bastards is carrying tools designed to cut through wire, and you're saying I can't touch them?" Mac glanced toward Dink and rolled his eyes.

She wondered what Dink was thinking, what it would be like to be a famous investigative reporter, sitting on top of a story like theirs and not able to tell a soul what was going on. Dink actually seemed pretty cool about it, though. He'd spent the last few hours talking to the different Nyrians, writing down their stories, taking pictures.

Mac cursed, drawing Kiera's attention again.

"Damn it all, Ted. Yes, but mine is a very small security force. My men are armed, but this isn't a game. I've got millions of dollars' worth of equipment here and we're reaching a critical point in the project. I can't afford any downtime at all. Okay. Thank you. Air patrol would be much appreciated. You know I'm good for any expenses incurred."

He slammed the phone down and focused on Kiera. "Do your guys know shoes? Can they form shoes?"

Bane squeezed her fingers before she could answer. "Yes, Mac. How do you need us dressed?" He gestured at the rest of the Nyrians. "All of us can help your security people watch the perimeter, but we can do it invisibly from the air a lot more effectively."

As he spoke, Bane and the others moved over to the big table where Mac and Dink had been sitting most of the morning. Kiera followed them, wondering what would come next, but she was proud of her guys, proud of the way they were so quick to respond.

Mac chuckled and glanced at Dink, who merely shook his head as if he wasn't quite sure what he was hearing. "I imagine you can," Mac said, "but what I want is a show of force. I've only got four security people here right now, and there are at least a dozen or more men outside the fence, along with our usual contingent of protestors at the front gate. What I want is more bodies. Big, tough-looking bodies, like you guys, only dressed in denim pants, flannel shirts, heavy boots." He cocked his head and stared at Bane. "Can you do that?"

Bane stood, disassembled, and then reassembled within the scope of a few seconds. He wore snug-fitting denim jeans, a red and black plaid flannel shirt like Mac's, and heavy work boots.

"Amazing." Mac shook his head as he stood and walked around Bane, checking out the clothing. "Someday, when things slow down to normal, you're going to have to show me how that works."

Bane cocked his head to one side as if listening to a distant voice, and then smiled at Mac. "Duran says he and Bolt have succeeded in teaching Morgan and Finn. There's no reason you can't learn as well."

"I wonder why Zianne never showed me how?"

"She didn't know. We've only just learned it's possible. Nattoch was the one who recognized the ability in Cameron, but until he was here and had accessed a human body and had the time to study it, we didn't know that some humans have the ability while others don't."

"Is it something that all of us can do?" Kiera wasn't all that sure that she wanted to turn her body into nothing more than sparkles of light, but it was definitely cool.

Bane glanced at Ankar. "You've done more exploring among the humans here. Can all of them disassemble?"

"Only the ones Mac calls the dream team can do it." He glanced toward Dink. "That one cannot. He lacks the switch."

"Gee, thanks." Dink frowned. It was obvious he was teasing, but Kiera was sure he was disappointed. He'd been following the conversation with avid interest.

"It's somehow tied into telepathic ability," Dake said. "You are not telepathic. The others are."

"Interesting." Mac studied Dink. "I wonder if telepathy is a genetic thing, or if it's just an anomaly?"

Dink laughed. "Lord knows, if there's an anomaly, it's you."

Kiera studied Dink's face. His laughter didn't ring true. She knew she'd be really upset if she thought she couldn't learn to do the disassemble thing, even though she didn't really want to learn because the whole idea totally terrified her. Still, it was the sense of being kept out of the game everyone else could play.

The door to the lodge swung open. Morgan, Rodie, and Finn walked in with Duran and Bolt right behind them, all wearing huge grins. They headed straight to the buffet counter, grabbed sandwiches and drinks, and then headed directly to the table.

It was already crowded, but everyone scooted around and made room for them. Rodie glanced at the group and her eyes practically glowed. "I saw Morgan do it. He turned into little sparkly stuff and disappeared." She turned and gazed at Morgan, and it was hard for Kiera to stay out of her head, because she was dying to know what put that look on Rodie's face.

The girl obviously had it bad, but Morgan didn't appear to be any better. Kiera felt a small twinge of jealousy. She certainly wasn't interested in Morgan, but she really wanted to experience the feelings the two of them appeared to have for one another. What would it feel like to care that much?

To have those feelings shared, because there was no doubt in her mind—whatever Rodie was feeling, Morgan was in just as deep. She tore her gaze away from the two of them and glanced at her guys. She felt so much for them, but love? How the hell would she ever figure that one out?

This morning, she'd felt an intense connection with Tor, but it was just on the cusp of developing into something more.

They weren't there yet—not in the same emotional place as Rodie and Morgan.

She wondered if she'd ever be, wondered if she'd know love even if it smacked her upside the head. Enough, already. It was almost noon, thank goodness. Time to start her shift in the dream shack where she'd be too busy to dissect her emotions.

Maybe her final shift.

She wasn't sure whether to feel happy, sad, or just flat-out terrified about that.

5

Mac checked out the five huge, very human-appearing men standing shoulder to shoulder in the lodge dining room. Decked out in worn jeans, heavy work boots, dark plaid flannel shirts—which looked much better now that they weren't all wearing the same plaid—and decided this was a lot more than he'd expected.

"You guys look great." He glanced over his shoulder. "Morgan, you said you and Finn need to work on disassembling, so I'll have Cameron show these guys where I want them to stand guard." He turned once again to the Nyrians. "You shouldn't have to do anything but just stand there. I think merely having you present will discourage anyone from trying to cut through the fence. You're all big enough; you'd sure as hell discourage me." He raised his head, looking for Cam. Where the hell was he?

"Anyone know where Cam went? He was here a minute ago."

"I'm here, Mac."

Cam pushed open the door into the lodge. Mir slipped past and held it for him while Cam backed in, hanging on to one end of a huge canvas with Niah holding the other end. They carried it across the dining room and the two of them carefully leaned it against a table about ten feet away.

Frowning, Mac stared at the dark and dramatic painting. This was nothing like Cam's usual mystical, fantastical, dream-like art. He glanced at the one over the fireplace that Cam had done after his first night—a painting of Nyria as the Nyrians remembered their planet. Nyria before the Gar attacked. The work was bright and beautiful, a memory of a world that only existed in the minds of the few remaining Nyrians.

Not this new painting. It was all dark energy and anger, and it spoke of endings, not beginnings. Still, there was something vaguely familiar about the scene. Mac stepped around the Nyrians and walked closer, still frowning. He squatted down in front of the canvas, though this close it was hard to tell exactly what he was looking at. Broad strokes, dark colors, a bright slash here and there. An overall sense of darkness and anger. Of doom.

Finally, Mac shook his head and stood. "I haven't got any idea at all what you've done here." He glanced over his shoulder. The Nyrian men looked anywhere but at the painting. "Aza? Do you know what this is? Bane? Jesat? Any idea?"

Dake was the one who stepped forward and stood beside Mac. He stared at the painting for a long moment with his arms folded tightly against his chest. Obviously, something about the art made him very uncomfortable. Without looking at Mac, he said, "It's the planet you call Mars. The way it looked the last time we were in this solar system. This is a view of that world during the attack." He sighed, glanced away, and then focused on Mac, not the painting. "When the Gar take every-thing from a world, it's done quickly. The people have no time to escape. Nothing survives. Not the smallest microbe, not the largest, strongest creatures. All die. All are utilized, either as energy or, in some cases, as food. We . . ." He glanced over his shoulder at his four companions and then focused again on Mac and took a deep breath. Let it out.

"We power the ship during the process—it takes a lot of energy to plunder a world, so all of us are needed in the engine room at the same time. It's bad enough knowing what our energy is being used for, but we're also forced to watch. To witness the death of entire worlds. Death by order of the Gar. It's meant to teach us fear, so that we will recognize their superior strength. They want us afraid of them."

He lowered his head and looked away, but Mac couldn't take his eyes off the man. Anger built, starting deep inside and forcing its way to the surface. Why hadn't he realized? How could he possibly have missed their reality?

Zianne had told him much the same, but he hadn't thought beyond her fear, her terrible circumstances as a slave. He'd not truly considered what she'd admitted, that the Nyrians had been the power behind the deaths of entire civilizations. Their energy had enabled the destruction of uncounted worlds, had caused unimaginable horror. Rage had him clenching his fists and his jaw when he asked, "Does it work? This method of the Gar's to put fear in the hearts of their captives?"

Dake shook his head. "Your anger is valid. All of us would understand, should you choose not to help us further, but the Gar's orders do not always work the way they want. All they've done is harden our resolve to find a way out, though until now, until you gave us this opportunity, we've been unable to escape. It is a sin against Nyria for us to take our own lives, but we had finally decided that was our only recourse after trying unsuccessfully for so long to find freedom. Many of our people made that choice on their own. They scattered their energy rather than power the Gar ship. In that respect, those of us who remain are cowards. We were not willing to die, which made us complicit in the murder of too many worlds."

He broke eye contact with Mac and stared toward the big windows looking out over the array. "Thank Nyria, many of the worlds were already barren of living forms. Not all worlds support life." He shook his head and sighed before gesturing at Cam's painting. "But too many were like this one. Too many were peopled by sentient beings with well-developed civilizations. We left them as nothing more than empty shells."

Jesat stepped up and put his hand on Dake's shoulder. Ankar, Bane, and Aza joined him, standing on either side of the two. "Dake leaves out an important part of the tale," he said. "We did not act because we were not willing to die uselessly. When we were first captured, the Gar still had engines and power to run their ship without us. Our deaths would have had only a minor impact on them. They would have continued destroying worlds and our deaths would have solved nothing. Now they are totally dependent upon us to run their ships and keep their people alive."

Dake glanced at Jesat and nodded. "What Jesat says is true. Before, if we'd suddenly disappeared, the Gar would have continued on with very little trouble. Now?" His smile sent chills along Mac's spine. "Now, when the last of us leave, the ship will implode and they will die."

"You're sure of this?" Mac realized his gaze had been drawn away from the Nyrians. He couldn't take his eyes off Cam's painting. This was the future that awaited mankind should their plans fail, and yet he was putting all his trust into creatures he didn't even know.

Zianne was different, wasn't she? He loved and trusted her, but what of the rest of the Nyrians? Were they truly as honest, as honorable as she? Could he believe them without doubt? What choice did he have? His own government refused to listen. Someone had to pay attention.

He forced himself to stand, to turn his back on Cam's painting and look at the Nyrians. "Once you're gone, they can't return to their ship's original power source?"

"It's no longer functional." Aza glanced at the others. "Three of us infiltrated their aging power plant. It's been shut down for well over a hundred of your years, so no one noticed when we destroyed components necessary for its function. The last ones capable of repairing the machinery died generations ago. The Gar have grown lazy, their equipment is outmoded, and they are totally dependent upon us."

"I sure hope you're right." Mac stared once again at Cam's disturbing painting. "Because that could just as easily be the earth if things don't go as planned."

"After all the excitement this morning, it's been really quiet." Lizzie stepped aside as Kiera settled herself into the recliner and placed the mesh cap over her dark hair. "I actually napped for a while."

Kiera smiled softly. "Sounds good. I didn't sleep much last night. Too many things to worry about."

Lizzie punched her lightly on the shoulder. "Too many good-looking guys in your bed's more like it." She stared at Kiera and laughed out loud. "Good gods, girl. You're blushing. I didn't know black chicks could blush."

Kiera rolled her head to one side and glared at Lizzie. She held that look for a few seconds and then burst into giggles. "That, my dear, is not a blush. Trust me, because I'm not one bit embarrassed about what I did with my guys. It's heat. Pure heat, just thinking of what went on in my bed last night. It's been nothing but women for me for so long, I forgot what a man could do for a girl." She fanned her fingers in front of her face. "Every single one of those guys is so damned hot."

Lizzie leaned over and gave Kiera a hug. Funny how she'd thought this one was sort of stuck up and not all that friendly when they'd first met. Amazing how first impressions could change. "I hope everything goes okay. Arnec's going to be in that final fight against the Gar, and I know Tor's chosen to stay, too."

"Teev and Sakel aren't back yet, either." Kiera sighed. "I hardly know them, but I can't stop worrying. How can they matter so much to us, so fast?"

"I think it's because they've been in our heads as well as our bodies. They've taken their forms from our minds, which makes them familiar to us. And face it, we've probably been more intimate with these guys than we ever have with any human lovers, male or female. I know I've never been so uninhibited in my life. Not that I'm complaining, mind you!"

Lizzie leaned over and picked up Zianne's tote. The tiny squirrel slept soundly. She'd not moved at all during Lizzie's shift and hadn't awakened when Kiera came into the shack. Poor thing, and poor Mac. She couldn't imagine what he was going through right now. So much riding on their success, and so many things that could go wrong.

"I'm taking Zianne with me," she said. "We've got enough Nyrians here with their soulstones; they should be able to share more energy with her."

"I hope so." Kiera ran her fingers over the squirrel's fluffy tail. "It would be horrible if we managed to save everyone but Zianne. I don't know if Mac could handle that."

"Dink, either. He loves her as much as Mac does." Lizzie took a step toward the door and thought of one more thing. "I guess Morgan's probably not going to be relieving you."

Kiera nodded. "I know. He and Finn should be leaving about then. Can you believe those two? It still seems impossible that they're going to somehow get transported to a spaceship that's on its way to attack the earth. I mean, a week ago I thought aliens were a bunch of hooey." She sucked in a deep breath, slowly let it out, and cocked her head to one side as she looked at Liz. "Remind me to keep an open mind about shit, okay?

Lizzie just laughed at the perplexed look on Kiera's face.

"Anyway," Kiera said, "I imagine they'll leave from here. If Mac asks, tell him I'll stay on duty as long as they need me."

"Okay. We'll probably all end up in here by this afternoon, anyway. I know I want to be as close to the action as I can get. And I'll admit I never thought the idea of aliens was hooey. I always figured there had to be someone out there, but to actually meet them? To be involved in a rescue and a fight against some really scary aliens? Not in this lifetime."

Except it was all much too true. Liz opened the door and a bright shaft of sunlight spilled into the small building. She glanced at the tote she'd slung over her arm to check on the squirrel. Zianne slept on. Then she shot a quick glance over her shoulder at Kiera. "Boggles the mind, ya know? I'll see ya later."

She closed the door behind her and took a deep, controlled breath. The August heat reflected off the rocky ground and shimmered in waves across the plateau. The nights were so clear and cold, it was hard to believe how warm it could get during the day. The smell of burned wood lingered, a reminder just how volatile the forest was this late in the summer.

And just how volatile and dangerous their position had become. She wondered about the guys that had been spotted on the back side of the plateau. Wondered what they really wanted, because no one believed all the crap about it being a religious protest. She didn't think your average religious protester carried rifles with night scopes or tried to cut through chain link fences.

Or set fires on windy days in a dry forest.

She looked around the area once again. There'd been no sign at all of that helicopter from the sheriff's department. Shouldn't they be showing up by now?

Tucking Zianne close against her side, Lizzie headed over to the lodge. That seemed to be where everyone was gathering, and she wondered if she'd missed anything important this morning.

The door into the dining room opened. Mac raised his head as Lizzie stepped into the room with Zianne's tote over her shoulder. "Is she okay?" He was on his feet and halfway across the room before he realized he'd even moved. Damn. Exhaustion was taking its toll. No sleep at all last night, and there was too much on his mind today.

"She's fine." Liz walked right past him and set the bag on the table. "I just thought that since we've got so many Nyrians here with soulstones, maybe they'd be able set up a schedule to give her power on a regular basis. It might keep her going longer, at least until we get her soulstone."

Why hadn't he thought of that? Mac shook his head. "Makes sense. Thank you for thinking of her. I . . ." He swept his hand over his eyes. Corin and Satza, two women Rodie had helped to gain their human forms, sort of eased Mac out of the way.

Both were beautiful, but Corin had chosen a petite, almost boyish frame and she had short, dark red spiky hair that set her apart from most of the other women who'd chosen a more traditional look. Satza was just the opposite of Corin—a voluptuous earth mother if he could call her that, with thick brown hair falling in loose curls to her waist and brilliant blue eyes. Satza picked up the tote and cradled it in her arms.

Corin placed a restraining hand on Mac's arm when he automatically reached for the tote. "We have our soulstones and our energy is strong. Let us take Zianne. We can give her a continuous feed, keep the flow of energy constant so that her system isn't jolted with too much at once. I think it will help her keep this form longer, at least until she has her own soulstone once again."

Mac raised his head and looked into Corin's dark brown eyes. After a moment, he nodded, but it killed him to step away. He hated giving up control, turning Zianne over to someone he didn't know, but they knew her even better than he could. They'd been with her for her entire life. "Do you need a quiet room? Someplace where you can rest?"

Staring at the small creature in the bag in her arms, Satza nodded. "That would be wonderful." She sighed. "This is all so difficult—coming to this new world, not knowing if the rest of us will survive, how this will end. As beings of energy, we don't actually eat or sleep, but this body requires food and rest." She shook her head and her blue eyes glistened with tears. "Corin and I were among the last to visit because we were afraid."

Corin leaned against Satza's arm, staring at Zianne. "I don't know about you, Satza, but I am still afraid. At least, under the Gar, we knew what to expect. It was horrible, but we learned to cope, to wall off our feelings. Here..." She stopped and glanced around the large dining room. "We have no idea what to expect, what our welcome will be."

Satza shook her head. "Our work for the Gar was wrong, no matter that we were captives. We know it was wrong, but we lied to ourselves, to one another. We told ourselves that our world was gone, that we didn't care what happened to others."

"But we do care," Corin said. "I hope Nyria will find it in her heart to forgive us." She straightened and looked directly at Mac. "If you have a quiet room, we would like to take Zianne there. We'll lie down on either side of her and let our energy drift over the squirrel's body. It's a slow and easy way to share. I promise we will do only good."

Mac nodded and led the two women toward the stairs. The lodge had been the first building, designed with rooms for the workers who stayed on site while the rest of the buildings were under construction and the satellite dishes assembled. There was more than enough room for all the Nyrians, as long as they didn't mind sharing.

He opened the door on a room down the hall from his. It had a single large bed, a bathroom, and closet, but not much else. "Will this be okay?"

The women walked in, wide-eyed. "It's beautiful. So big. And look!" Corin rushed to the window and lifted the shades. Mac stepped up and showed her how to raise them. "We can see outside. Look, Satza. Mountains and trees . . ."

"And blue sky and sunshine. I remember sunshine on Nyria. And growing plants." Satza let out a huge sigh. "So long ago. Leave the shades open, Corin. We can look outside from the bed."

She set Zianne's tote down in the middle of the king-sized bed and lay down beside her. Corin slowly pulled herself away from the window and stretched out on the opposite side.

Mac quietly left the room, shutting the door behind him. He hadn't really thought much about what the Nyrians were going through. He'd been so caught up in worry about Zianne, about Finn and Morgan, and the idiots trying to come through the fence that he'd essentially put the Nyrians and their personal issues out of his mind. They had every right to be terrified. What did they know of this new world they'd suddenly aligned themselves with?

He heard his cell phone ring and slapped his back pocket. Shit. The damned thing was still in his room on the charger. He did a quick one-eighty and reached his door, threw it open, and grabbed the phone off the charger on the bedside table.

The number was blocked. He answered anyway. "Mac Dugan here. General Adams?" Now why the hell was the Pentagon calling him? Last time they'd spoken, he'd essentially been not too politely shown the door.

But as he listened to the general, Mac realized that if he'd been a lesser man, he might actually be smiling. But he wasn't.

He couldn't, because it appeared the Gar's ship had been spotted by more than one amateur astronomer, and the shit had already hit the fan. By the time he hung up the phone, neither Mac nor the general were entirely satisfied with the result of their conversation.

"Dink? How long before you can get a news crew up here?" Mac planted his palms on the table and focused on his ace in the hole. If anyone could take this public and do it right, it was Nils Dinkemann.

"It'll take a few hours to get a full crew. Sacramento's got a chopper and everything we need. What's happened?"

"I just heard from the Pentagon. They've finally decided I'm not nuts after all. I haven't had the news on or even been online, but it appears that more than one amateur astronomer has spotted the Gar ship. They've just come around the far side of the moon and the ship is huge—big enough that stations all over the world are running some pretty clear pictures."

"Holy shit." Dink was up and heading for the flat-screen TV on the dining room wall, but Rodie was already there, turning the thing on and finding a twenty-four-hour news channel.

"I'll be damned." Mac stared at the grainy image on the screen. The distance was so great that the photos lacked a lot of definition, but there was no denying they were looking at some kind of vessel, that it was obviously directed by sentient creatures, and that the cat was, quite literally, out of the bag.

"What's the Pentagon's take? Have you heard from the secretary of defense or the White House?" Dink stared at the screen as he fired questions at Mac.

"Not yet. Just the general so far. He says the first reaction from the population as a whole is that it's real exciting stuff—a chance to meet some authentic aliens. People with SETI are over the moon, but I told General Adams that it isn't quite like that. I also told him exactly what we know and what the threat is, that we're planning a counterattack with the Nyrians' help, though I didn't give him the details. He's going to check in with the secretary of defense and the president and get back to me, but essentially he wants us ready to go public with the Nyrians' plight, the planned rescue, the whole thing. Too many people know about the ship to keep it secret."

"He's leaving us in charge?" Dink turned away from the screen and frowned at Mac. "You're telling me that General Arthur Alfonse Adams, the same guy who told you that you needed a good psychiatrist, is now turning the defense of the entire world over to you?"

Mac chuckled. "I think he's in shock, especially since everything is happening exactly as I said it would. I explained that the attack has to come tonight or we're screwed, that if we wait, the ship will be too close to Earth's atmosphere to blow the thing without a whole lot of collateral damage. Now that he's seen how big the sucker is, he's inclined to believe me."

"Any chance of them getting some troops here to stop your neighbor? Bane checked in while you were gone and said they appear to be gathering on the downside of the plateau. He needs to know if you want him to stop them."

Mac shook his head. "Not until they trespass. We go after them on Bart Roberts's property and we're screwed."

"Even now, with the government involved? Don't you think they'd want you to do everything in your power to secure a successful mission?" Dink turned and stared at Mac with one eyebrow cocked, just the way he'd perfected it for the camera. "We're talking about an attack on the world, Mac, not merely something that's got a group of religious nuts up in arms." He frowned. "You sure the religious angle is all that's behind them?"

Mac shook his head. He hadn't believed that for quite some time, and definitely not anymore. "Not after the research Morgan did—the religious protest is just a cover. Morgan did some poking around the Internet and discovered that Bart Roberts, the guy who's spearheading all the protests, was Patrick Randle's brother. Randle's the guy who almost gutted you that night in '92. Bart must have seen Zianne turn into energy when she dragged Randle out of my apartment and tossed him over the balcony. Not only did she kill his brother, she turned into something impossible in order to do it. I think he's after Zianne, whether to avenge his brother's death or because he figures she's an alien and he's totally xenophobic. For whatever reason, he's been planning this for twenty years."

"Well that certainly changes things. Have you thought of calling the Pentagon back, requesting a little help here?" Dink ran his fingers through his hair before leveling a sharp eye on Mac. "Where the hell is the sheriff? Didn't he agree to provide air support?"

"He did, Dink. I'll check." Mac dialed the number for the sheriff's cell and left a message. "No answer. And as far as the government stepping in to help, there's really no provision for getting troops up here. No proof of wrongdoing. Nothing but the word of a guy who was labeled a crackpot not more than a few weeks ago. Adams might believe me, but he's really the only one I've ever confided any of this story to. He's going to have a hell of a job convincing the Department of Defense and the president that I've gone from being a total nutcase to actually knowing what I'm talking about."

"So you want me to take it public, get the people behind us?"

Mac nodded. "Pretty much. I thought we'd have more time, that once we made contact, we'd have months, or at the very least, weeks, not hours, to figure out how to deal with freeing the Nyrians. I knew the Gar were dangerous, but Zianne said they were also very systematic in their process of stripping planets. Meticulous about determining risk. Sometimes they'd spend years studying a planet before actually siphoning off the atmosphere and then going for other resources. They've only been here a few months."

"Maybe it's been a long time since they've found a planet worth plundering," Dink said. "Could be they're growing short of stuff they need to keep their ship alive."

"Could be. You might want to talk to more of the Nyrians, get as much background as you can so you're ready when the news crew shows up. We have to break this in such a way that there is absolutely no sympathy for the Gar."

Dink folded his arms across his chest. "That shouldn't be all that difficult. How do you sympathize with a race of beings intent on the destruction or enslavement of everyone else they meet?"

"Good point." Mac glanced around the dining hall. Liz and two women whose names Mac hadn't caught sat by the window. Rodie had taken a seat near them. "Rodie? Where is everyone?"

"Cam's got Mir and Niah resting in his cabin. He's down at the fence line with Bane and his guys and Ralph and the security team. I just got all five of Morgan's women settled in a couple of the extra rooms upstairs. Tara's with Morgan, Finn, Bolt, and Duran. She's helping the guys with their disassembling. Disincorporating. Whatever." She gave an exaggerated shudder. "I can't watch. It scares the crap out of me, thinking something could go wrong."

"I know." Mac glanced at Dink. "Okay. Here's what we need to do. See if you can get a news crew up here ASAP. Promise them an exclusive, and let 'em know we've got aliens here willing to help us fight the ship that's headed our way. Rodie, how were Morgan and Finn doing with their . . . shit. I hate to even say disassembling or disincorporating. It just sounds bad."

She gave him a thumbs-up and he nodded.

"Good. Dink, why don't you start with Liz's two women, find out anything they can tell you, especially anything that makes them look even more sympathetic. Maybe you can use Cam's paintings to illustrate things."

"Like the destruction of the Nyrian's planet? What turned Mars into a dead, red planet? Gotcha."

"I knew you would. Publicity is all yours. I'm going down to the fence line to see how things are looking. I think it's about time we tell Meg and Ralph and the rest of the crew exactly what they've gotten themselves into." He glanced at the big double doors to the kitchen. "Meg first."

Dink reached for the phone as Mac spun around and headed for the kitchen. Meg was in there, frying up chicken for tonight's dinner. She raised her head and stared at him, and he wished he knew what she was thinking. He'd always liked Meg. She and Ralph were close to retirement age—in their early sixties—but both of them had way too much energy and drive to sit back and watch the world go by.

Using tongs, Meg lifted a perfectly browned chicken thigh out of the pan of hot grease and carefully added more pieces. Once it was filled, she raised her head and focused on Mac. "I hope you're going to tell me what's going on up here, Mac Dugan." She wiped her hands on a towel and planted them on her hips. "I've tried really hard not to ask questions, but all of a sudden we've got a huge crowd of people who just appeared out of nowhere. People who don't seem to know a lot of things a normal person would know."

"I figured you'd probably guessed something was up." He leaned against the counter and crossed his arms over his chest. "Smells awfully good in here."

Meg surprised him with a big smile. "Of course it does. Don't change the subject." She checked the pan filled with sizzling pieces of chicken and covered them with a mesh lid to catch the spattering grease. "I take it those satellite dishes worked, then? We all figured you were using them to talk to aliens, just like that SETI project down in Hat Creek. Except yours worked and his didn't. Am I right?"

Mac just nodded his head. He knew there'd been a lot of conjecture going on among the staff members, and they were all intelligent enough to figure out something weird was taking place. "That you are. And, yes, all of those new faces belong to people called Nyrians. They're peaceful, obviously intelligent, and we're helping them escape from some aliens who aren't. Have you had the news on at all today?"

Meg just shook her head, but he could feel her excitement even though she wasn't the least bit telepathic.

"Well, if you had, you'd know that astronomers have spotted a large spaceship headed this way. They don't know what we know, so right now everyone is really excited about meeting aliens. Unfortunately, these particular aliens intend to steal just about everything that keeps our planet and everyone on it alive."

Meg gasped, but Mac shook his head. "Don't worry. I'm telling you this so you'll understand why we're not planning to greet them with open arms. Our goal is to stop them from getting close to us. They've held the Nyrians captive as slaves for a long time, but we think we know a way to stop them."

"Does Ralph know what's going on?"

"Your husband's pretty sharp, Meg. I think he has a good idea. He's working with a team of security guys he just met today—they're all Nyrians. I'm headed down to the fence line so I can officially let everyone know all the details. There will be reporters showing up before too long, and hopefully the rest of the Nyrians."

"That little squirrel is special. She's not really a squirrel, is she? Is she one of them?"

Mac bowed his head and closed his eyes for a moment. Damn. So much could go wrong. "Yes, Meg. She's one of them, and she really is a squirrel, but the squirrel's hosting the consciousness and energy of one of the Nyrians. She's growing weaker by the hour. In fact, she's dying, but she's the whole reason I built this array, the entire reason we're all here. Say a prayer for her, Meg. I'm not sure how I'll handle it if we save everyone but the woman I love."

He turned away but Meg stepped up and grabbed his arm. "I'll fix a lot of extra food for tonight, Mac. You'll want to feed all these folks once you get 'em off that ship. And you will get them all off. I have faith in you. And you'll save your girl, too."

"Thanks, Meg. I hope you're right."

"What's her name?" She looked at him with twinkling eyes.

"Zianne. Her name's Zianne."

"I like that. I sure hope she knows what a treasure she's getting with you, Mac Dugan." She patted his cheek.

Meg was only about fifteen years older than he was, but she'd been trying to mother Mac since the day he'd hired Ralph and this wife of his who could cook like a five-star chef and keep everything running like clockwork. At first it had really bugged him. Right now he welcomed her easy warmth and honest concern.

"Thanks, Meg. I'll have to tell Zianne you said that." He grabbed her hand, kissed her fingertips, and headed back to the dining room.

Exhaustion beat at him from all directions, but there was no time to sleep. Not even to think about sleeping. He wondered how Corin and Satza were doing, if they'd been able to help Zianne, but there was no one else right now and he had to trust them.

He walked through the dining area. Dink was on the phone, speaking quietly but with obvious intent, and Mac had no doubt he'd have his news crew sooner rather than later. Rodie and Liz and the two Nyrian women sat on the couch beside him, all of them sipping iced tea. Rodie and Liz looked wound tight, but the two Nyrians appeared to be relaxed and ready to talk. He hoped like hell Dink got the information he needed to make this story work.

He waved at them on his way outside, then paused on the deck, blinking against the glare of the afternoon sun. He checked his watch, shocked to discover it was almost two. In just about three more hours, if all worked according to plan, Finn, Morgan, Bolt, and Duran would all be on the Gar ship.

He wished he didn't have this damned knot in his gut. Wished it was already tomorrow and the job was done, the soulstones recovered, and all the Nyrians safe. He wanted Zianne in his arms, Dink curled up beside them, and his world back in order again.

Sounded great. Sounded fucking impossible.

He climbed into one of the little four-wheeler ATVs and pointed the thing due east to the fence line where Bart Roberts was creating just one more problem for them to deal with. At least Roberts was something solid and familiar. Something Mac could focus his anger on.

Maybe, if he was lucky, he'd even get in a punch or two.

6

Finn went deep inside his mind, found the switch, and flipped it. His body disappeared and he was suddenly nothing more than a swirl of energy and spinning molecules. Morgan made the change as well. Once again they tried to move about without their Nyrian hosts. They needed the ability to travel under their own power in case anything happened to either Duran or Bolt, but so far, they'd had trouble directing their molecular parts in any particular direction without help from the Nyrians.

Morgan had managed a short move across the room the first time he disassembled, but he had no idea how he'd done it, couldn't seem to repeat it, or explain it to Finn. Duran and Bolt—even Tara—had been unable to describe the process. They couldn't find the right words in a language still new to them, but that was the only language Finn and Morgan understood. As irritated as Finn was over his inability to learn something that, when compared to turning himself into a cloud of molecules without a corporate body seemed so damned simple, he had to keep reminding himself that the Nyrians were doing an amazing job just to be able to function as humans and speak a language they were still learning.

Still, there had to be a way. Somehow . . .

This is so damned frustrating.

Obviously, Morgan agreed with Finn's take on the matter. *I know. I can hover in one spot, but I can't go anywhere.*

Finn watched the three Nyrians, sitting together on the couch—Tara and Duran holding hands, Bolt beside them, all staring at the spot where the two humans now spun in what seemed to be nothing more than molecular disarray. *What's even more frustrating is that we can't communicate with them when we're like this and they're solid.*

Morgan's thoughts slipped easily into Finn's mind. *Bolt said it's the time element. We're moving so much faster that our thoughts don't register in their human minds.*

It shouldn't be this hard, Morgan. I thought shifting would be tough. It's simple compared to trying to move! Duran said I should be able to think myself somewhere, and just go there.

I've been trying. Obviously it's not working.

That was definitely a mental snort from Morgan.

Try someplace you've been already.

Made sense to Finn. So why wasn't he going into the bedroom? Maybe somewhere he'd been in this form? *The fence line?*

That's pretty ambitious. Maybe you should . . .

Morgan's suggestion disappeared as the ground sped by beneath Finn. Holy shit! He was moving, zipping over the ground so damned fast that everything was a complete blur beneath him until he came to an abrupt stop. The fence line. Go figure. He looked ahead and saw men standing guard at the edge of the plateau.

Now that he'd done it, moving wasn't nearly as complicated as he'd been trying to make it, so he moved a bit closer and stopped instantly when he thought of stopping. He felt like an idiot, but that's what happened when you tried to overthink the simple stuff. Think of a place, go there. Think of stopping, stop. What could be easier?

Curious, he flashed beyond the fence and slipped through the heavy undergrowth along the steep hillside.

He hadn't been here before but he was going where he wanted to go. How? He had no idea, but that didn't really matter as long as it worked, because they were supposed to be heading for the Gar ship in about three more hours.

He stopped and hovered over a level spot behind a wall of boulders and brush. The small clearing was filled with heavily armed men dressed in camo gear, at least a dozen of them sitting around as if they were waiting for something to happen. A few guards were posted, but they weren't going anywhere. Just waiting.

But why? What were they planning? He couldn't hear them like this, so he slipped behind a large boulder and regained his human form. *Shit, yes!* He was dressed! At least he'd gotten that part of the training right.

Moving quietly, Finn crept as close as he could. The men's voices were still hard to understand, but he pressed close against the warm boulder and listened. They were talking about the number of new guards, the fact that their leader had said the site would be poorly defended but had a lot more guards than any of them had been led to believe.

That meant the Nyrians in human form had these idiots fooled, which was a good thing. Maybe it would keep them on their side of the fence until he and Morgan finished tonight's mission.

For a brief moment, Finn actually began to relax.

"Hey! Who the hell are you?"

Shit! Finn spun around as two men burst through the brush about ten yards away with weapons drawn. Big weapons—automatic rifles of some kind—and they were pointed right at him. He dove into the thick tangle of bitterbrush growing beside the boulder as the camp erupted into action. Bullets cut through the leaves, bounced off rocks, and shattered a thick branch on a juniper tree next to his face. Shards of splintered bark sprayed him as he frantically reached for that mental switch.

Something punched into his left leg and spun him around. Before he hit the ground, a bolt of pure fire crossed over his shoulders. Adrenaline poured into his system and Finn managed to find the damned switch in his brain and flip the blasted thing.

He was aware of blood spraying in a fine mist, swirling around him as everything else went totally still. He didn't take time to see what else was going on. Instead, he pictured the peace and quiet of his cabin and thought himself home.

Morgan shifted back to his human self. Where the hell was Finn? One minute they'd been communicating just fine and then the damned guy just disappeared. He hoped like hell Finn was out there traveling around and could tell him how it was done.

"Where's Finn?" Duran leapt to his feet and headed for the door with Bolt and Tara right behind him.

"I was hoping you'd know." Morgan caught his bearings and stepped outside with the three Nyrians. The afternoon was warm, the air redolent with the aromatic scent of sage and sun-warmed rock. The sky shimmered clear and blue and, other than a couple of turkey vultures circling high, was totally empty.

There was absolutely no sign of Finnegan O'Toole.

"You both made the shift perfectly." Duran glanced over at Morgan. "Were you able to move this time?"

"I didn't but I have a feeling that Finn might have figured it out." Where the hell was he?

Gunshots echoed off the surrounding hills. The distant sound of men shouting. More gunshots. Duran flashed out of sight. Tara screamed. Bolt grabbed Morgan's arm. "What is that?"

"Gunshots. Weapons. The idiots on the down side of the plateau must be shooting at someone." Good lord, he hoped Rodie was okay. He couldn't recall if she'd planned to go down to the fence line or not, but damn it all, that was the last thing Finn had said. *Fence line.*

He heard a soft moan inside the cabin. Finn! Morgan shoved past Bolt and reached Finn as the man toppled to the ground. Blood soaked the denim covering his left leg and was already staining the wood floor. He was bleeding just as heavily from a long, narrow slice across his shoulders.

"What the hell happened to you?" Kneeling beside Finn, Morgan checked his injuries. Scratches on his face and neck, probably from brush or possibly ricochets, a deep furrow across his shoulders where it looked as if he'd been grazed by a bullet, and what appeared to be a serious gunshot wound in his left calf, just below the back of his knee.

There was no sign the bullet had gone through.

"Fuck. Fuck this. Damn it all to hell, Morgan." Finn raised his head and stared at Morgan, and there were tears in his eyes. "I didn't intend to get shot. We need to get this taken care of. We're scheduled to leave in . . ."

Morgan shook his head. "You're not going anywhere, Finn. Not with injuries like this. We need to deal with that wound in your leg. It's bleeding like crazy. You need a doctor."

"I can help." Bolt knelt beside Finn and gently placed his hand on Finn's forehead. "Lie back. Be still. I'll heal what I can."

He shimmered into pure energy and disappeared inside Finn, who lay back with his eyes shut. Duran suddenly appeared next to Morgan. "Is he badly hurt?"

Morgan shook his head. "He's been shot. Bolt went in to fix things. I know Zianne did this for that news guy a long time ago, though I don't think there was a bullet involved."

Duran smiled and shook his head. "No, but a knife wound isn't an easy fix, either."

Tara knelt beside Duran and held Finn's hand. The two of them seemed to be praying, and Morgan wasn't sure if that was a good or bad sign. He heard footsteps behind him and glanced over his shoulder as Rodie raced into the room. Her wild-eyed gaze flew to Morgan.

"You just popped into my head. I wasn't sure what was going on—just a strong sense that you needed me. What happened to Finn?"

Morgan shook his head. "I don't know for sure. We were practicing moving around while in energy form and he took off. Next thing I know, I'm hearing gunshots, and he shows up bleeding like a stuck pig."

"Where's Bolt?" She sat beside Finn with her legs crossed and took his limp hand in hers.

"Bolt's inside Finn. He's repairing damage from the inside."

"Oh."

They all heard a soft *plop* as a bullet landed on the floor beside Finn's leg. Duran reached for the slug and handed it to Morgan. "It's good that Bolt has gotten the projectile out. That will help Finnegan heal."

Morgan turned the bloody lump of metal over in his fingers. "That's a damned big shell. It should have gone clear through, unless it lodged in the bone."

Finn moaned. His body stiffened, and then relaxed. Morgan immediately placed his fingers against the big artery in Finn's neck. His pulse was rapid, but strong and steady. Sighing with relief, Morgan glanced at Rodie. "Shit. I thought something worse had happened."

Duran stroked Finn's forehead. "I imagine Bolt is repairing

the bones in his leg. The bullet might have shattered them. He has probably passed out from the pain. Healing serious injuries in corporeal bodies this quickly is not a painless process."

Tara held tightly to Finn's other hand. She'd not said a word, but tears ran slowly down her cheeks. "He is in much pain. I'm in his mind and doing my best to take him away from what Bolt is doing for him." She stared at Duran for a long moment and then focused on Rodie. "He may still be able to help with the rescue, but in case he isn't strong enough, would you be able to go?"

"Me?" Rodie squeaked, and stared at Tara.

Tara nodded. "I know it's asking a lot, but we can't expect Morgan to do this on his own, and we need another human. The Gar weapons can disrupt our Nyrian energy fields, no matter what form we take."

"Rodie's not going on that ship." Morgan glared at Tara. "We'll get Mac. Or Cameron. Anyone else but Rodie. It's too dangerous."

"Excuse me?"

Rodie stared at Morgan like she might want to take his head off. "Did I actually hear you answering for me?" She shook her head and smiled at Tara. "All I need is for someone to show me what to do. I'm perfectly willing to go." Turning back to Morgan, she gave him a look that should have left him dodging daggers. "I will admit I was surprised when you asked me, Tara, but I'm more than capable, and I'm sure Morgan can teach me how to make the shift."

Finn moaned, his eyes flickered and slowly opened. Morgan realized that somehow, during the time he'd been sticking his foot in his mouth, Bolt had reappeared beside Finn and there was no longer any sign of blood on either Finn's shoulders or his leg.

Morgan raised his head and stared at Bolt. "How the hell did you do that?"

"I go inside and draw the blood back in, remove impurities so it can be replaced, and also repair and replace the tissue and bone cells so I can put them back where they belong. Because I'm in my energy form, what would normally take hours is done fairly quickly, at least in your perception. That's all." Bolt shrugged.

That's all. Crap. And that simple shrug. Such a human gesture from someone so obviously not human, but whatever he'd done must have worked. Finn was blinking his eyes and looking around at everyone staring back at him. He focused on Morgan. "What the shit just happened?"

Morgan shook his head. "I was going to ask you the same thing."

Finn struggled to sit up. Before Morgan could move to help him, both Tara and Duran were supporting his back and then standing with him. Leaning heavily on the Nyrians, Finn stood there a minute and stared at his leg, at the neat hole in the denim just beneath the back of his knee. He raised his head and stared at Duran. "Did you . . . ?"

Duran smiled at Bolt. "It was Bolt. He's a more accomplished healer than either Tara or I. Are you all right?"

Finn stepped away from their support, tested his weight on his left leg, and frowned just as his knee buckled. Tara caught him, and with Duran's support, they got him to the couch.

"You must give yourself time." Tara stood over him, hands planted on her hips, green eyes flashing, and lips firm. "What Bolt has done repaired the physical damage but it does not replace the energy lost or immediately heal the trauma to your system. You must rest!"

Bolt slapped Finn's shoulder. "I'm good, but not a miracle worker. Give yourself some time to get your strength back." He winked at Tara. "Or suffer the wrath of Tara."

Morgan felt as if he'd fallen down the proverbial rabbit hole. Tara could have been any human woman, and Bolt's comment was right out of American slang. How the hell did they do that?

Bolt raised his head. "We've mined the thoughts of everyone we've come in contact with, knowing we must assimilate into your world if we're to succeed. We are all a combination of everyone here, though what we say and do will always be colored by our own personalities." He smiled affectionately at Tara. "This one has always been bossy. Right, Duran?"

Duran held his hands up. "I'm not going there. I value my life too much, but, Finn, Tara is right. Give yourself time."

Finn closed his eyes and bowed his head. "I can't stand this. How much time?"

Duran plopped down on the couch beside him. "A couple of hours and a good meal. You might be ready to go by the time we return to the ship, but we'll teach Rodie what we can, just in case. Are you okay with that?"

This time, Finn looked at Morgan. "What about you, Morgan?"

"Excuse me?" This time, Rodie glared at Finn. Morgan kept his mouth shut.

Finn took her hand in his. "Rodie, if Morgan's more afraid for your safety than he is for his own, he could end up making mistakes. Screwing up the whole operation. I need to know he'll be okay with you there. I know I'd be a wreck if you were mine."

She took a deep breath and stared at Morgan. He felt the questions in her eyes, the attempt to understand the depth of feelings even Morgan wasn't sure of. After a brief moment, she looked away.

"I don't belong to anyone, Finn. I care very much for Morgan, but my feelings won't get in the way of doing whatever job I'm supposed to do." She glanced at Morgan once again. "And I doubt Morgan's feelings for me would interfere, either. Right, Morgan?"

Crap. Was this a test? Did it matter? He'd probably fail no matter how he answered, so he gave her the truth. "You're your own woman, Rodie. I think you can do anything you put your mind to. I think I can, too, though I might have to work at it. We can do this, no matter what our relationship—or lack thereof—might be."

She gave an affirmative jerk to her head. "Fine. We're okay, then. I want to know whatever you've learned. That way I'll be ready. And, Finn, you should probably get over to the lodge as soon as you can and fill up on some of Meg's sandwiches. She's keeping the counter loaded with food so we can grab stuff when we have the chance. The entire staff is aware of what's going on now, and they're doing their best to help Mac in any way they can."

Morgan stood and reached for Rodie's hand. "Let's go over to my cabin where it's quiet. Bolt? Do you think I can teach Rodie on my own, or should you come with us?"

"You start. I'm going to help Finn to the lodge as I need to feed this body as well. Healing takes a great deal of energy. I'll come to your cabin once I've eaten."

"Good." Giving Rodie a gentle tug, Morgan headed toward the door. It was almost two thirty. Damn but he hoped Finn was strong enough to go in a couple of hours. Morgan knew he was so full of shit. No way in hell was he ready to let Rodie board the Gar ship.

"Okay. So how do we do this?" Rodie sat cross-legged in the middle of Morgan's bed. He lounged shirtless and shoeless against the headboard, looking so damned sexy she had trouble focusing on anything beyond the washboard abs and broad shoulders, the way that dark little happy trail disappeared beneath the waistband of his snug jeans. She'd much rather be following that furry little trail than the one she was currently pursuing.

Morgan huffed out a big breath and focused on her. "With Duran and Bolt, we used sex to allow them into a part of my mind I hadn't been able to access before. They tried, but it didn't work until they brought you in, which is why I think you and I can probably do this on our own."

"Okay." That fit her plans. She liked the idea of just her and Morgan. She leaned forward and reached for the snap on his jeans.

He caught her wrist in his hand. She raised her head and looked into his eyes, but she couldn't read anything in his expression. It was as if he'd shut down.

Shut down and shut her out.

"I don't want to do this, damn it." He let out a deep breath.

Rodie didn't move, though it was awkward, leaning forward with her wrist tightly clasped in his strong hand. She glanced down and concentrated on the way his long fingers wrapped entirely around her arm. He was bigger, stronger, and 100 percent male, but she wasn't at all afraid of him. He'd never hurt her, but by god, he was going to help her whether he wanted to or not.

She raised her head and stared into those dark, enigmatic eyes. "You said you would."

"I know. And I will. I just want you to know I don't like it." He scowled at her.

She burst out laughing. "Duh. That's more than obvious. Morgan? I'm not an idiot. I know this is dangerous, but like you, I believe in the Nyrians. I believe they need our help and that if we don't give it, the Gar will have won, even if the Nyrians stop them on their own and the Gar all die. We can't let them have even one more innocent life, and if my going aboard that ship helps save the remaining slaves on board, even if I don't make it, then it's worth it."

He snarled and released her wrist. She grabbed his hand and held on tightly when he tried to tug loose. "Morgan, just because I'm a woman doesn't mean I'm not brave. It doesn't mean I don't care as deeply, or feel as much, or understand the meaning of sacrifice. I know it's your nature to protect those weaker, but who's to say I don't have my own strengths? That maybe I can bring something to this mission that would be missing with just you and Finn."

Morgan just glared at her for a minute. Then his lips curved up in a sexy grin and his eyes twinkled. He tugged her close and kissed the end of her nose. Sputtering, Rodie pulled away.

"What's that supposed to mean?"

He laughed. "Just thinking of that video I saw on YouTube; the one of you chasing those three naked cretins down the hallway in your apartment building, firing your Taser. I've got to quit underestimating your abilities."

Rodie slapped her forehead with her palm. "Will I *never* live that down?" Finding her boyfriend in her bed, with not only another woman but another man, too, had been bad enough. Chasing all of them stark naked and screaming bloody murder down the hall, armed with her Taser, had felt wonderful—until it all showed up on YouTube in glorious high-def color.

Her neighbor and his smartphone had done an amazing job filming what was probably not her brightest moment. But, it had made Morgan laugh, and Rodie, too, now that she thought of it. "I got the ex right in his skinny ass with both darts," she said. "He went down like a ton of bricks, peed all over himself, and was still twitching when I pulled the leads free and went back to my apartment."

"You mean you just left him there?"

"I did." She chuckled and actually hugged herself. That had felt so good, watching that jerk go down. "He screamed like a little girl when I zapped him. The others kept running but they must have come back and gotten him, because when I looked out a few minutes later, he was gone."

"He didn't file charges?"

She shook her head. She'd worried about it for a while, but then she realized that the apartment was in her name and she could charge him with trespassing if she wanted. He must have figured it out, because he'd stayed away. "I boxed up his things and left them in the hallway, sent him a message on Facebook to pick up his shit, and then unfriended him. His stuff was gone within an hour and I changed the locks. Done deal."

"I think the Gar should run in fear." He wrapped his big hands around her neck and tugged her close. Kissed her with such tenderness that her breath literally caught in her lungs.

So, who needs to breathe? She wasn't sure how it happened, but somehow she was lying across Morgan's thighs, curled against the deliciously solid wall of his warm chest, and his lips were giving a new meaning to the description of a kiss.

Good lord, but she could kiss this man forever. His lips were soft, then hard, then sliding over hers with the barest brush of sensation. His tongue swept across hers and then tickled the sensitive roof of her mouth and she felt her entire body drawing up close and tight against him.

The thick ridge of his erection brushed against her hip, and she sucked in her belly against the slide of his fingers slipping beneath the waistband on her yoga pants. She'd skipped wearing either a bra or panties this morning, and right now she was damned thankful she'd been in such a hurry that she hadn't gotten around to putting any on.

It was so easy to let Morgan take control, so easy to open to him and follow where he led, but wasn't this supposed to be about showing him how strong she was? How formidable she could be if they needed her to go on board the Gar ship?

Without breaking their kiss, Rodie shifted until she was straddling Morgan's hips. His hands slid up and down her back, sliding easily beneath her loose crop top while she reached for the fly of his jeans, unbuttoned the metal button at the waist, and slowly pulled the zipper down.

The pressure of his erection swelling against his zipper forced the fly open. She smiled against his lips when she noticed he'd skipped wearing boxers this morning. How convenient was that? Both of them so obviously thinking alike. She slipped her hand through the opening in his jeans and lifted the heavy weight of his erection free, loving the sound of his groan against her mouth as she wrapped her fingers around his thick shaft. His cock filled her hands, hard, hot, and damp with perspiration, and yet his skin felt smooth as silk. Such an incongruity, that satiny skin over a shaft so hard and strong.

Resting his full length across the palm of her hand, she slipped her other hand beneath to cup the firm weight of his testicles. He ripped his mouth from hers, sucking in a deep breath as she fondled the heavy orbs in her hand, running her middle finger back along his perineum while squeezing his shaft in a slow and steady rhythm.

"Crap, Rodie." Air whistled between his lips. "You're trying to kill me, aren't you?"

"I can't. You're wearing too many clothes." She shot him a cocky grin as she leaned forward and ran her tongue across the bulbous crown, dipping into the tiny slit to taste the salty drops she found. Morgan jerked. She barely heard the whispered, "Damn," as he sucked in another sharp breath. She breathed deep, inhaling the clean, male smell of him, the scent she would always associate with Morgan.

"Okay. You win." He lifted Rodie off and tumbled her to the bed beside him. Then he shoved his pants down over his feet while she tugged the crop top off and removed her stretchy pants.

Naked, she knelt on the bed in front of him and lifted her breasts in her hands. She'd never done anything like this before, but somehow, over the past few days, she'd begun to see herself as a more sensual woman. Whether it was Morgan or Bolt or just being here where sex was so much a part of every single thing they did, Rodie wasn't sure.

But she knew she liked this. Loved it, actually. Loved the light in Morgan's eyes as he focused on her beaded nipples. Loved the way he reached for her. That possessive glitter in his eyes, so determined, and with so much need that it washed over her, a psychic storm of almost overwhelming desire.

He leaned forward and took first one nipple and then the other between his lips. She felt the sharp edges of his teeth, the flat lick of his tongue, the hot brush of his breath against her skin. Opening her mind to his, she fell into a maelstrom of need and desire, both Morgan's and hers. He lifted her, turned her on the bed until she lay with her head on the pillow, and he knelt between her knees.

Then he crawled forward until the thick head of his penis rested against her swollen lips, teasing her but not entering. He pressed forward just a fraction of an inch and she whimpered. Reaching behind her, Rodie clung to the rungs of the headboard, arching her hips closer.

"You have to want me, Rodie." The harsh sound of his voice told her just how much Morgan wanted her. She heard the need in his words, felt the push of his desire in every heated breath. "You have to want me so desperately," he said. "So completely, that you're going to open your mind, your heart, and your soul to me. You're going to let me in, so deep inside your mind that I can show you how to make the shift."

"I'm not keeping you out, damn it!" She hadn't meant to snarl at him, but her vaginal muscles were clenching at nothing and her entire body ached with need.

Morgan swept his fingertip across her clit and she bucked against him, her hips lifting of their own volition. "Damn you."

She thought she'd laughed. She meant to laugh . . . so why did it sound more like a growl?

He kept it up, touching and teasing her, drawing her body tighter and then tighter still until she thought she might fly apart, all bits and pieces of her going in every direction, but when she reached a point where she knew she couldn't take any more, knew she was going to scream her frustration to the heavens, Morgan lifted her hips in his big, warm hands, held her up to him as he knelt between her thighs, and drove in, deep. Hard. So hard that his balls slapped against her butt and his coarse, dark pubic hair scratched across her mound.

She was ripe and so ready, but Morgan was more than she expected. Bigger, harder, filling her beyond her ability to take, but take him she did.

And the pain was sweet, the climax sweeter still.

He was there, deep in her mind. Every bit as much a part of her thoughts as he was of her body, and he was showing her a place in her brain that she'd never guessed existed. And while she wouldn't exactly call it a switch, it was definitely something she could physically change.

And change it she did.

Rodie? Are you okay? Can you hear me?

Ohmygawd. Yes! Yes, I can hear you, but all I can see is a spinning swirl of little lights. Is that you?

Yes! You did it, Rodie. Wow. Can you move around?

I don't know. How?

Think of a place, but let me know so I can go with you.

The lodge. I want to see if anyone's over there.

He almost lost her, because the thought had no more than entered her mind than she was headed that way, right through the bedroom wall and then through the front door, with Morgan hot on her heels.

So to speak.

They reached the lodge in a fraction of a second.

How come they're not moving?

Weird, isn't it? It's because we're moving so much faster that they seem to be sitting still.

Mac, Cam, and Dink were huddled in one corner with a bunch of papers spread out on the table. Liz and the two Nyrian women she'd brought to Earth had gone, probably resting in Liz's cabin.

Let's see if we can rematerialize in front of Mac and the others.

You're sure?

Yeah, but remember, we were naked when we disassembled. Think clothes.

Just think them?

That's what Bolt said. Something simple, but be specific.

Okay. If this doesn't work, you know I'm going to kill you, Morgan. No doubt about it.

Morgan heard what had to be a giggle. And then both of them were standing beside the table. A quick glance showed him Rodie in a short tunic that barely covered her ass, and he'd managed a pair of jogging shorts, but Mac cursed, Dink knocked over his iced tea, and Cameron scooted his chair back so fast he almost toppled.

It was probably a good thing they hadn't appeared naked.

"Holy shit." Mac lurched to his feet. "Rodie? When did you learn to . . . ? Where's Finn?"

Rodie shot a quick look at Mac. "He didn't tell you? I thought he was on his way over here."

"Tell us what?" Mac glanced at Cam and Dink. "We just got here a couple of minutes ago and the lodge was empty. We were checking out the gunfire but couldn't figure out what they were shooting at."

"Idiots," Dink muttered. "At least I've got some good film of them firing at our guys."

"They were firing at Finn." Morgan glanced at Rodie. "They shot him."

"He's okay," Rodie said, interrupting. "Bolt healed him." She glanced at Dink. "Bolt changed to his energy form, went inside Finn, and got the bullet out of his leg and patched up a deep graze across his shoulders, just the way Zianne healed you, Dink."

Mac threw his hands in the air. "Whoa! Wait. Wait a minute. How the hell did Finn end up getting shot?"

"We were trying to learn how to move around when we were just molecules. It's not easy to figure it out, moving without a corporeal body." He glanced at Rodie and shook his head. "Well, it was easy for Rodie, but not for Finn and me. Finn suddenly got it and disappeared. Turns out, he decided to check out the guys on the other side of the fence line, but he forgot that when we're disassembled, we move so fast that we can't understand human speech. He shifted back so he could hear what they were planning."

"Are you saying he took his form back while he was down there on the back side of the plateau? In the middle of those idiots? What the fuck was he thinking?"

Mac was pulling his alpha shit, and for some reason it really pissed Morgan off, but before he could reply, Rodie beat him to it.

"Damn it, Mac! He was thinking he could get us some information. There's a big group waiting down there, all of them heavily armed. He didn't expect anyone to come up behind him, and he got shot." Rodie's indignant reply had Mac spinning her way.

A slow grin spread across his face. "Okay, so Finn got shot, Bolt healed him, but you're now flying around all disassembled. Why do I see a connection here?"

Morgan sighed as he shot a glance at Rodie. "Because Rodie's ready to go in Finn's place if he's not feeling strong enough when it's time to head for the Gar ship. And, no, it was most definitely not my idea."

Rodie's smile lit up the room. "Tara suggested it. Even if Finn's better and he goes, I'll still go with them. It's dangerous for the Nyrians to fight against the Gar because the Gar have weapons that totally immobilize them. They need us."

"She's deadly with a Taser, boss." Morgan caught Mac's eye and shrugged. "I think I want her on my side."

Mac merely shook his head. "This is certainly not something I was planning on, but if you guys are comfortable with the arrangement, I'm fine with it."

Morgan wrapped his fingers around Rodie's. "I'm not particularly comfortable with anything that puts Rodie in danger, but she's right when she says she has skills we might need. If nothing else, she's always got a different perspective on things. We're going into a totally alien situation, no pun intended, and I think the more minds working toward the same end, the better."

"I agree." Mac glanced at Dink and Cam. "That's why we're putting together everything we know about the Nyrians that we can share during the broadcast. We're going to want to show you guys leaving, if we can."

"You're planning to broadcast before we know if we'll succeed? Crap, Mac. What if we fail? What if the Gar win?" Morgan felt Rodie's fingers tighten around his.

Dink shuffled the papers on the table in front of him. "I'm going to tell you the same thing I told Mac, that failure's not an option." He glanced at his watch and shoved the hair out of his eyes. "It's almost four. I'd suggest you get something to eat and kick back for a bit. You've got about an hour before you go. I want you looking your best for the evening news." He grinned at both of them, that professional smile they'd all seen on the nightly news, and added, "You wouldn't dare screw up the biggest story of my life. Would you?"

Rodie snorted, and glanced at her short tunic. "I need to think more clothes next time. The whole world will be watching."

"But you've got such a cute ass, sweetheart."

"I'm bringing my Taser with me, darling." She smiled sweetly.

Morgan was suddenly all business. "Yeah. Okay. Let's get something to eat. Looks like Meg's putting out fried chicken."

7

Lizzie quietly crawled out of bed and opened the bedroom door without waking either Reiah or Seri. The two Nyrians slept soundly, curled up like a pair of puppies in the middle of the big bed. She'd helped them strengthen their corporeal bodies during a most amazing all-girls orgy just the night before. It was fascinating how they drew energy from not only sexual fantasy, but from the act itself.

Or acts. Damn. What a night! Lizzie felt a pleasant ache this afternoon, but Reiah and Seri were flat-out exhausted, in spite of the sexual energy. Exhausted both emotionally and physically, the two of them still scared to death of the sudden changes in their lives, the unexpected rush to escape the Gar ship this morning, and the fear that some of their fellow Nyrians might not survive.

Lizzie couldn't imagine coping with all the trauma the Nyrians had to deal with—trauma that went well beyond the actual escape. Even though they could download everything they needed to know from those human minds around them, the information was totally out of context in so many ways. Not only were they having to learn a new language but an entirely new way of thinking.

The adjustment to dealing with corporeal bodies alone was mind-boggling. Reiah had tried to explain that while sleep wasn't necessary to them in their energy form, they'd quickly learned that these human bodies required it, just as they required food and water and air to survive.

Taking food in, the mechanics of bodily functions—tears, sweat, elimination of waste—all were new to them. All something they knew how to deal with through mental osmosis and the natural instincts inherent in their human bodies, but still had to adjust to on an emotional and mental level.

It was a huge learning curve. Liz wondered what it would be like if or when the women experienced something as basic as a menstrual cycle. Crap. Had anyone discussed birth control with the Nyrians? Would that become an issue? She had no idea if they were fertile in their human bodies, or were they still essentially Nyrian? If they were fertile as humans, what would happen when they switched to their energy forms if any of them got pregnant?

The human women of project DEO-MAP all had birth control implants. The human men were as fertile as always. And sexually active. Very sexually active, and the Nyrian women loved that activity. Needed it to keep them strong.

But would that change if they stayed in their human forms? Would they still need sexual energy when they were complete with their soulstones and corporeal forms? Damn, but there were so many more questions than answers. Lizzie figured she'd better start a list. That was something she was good at—organizing thoughts, figuring out what needed to be dealt with first. Sort of a mental triage of issues.

After the rescue. After they got through tonight. There was only so much her mind could handle, no matter how brilliant she was supposed to be. Opening the front door and then staring across the vast plateau, Liz stopped dead in her tracks and sighed.

Pregnant Nyrians? *Holy shit.* Hopefully that wouldn't be an issue, at least not right away. Nattoch had cautioned all of his people that once they had their human bodies and their soulstones, they must remember to sleep, that it was during sleep that the human subconscious could effectively integrate their new knowledge with their Nyrian minds.

Unfortunately, Lizzie doubted birth control was tops on anyone's list of issues. Besides, could the subconscious handle everything? When this crisis was over, when life returned to normal, they really did have to sit down and talk. For now, they just needed to get the basics.

Basic number one—she really needed to let Reiah and Seri get some sleep. Maybe by the time they woke up, they'd be more comfortable with all the changes in their lives. "With luck," she whispered, taking a quick glance over her shoulder at the bedroom door, "you'll sleep until this nightmare ends and everyone's safe. Then we can work on the details." There was nothing else they could do. Not now.

Quietly, Lizzie closed the door and stepped outside.

She stood there on her front porch for a moment, taking slow, deep breaths and searching for some calm. The minute she started thinking of details, she felt herself going into automatic overload. What she needed was some quiet time on the beach, maybe even a Zen moment, but that wasn't going to happen.

She wasn't sure where she was going, but her feet seemed determined to take her to the lodge by way of Finn's cabin next door. She definitely had an overdeveloped worry gene. Not only was she freaking out about the Nyrians, she couldn't get Finnegan O'Toole off her mind. Morgan had Rodie but Finn had only Tara and Duran. She knew they were really close and that he cared deeply for them, but had any human ever really cared for Finn?

He'd changed so much over the past few days and she'd seen a totally different side of the man. He was a good person, not nearly the jerk they'd all pegged him for in the beginning, and in a few more hours he'd be risking his life, going on board the alien Gar ship to rescue even more aliens. Pretty amazing, when she thought about it. How many men would be so brave? So selfless.

She stood on rocky ground in front of his cabin for a moment, wondering why she felt this need to at least wish him well, to let him know she cared that he come back safely. It wasn't like they had anything going between them, or even that they ever would, but she wanted Finn to know he mattered. That she cared about him. That his safety was important to her, that his bravery honored all of them.

That was all. No big deal in the scheme of things, but she hoped it mattered to Finn, because it sure felt important to her. Slowly, she walked up the steps and peeked in the open window. The front room was empty, so she knocked quietly. A moment later, Tara opened the door. Duran stood just behind her.

"Lizzie. Hello. Were you coming to check on Finn?"

She felt small and awkward, staring up at the gorgeous Nyrian woman. Being the youngest and the shortest of the entire dream team had its drawbacks, like now, when she felt about eight years old. She glanced beyond the two Nyrians, but there was no sign of Finn, so she merely smiled and said, "I just wanted to wish him luck."

Duran reached around Tara and opened the door wider. "Please, Lizzie. Come in. That's very kind of you, but we still don't know if he'll be able to go."

She'd just stepped inside, but Duran's comment brought all

forward momentum to a halt. Spinning around, her gaze flew from Duran to Tara and back to Duran. "What? Why not? What happened?"

"You did not hear the gunshots? He was injured." Tara's voice cracked on the last word.

Injured?

For the first time, Lizzie noticed dried tears streaking the Nyrian woman's cheeks. "Finn? Shot? But when? How is he?"

Tara took one of Lizzie's hands in both of hers. "One of those men down by the fence, the ones with guns. Finn said it was a bullet that tore into his leg and another that cut across his back. Bolt has repaired the damage, but Finn is still very weak."

Finn? She couldn't imagine him hurt. Couldn't picture him as anything but the strong, cocky guy she knew. "Will he be okay? Does he need anything?"

Duran shrugged. "I imagine your concern would help. I think sometimes that Finn is too much alone."

What an odd thing for the man to say. Wasn't he Finn's lover? Both he and Tara? She glanced at the clock on the wall. It was almost four, which meant only about an hour until the rescue team was scheduled to leave. She gripped Tara's hands with both of hers. "But what of the rescue? If Finn can't go, who will? Don't you need more people to help?"

Duran glanced toward Finn's bedroom, then returned his attention to Lizzie. "Rodie will go with Morgan, Bolt, and me. If Finn is able, he will go with us as well." He took Tara's arm and looked once again toward Finn's bedroom, but it was hard to process what she'd just heard. Rodie going instead of Finn? That didn't make any sense, but Duran was still talking and edging his way toward the front door with Tara.

"Do you mind staying here while Tara and I go over to the lodge to get something to eat? We keep forgetting that these bodies need food, but we didn't want to leave Finn alone. Bolt took him to the lodge earlier, so he's eaten, and he's resting now." Duran paused to brush a hand over Lizzie's hair, then cupped her chin in his palm. "Go to him. I think your concern will help strengthen the man."

Liz wasn't quite sure how to respond to that, but she stood there quietly as Tara and Duran left. That was probably the oddest conversation she'd had in a while. Rodie going to the Gar ship? Now that was bizarre. But, Finn hurt? She hadn't heard anything.

Not gunshots. Not a mental warning, nothing.

She went to his bedroom door and peeked inside. Finn lay in the middle of the big bed, one arm flung over his eyes, sheets tangled around his legs and barely covering his groin. At least he was almost decent. Liz stood there, staring at him for what felt like the longest time, but she'd never really had a chance to look at Finn without him looking back and making some smartass comment.

Except last night, when they'd talked, when he'd told her that being with Tara and Duran was the first time he'd ever experienced intimacy that mattered. She'd felt so sad when he told her that, to think he'd never known love until he'd made love with them, something so far beyond just plain old sex that he'd said he didn't think he could ever go back.

That simple conversation had changed everything Liz thought about him. She'd suddenly seen Finn as someone who was thoughtful and kind, a man who had been very much alone in spite of all the women he'd bedded. It made her wonder how much of his personality and predatory ways were born of a need to protect himself.

And, with her new understanding of Finnegan O'Toole, Lizzie realized she cared more than she thought she had. She wasn't in love with Finn, but she loved him as a friend. She cared what happened to him and she wanted him to be safe. More important, she needed for him to know that before he left tonight.

Standing there, watching him sleep, she had no doubt he'd go. He was too hardheaded to let an injury hold him back. He shifted his position in the bed and then slowly, as if he'd just become aware of her steady perusal, Finn turned his head, blinked owlishly, and then focused on her. "Lizzie? What are you doing here?"

"Are you okay?" She took a step closer. "I didn't know you'd been hurt. I just came by to wish you luck tonight." Another step. "When I got here, Tara and Duran wanted to go have dinner, but they didn't want to leave you alone. Sorry, bud, you got me."

She stood beside the bed, gazing down at him.

His smile spread slowly, and damn but he was one gorgeous guy. Even lying relaxed in his bed, his belly rippled with a perfect six-pack and his pecs were so perfectly defined she clasped her hands together to keep from touching. She was not going there. This was Finn.

Damn. This was definitely Finn. He scooted up against the headboard and patted the mattress beside him. "So, you're the babysitter, eh?" He winked. "Stay and talk to me. Please?"

She flopped down on the bed closer to the foot, next to his legs. No reason to get closer. Sleep-rumpled and sexy, he was way too much temptation. More temptation than she would have expected, considering she was only now changing her opinion of him from jerk to more of a friend. "How are you feeling? I didn't realize you'd gotten hurt."

He glanced at the spot he'd patted, directly beside him, then cocked one eyebrow in her direction before nodding his head. "Yeah, leave it to me to screw things up. But, Lizzie, disassembling was so damned cool. Duran was right—it's like this little switch in your brain and you can flip it and just disappear! I figured out how to move, and believe me, it's not easy at first, but when I did, I headed down to the plateau to check out the idiots along the fence. Only thing is, in that form I realized I couldn't understand them, so I switched back to my regular self and hid behind a rock."

She'd covered her lips with her fingers without even realizing it. "They saw you?"

"Not the ones I was spying on. A new group I hadn't seen coming up the side of the hill spotted me and started shooting. I was so rattled, I couldn't remember how to shift back to molecules. Caught a bullet in my calf and another one grazed my shoulders before I was able to disappear. I'm just damned lucky they're such crappy shots, or I'd be dead." He laughed, leaned forward, and grabbed her hand. "Lizzie, my biggest regret is that I didn't get to see their faces when I disappeared. They're probably still scratching their heads, but I knew I'd been hit and wanted to get the hell out of Dodge. Next thing I know, I'm back here and Bolt's climbing around inside me, fixing my leg and patching up my back."

He turned and patted his shoulder. "Do you see anything?"

She leaned forward and traced a long, pink slash that ran across his shoulders, running her fingers from right to left, over muscle and bone and new, pink skin. "This must have been awful. It's about two feet across and half an inch wide of new skin. Does it hurt?"

He shook his head. "Not now. Burned like a son of a bitch when it happened." He pulled the sheet back from his left leg and touched a round, quarter-sized spot of pink flesh on the back of his calf just below the bend of his knee. "This is where a round went in. Bolt said it shattered the bone." Sighing, he slipped his leg back under the sheets. "Bolt repaired it. He even managed to decontaminate the blood that was all over the floor and on my clothes and put it back. Totally mind-blowing, ya know? It's not hurting, but I'm still kind of weak." Chuckling softly, he shook his head and added, "I feel like a wuss."

Lizzie started to push herself away from the bed. "Do you want me to leave so you can rest?"

An almost frantic look passed across his face. He grabbed her hand. "Will you stay? I'm not putting the make on you, Liz. Really. I promise."

Laughter bubbled out before Liz even tried to control it. She'd never seen Finn looking quite so desperate. She squeezed his fingers. "This is so not you. At least not the you I first met, but, yes, Finn. I'll stay if you promise to try and sleep. You've still got an hour, and Duran said every little bit will help."

He put a pillow beside his. "Lie down with me, Liz. Please?"

She leaned over and kissed him. Nothing sexy, but he tasted good and it felt right. Then she stretched out beside him, and turned her head so she could see his face. "I will. I want you healthy and strong, Finn. Not because I want you going to that damned spaceship, but because I know you want to go so badly. I can feel it. You'll never be happy unless you get this chance."

He lay down beside her and tangled his fingers with hers. "Thanks, Liz. You're right, you know. I really do have to go."

"Rest," she said. She snuggled close against his side and he wrapped his arm around her. It felt good here, as if she belonged beside him. She closed her eyes, felt Finn's body relaxing beside hers, and thought how special this moment felt. The two of them were friends. They'd never had sex and probably never would, but she loved him.

And right now, lying beside him, Liz knew Finn loved her every bit as much. It made this whole thing seem even more important, somehow, knowing she mattered to him. That they both mattered to each other.

Lost in thoughts of all the bad things that could happen when the final bid to rescue the last of the Nyrians began, Cam almost missed Mac's question.

"Cam, do you have any other paintings that might help add color to Dink's story?"

He dropped the front legs of his chair back to the floor and thought of the few small projects he'd had time for. Not much, considering. "I've got a few things you might be able to use. Scenes from inside the Gar ship, stuff that Mir and Niah remembered and shared with me. They're not paintings; pen and pencil sketches more than anything, with a little watercolor added." He shrugged. "You know, like court drawings of trials where the press isn't allowed access with cameras?"

Dink turned to Mac and a slow smile crossed his face. "Perfect. Do you think you and the girls would be comfortable describing what you've drawn?"

"In front of a camera?"

Nodding, Dink said, "Of course."

"I'll have to ask Niah and Mir. They're resting, but I was about ready to get them up, anyway. They want to be here when the rescue begins."

The heavy *whump, whump, whump* of a helicopter coming in close had everyone headed for the front door of the lodge. "That's either the sheriff or the news crew," Mac said. He flung open the door as a small helicopter painted with a bright blue news station logo touched down for a graceful landing in the open expanse between the lodge and the dream shack.

Cam followed Mac and Dink out onto the porch, and the three of them stood and watched as the rotors continued to spin and the two men inside went through the process of grabbing their gear.

"It appears my news crew has beat out the sheriff's department." Dink stepped past Cam and started down the steps.

"Uh, Dink?"

Dink turned around and looked at Mac. "Yeah? What?"

"That's a Eurocopter AS350, right?"

Dink studied the chopper for a minute. "I think so. Why?"

"It's called a Squirrel." Mac shrugged. "Just thought it was terribly apropos, ya know?"

Chuckling, Dink slapped Mac on the shoulder. "Only you, Dugan. Only you." He turned away and walked toward the two men climbing out of the small helicopter.

Terribly apropos was right. Cam turned, prepared to tease Mac, but the tears sparkling in the man's eyes stopped him cold.

Mac cleared his throat. "I need to go check on Zianne," he said. Before Cam could reply, Mac was through the door and headed up the stairs.

"Cam?" Dink paused, halfway to the helicopter. "Can you get Mir and Niah and be ready by quarter to five? That's about forty minutes from now."

"No problem." He started for his cabin and then thought of something else. "Dink? Will you check on Kiera? She's been in the dream shack since noon, and Morgan's not going to relieve her."

"Right now." Dink waved, changed course, and headed for the dream shack.

Cam circled around the side of the lodge to go back to his cabin. He'd left Niah and Mir sleeping soundly, but it was time for all of them to get moving. In less than an hour, things were going to start popping. Damn but he was glad he wasn't going on board the Gar ship. From what the girls had told him while he sketched their visions, the inside was dark and cluttered, the air thin, foul smelling, and hard to breathe.

He wondered if Mac had any kind of face masks the guys going aboard could use, but then he had no idea how you'd carry anything when it was time to disassemble, and that whole process left him cold. But, as he stepped into his cabin and glanced through to the bedroom, when he saw his beautiful Nyrian woman waiting for him on the bed, Cam decided he was actually quite warm.

They were naked. Both of them, and so perfect they not only raised his temperature, they made him ache. When Mir smiled, when Niah reached for him, Cam stopped in midstep.

He'd been planning to tell them to dress, that they needed to prepare to speak with members of the media, but they had over half an hour before they had to meet with Dink.

Plenty of time. Cam quickly undid the buttons on his flannel shirt and shrugged the thing off. It dropped to the floor as he stopped beside the bed. Mir flicked open the snap on his jeans and quickly lowered the zipper, reminding Cam he could accomplish an awful lot in half an hour.

And this did help raise Nyrian energy levels, right? Niah stroked his chest with just enough pressure from her fingernails to leave shivers in their wake. Mir shoved his pants down below his knees. Cam's cock leapt free, rising hard against his belly. He was so damned ready he ached.

Mir leaned forward and wrapped her lips around the sensitive crown and slowly sucked him deep. Niah's fingers cupped his sac. She gently rolled the two orbs inside, tugging just enough to pull him forward, closer, until he managed to crawl onto the rumpled bed between the women.

Mir swallowed him deep, then deeper still until her lips pressed against his groin and he felt the rippling constriction of her throat tightening around his shaft. Groaning, he fought the urge to drive into her and instead pulled Niah around so that he could reach her with his lips and tongue. Sweet liquid filled his mouth, her amazing ambrosia tasting of honey and vanilla. He wondered if this was unique to all Nyrian women. It certainly was to these two.

His tongue swept deep and Niah arched against him, filling his senses with her sweet aroma, teasing his tongue with her addictive taste. He licked again as Mir's lips tightened around the base of his shaft and Niah's fingers continued to stroke his aching balls.

Half an hour, hell. He'd be lucky to last ten minutes.

* * *

Mac stood outside the door to the room where he'd left Zianne with Satza and Corin. He'd had to force himself not to worry about Zianne today. Not to come up here every ten minutes and check on her, but at the same time, he'd been terrified of what he might find.

She was growing so weak, and according to Bolt, she'd gone without her soulstone now far longer than any Nyrian ever had—and survived. He held his fist up to knock, but the door swung open.

Satza stood in the doorway, her long, curly brown hair tumbling to her waist, and a smile of welcome on her lips. "Zianne sensed your arrival." Stepping aside, she opened the door and invited him inside.

"Zianne?" She sat on the bed beside Corin, looking healthy and rested. Mac rushed across the room and pulled her into his arms, but the moment he lifted her, his breath caught in his throat. She felt lighter than air, insubstantial, almost as if he lifted a child. Dear lord, but she was so fragile, her fair skin almost translucent, her life force a quiet hum where he'd always felt a surge of energy whenever they touched.

He was losing her. She'd spent hours with Corin and Satza and it hadn't been enough. Nothing would be, until she was reunited with her soulstone. Impossible as it seemed, as frustrating as it was, that tiny bit of carbon held prisoner by the Gar was her only chance at life.

He kissed her gently and then sat on the edge of the bed and settled her comfortably in his lap. Her arm looped around his waist and her head pillowed against his shoulder. He nuzzled her ebony hair, kissed her gently. "Are you all right? Did you rest well?"

She nodded. "Corin and Satza shared energy with me, though I fear it doesn't last me very long." She ran her fingers over his unshaved chin. "That shouldn't matter, once I have my stone back." She smiled at him, but there was no sense of joy, none of her usual sparkle. "I will get it back, Mac. I believe in you and your team. Please, don't despair. How are plans for the rescue going?"

He swallowed past the lump in his throat. How the hell could she remain so damned positive? "It's after four." He turned his head just enough to kiss her fingertips. "Duran, Bolt, Morgan, Rodie, and, if he recovers in time, Finn, will board the Gar ship at five o'clock."

She slowly lifted her head away from his shoulder and frowned. "Rodie? But why? And what happened to Finn?"

"Finn was injured and Rodie intends to take his place. She's brave and smart and there's no stopping her. Even Morgan approves, though he's not entirely happy about it."

She smiled, and this time her beautiful amethyst eyes had the sparkle he remembered, no matter how fragile her form. "Tell me, my love. Would you be happy if I were the one going on board an alien star cruiser to save people you hardly knew?"

"I'd be fine, because I would tie you up and lock you in a closet so you couldn't go." He kissed her nose, her cheeks, and finally her lips. The sweet scent of honey and vanilla, the taste of her on his tongue brought tears to Mac's eyes. They were so close to saving her, and yet so damned far away right now. If she didn't have her soulstone soon, Zianne would die. Even now he sensed her fading, so delicate, so insubstantial that she was little more than a wraith in his arms. Even with Satza and Corin's generous help, Zianne's condition continued to deteriorate.

"Would it be easier for you to stay in the squirrel?" He brushed her hair back from her face, tangling his fingers in the long, black strands. "I don't want to tire you."

She shook her head. "If the mission fails, if I have only hours left, I don't want to spend them as a little gray rodent." She reached over and ran her fingers along the squirrel's fluffy tail, but the tiny creature slept soundly. "She's been a sweet and willing hostess, but it's time for her to return to her life as a squirrel."

"I think that's going to be difficult. She's grown too fond of all the goodies we've been feeding her." He traced Zianne's lips with his fingertips and watched them curve slightly into a smile. "She's been willing because she's been fed like a little princess."

"Mac?" Corin had been staring out the window. Now she turned to Mac, frowning. "What is going on below? The noise from that machine woke us, but now there is much activity."

Mac stood with Zianne in his arms and carried her across the room to the window. She weighed nothing at all, and he held her gently, worried he might bruise her tender skin. Together they looked at the scene below. The two men from the television station had set up their camera equipment and appeared to be talking to Rodie and Morgan.

They'd positioned it perfectly, filming with the massive array of huge satellite dishes in the background, the dream shack off to one side. Rodie was, as usual, talking with her hands, and he could just about guess what she was saying. Always so animated. So alive. He glanced at the woman in his arms and remembered a time when Zianne had been that filled with life. It made him ache to see her like this, so terribly fragile.

"Who are those people? I know Dink, but who are the men with cameras? Are they from the news station? Mac, people will know what's happening. Why? I don't understand what's going on."

He heard the fear in Zianne's voice and shoved his own aside. Damn, that's all he seemed to do anymore. Hope that if he didn't think about the crap it would all go away. Hell, he was living in a permanent state of denial, but he had to believe they'd made the right decision. He kissed her forehead, cleared his throat, and said, "It's starting, Zianne. While you slept, we discovered that the news was out, that astronomers had spotted the Gar ship heading for Earth."

She turned her head and gazed directly into his eyes, listening, realizing, as Mac did, that there was no turning back.

"One of our generals contacted me," he said. "I told him of our plan, that the Gar were not the peaceful aliens so many on Earth hoped for, even expected for our first contact with another sentient species."

"Does he believe you?"

"I don't know. I expected to hear back from him, but I haven't, yet. I told him we'd be sending humans to board the ship around five, but I didn't tell him how. I don't know what he thinks. Just a couple of weeks ago he told me I was nuts, that I needed a good psychiatrist. At least, in that respect, he seems to have changed his mind."

"The man is still a fool."

Mac smiled and kissed her nose. "He's coming around. A bit late, but at least now he's listening to me. In the meantime, we've got the news crew here to handle the public. We plan to follow the entire rescue as closely as we can and broadcast everything in real time. It's going out on network television as well as the Internet, so the world will know what's happening.

"People will be able to follow us during every step. Rodie's even going to try and take a small camera with her when she boards the Gar ship, but that will depend on her ability to include it when she disassembles. I'm hoping the sheriff arrives soon. We can use his help to control the protestors and the men harassing our guards near the fence line. I wish I knew what they were planning, but I don't, and I don't want to have to worry about them while this is going on. It's too distracting."

Mac sighed. So much they didn't know, so many things left to chance. This wasn't the way he worked. He'd always been a planner, a plotter, someone who knew what the next step would bring. This mission, the most important of his life—of anyone's life—and it was all just falling together as it happened.

He only hoped it didn't fall apart. He adjusted Zianne's soft weight in his arms, holding her even closer against his chest. She was the constant in his life. The one he'd counted on for twenty years. He'd trusted for two decades that she'd be here waiting for him, and even though her life might be forfeit, she'd been exactly where she said she'd be. He'd trusted Zianne, and he had to trust their plan would work. It had to.

"I don't know exactly when our guys are heading for the Gar ship," he said, "but it's all going to be happening very soon and very fast. I just hope they're ready."

His cell phone vibrated in his pocket. Mac reached around Zianne and pulled it free. The blocked number again. He walked across the room and sat on the edge of the bed before he answered.

When he ended the call a few minutes later, Mac wasn't sure if he'd just gotten good news or a death sentence for the few remaining Nyrians—Zianne included. He stood, adjusted Zianne in his arms, and walked back to the window. Stared at the news crew, at the helicopter squatting like a bug below, and thought of the conversation he'd just had, and of the stupidity of politicians in general.

"What is it? Tell me." Zianne's soft demand left no room for dissembling.

He let out a deep breath as he organized his thoughts. As if there was any reason to attempt to organize anything at this point. "That was General Adams from the Pentagon. He's spoken with the president and members of his cabinet, as well as the head of our Department of Defense. They're divided on what action to take. Too many people are excited about the huge spaceship coming closer to Earth. They don't believe any ship could do the kind of damage I warned them of, and they want to reach out to the Gar in friendship."

Zianne slowly shook her head. "The Gar do not understand friendship. They only understand domination, theft, and the total annihilation of other worlds. Until they find a planet that suits them for their own use, one they can take over, they'll want to continue their destruction of any world that offers what they need." Frowning, she shook her head, a short, sharp jerk. "I guess that's a moot point, though. There are no longer enough Nyrians aboard to power the ship during an attack, or run the machinery they use to rape worlds."

"That's what I told him. That the only thing we can do at this point is rescue the remaining slaves before the ship is too close to Earth, and hope that when it blows, it doesn't take us with it."

She shrugged. "Exactly. The one good thing is that, finally, there are not enough Nyrians aboard their ship to attack this world or any other. The only thing we can do now is retrieve as many of my people as we can and bring them to safety before the ship is too close to your atmosphere."

"General Adams said they intend to call in scientists from around the world and discuss what action they need to take. The general consensus is that at the speed the ship is moving, it won't reach Earth for another couple of days. When I tried to refute that, he asked me not to tell him any details of what we're planning, that what he didn't know, he couldn't try to stop. In that respect, he's doing what he can to help us. He also said we need to be careful in our dealings with the local sheriff, which may explain why we've not had the help we requested."

"The helicopter you asked for? I know it's not that one." She looked at the news helicopter parked in the open area below.

"Yeah. Ted Alvisa, the deputy sheriff I know, is all for helping us, but according to the general, the county board of supervisors has stepped in and told him he's not to interfere with anything Bart Roberts instigates until they know more about the situation. It appears Roberts has gotten to a couple of the supervisors. He's convinced them we're the bad guys here, that 'our' aliens are evil and the Gar are the good guys."

"What fools." Zianne sighed, and she seemed to shrink even smaller within his arms. "So what do we do?"

"Protect our perimeter and go ahead with our plan. Dink's working up the backstory and will go live as soon as Morgan and the rest leave for the Gar ship. He'll tell our story from twenty years ago and what's transpired since. He's good, Zianne. He'll know how to get your story out there and get people on our side. He'll make them care about Nyrians, the fact your planet was destroyed by the aliens coming closer by the hour. He's going to use the picture Cam painted of Nyria before the Gar destroyed it, one he did of Mars during the Gar attack, and some of his other work. We want the world to know what happened to your people, and what so easily could have happened here, if not for the Nyrian's bravery. Right now Dink and his crew are taping stuff to run while we're waiting for news after everyone heads for the ship."

Zianne clutched the front of his shirt in both hands. There was a frantic, desperate glitter in her eyes. "I want to be in the dream shack when they go. I know it's a small building, that we won't all fit, but I must be with you. Please?"

"Oh, sweetheart." Mac leaned forward, touching his forehead to hers. Her skin felt icy, as if all the life was leaving her, and it broke his heart. His voice sounded husky, and he realized his emotions were on the same, sharp edge as Zianne's. He was feeling what she felt, the fear, the utter despair, knowing that even though they were so close, it might be too late for her.

She'd been without her soulstone for so long now, the odds were growing stronger that, even if they managed to retrieve it, she wouldn't survive. "You will be wherever I am. Everything

I've done, all of this, is for you. I want to save your people, but don't you understand? I want to save them for you. I will always love you. I will never stop needing you. Hold on, please."

She shivered and he held her close, warming her as much as he could with his body. It was all he could do to hold himself together. They were so damned close, and yet success was such a fragile thing.

Even if everyone else survived, he could still lose Zianne. Mac felt a huge pressure in his chest, a horrible pain that stopped him in his tracks, and he wondered if he was having a heart attack, if twenty years of stress and worry had finally taken its toll.

And then he recognized it for what it was, the despair he'd kept buried for so long. The fear he'd not recognized, the sense of failure that hovered just out of reach. He couldn't see a thing through the window, through the tears flooding his eyes. Couldn't breathe through the lump in his throat, but he struggled to pull himself under control.

Dink's words sifted through his mind, the words that had been his mantra for the past twenty years.

Failure is not an option.

Not an option, but always, unfortunately, a possibility.

8

It was a possibility he couldn't ignore. As much as he hated the mere thought of it, Mac had to be prepared to deal with the fallout should their mission not succeed. He glanced around the room and wondered when Corin and Satza had left. The only ones here now were Zianne, Mac, and the squirrel, but when he looked out the window, he could see all the Nyrians gathering in the open area below, standing together with the members of his dream team.

Cameron was there with Mir and Niah, and all five of the women Morgan had given form. He tried to remember their names, surprised when they came to him so easily: Reneya, Deina, Lali, Tiram, Nala. Each an individual with hopes and dreams and fears they were doing their best to control.

As he watched, Corin and Satza joined the group, and then Liz showed up with Reiah and Seri. None of the men were there. No, they'd be along the fence line, guarding the perimeter. He glanced at the clock on the wall and wondered where the day had gone.

It was almost five. Kiera must still be in the dream shack. Rodie, Morgan, Finn, Bolt, and Duran would be preparing to leave for the Gar ship. He had no doubt Finn would be there. The guy was determined to be part of this mission, no matter what.

He rubbed his chin across the top of Zianne's head. Strands of her long hair tangled in his two-day growth of beard, reminding him he'd forgotten once again to shave. "C'mon, sweetheart. I think we need to get down there. We'll take your squirrel in case you need her," he said. "Are you ready?"

Zianne tilted her head back against his arm to better see his face. "Mac, I'm terrified. What if something happens to Rodie or Morgan or Finn? My people know the risk, but what of them? If they're hurt, I'll never forgive myself."

He planted a light kiss on her mouth. "Sweetheart, Morgan, Rodie, and Finn have made the choice to go. It's their decision, and I don't think we could stop them if we tried. If I didn't feel that my place was here, I'd be right there with them. Their choices are not something you should feel guilty about, no matter what happens. They want this."

Without giving Zianne time to answer him, Mac tightened his grasp around her and tilted her over the bed so she could grab the tote bag. She settled it in the crook of her body while Mac adjusted her slight weight in his arms. The squirrel opened her eyes and gazed at Zianne with what could only be affection and recognition. Then she sighed, curled up, and went back to sleep.

Mac stared at the squirrel. "I sure wish I felt as relaxed as this little girl."

"Maybe she knows something we don't." Zianne steadied the tote with her left hand and tightened her right arm around his neck so she could reach up and give him a quick kiss. "Maybe she's telling us not to worry, that all will be fine."

"One can only hope." He opened the door, and still carrying

his woman, Mac headed down the stairs and through the dining hall.

Meg was wrapping up leftover food on the buffet counter. "Hi, Mac. I'm just going to keep this in the refrigerator for later. It's all stuff that will make good leftovers, and I imagine you'll be hungry when this is over with."

"Good idea, Meg. Thank you." He paused for a moment. "Meg, this is Zianne, the woman I told you about."

"I know that, Mac." Meg smiled and stepped around the table. She took Zianne's hand in both of hers. "It's nice to meet you, Zianne. I hope everything works just the way you want. I'll be praying for you, and for all your people."

Zianne glanced at Mac. *I didn't know she knew. And she cares, Mac! Her feelings are genuine.* Then she smiled at Meg. "Thank you. Your prayers for all of us are most welcome."

Nodding, Meg backed away. Mac turned to leave but thought of something else. "Meg, if anything happens tonight, with those jerks trying to break through the fence or the ones at the front gate, remember that the basement here is a safe room. You get down there with as many of the Nyrians as you can and lock yourselves in. There's an intercom and it's got its own power source, so you'll still be able to communicate with us in the dream shack, but no one can get in, and even if the lodge burns to the ground, you'll be safe. Don't take any chances."

"Thanks, Mac. Let's hope it doesn't come to that." She lifted a couple of trays and turned toward the kitchen. "But if it does, I'll keep an eye on your Nyrians. Be safe, and good luck."

"Thanks, Meg." He walked quickly toward the door and the news crew waiting outside. It was time they met Zianne. Time the world knew about the woman who had changed his life.

Finn awoke, feeling more rested than he had in days. He lay there a moment, blinking slowly, pulling his mind from a dream he couldn't recall, when reality hit hard and fast. He sat up, heart pounding, sucking air as if he'd run a mile. Had he overslept? Did they go without him?

Where the hell was Lizzie?

He glanced at the pillow next to his, saw the indentation where she'd lain beside him, and smiled. She'd really been here. For a moment, he thought maybe he'd been dreaming. And it wasn't late. He took a second look at the bedside clock. Still twenty minutes before they were planning to go.

Duran walked into the room. "Good. You're awake. I was just coming to get you. How are you feeling?"

"Okay, I think." He frowned. "How long was Liz here?"

"She left just a few minutes ago. No matter. She's not important. I want to see you change. Disassemble now."

Well, maybe not to you, but . . . "Now?"

Duran nodded. "That's what I said."

This was a new side of the Nyrian, but if Duran was half as nervous about this mission as he was, Finn couldn't blame the guy. So he shrugged, went inside his head, and flipped the switch. He knew he wasn't really flipping anything, but the sensation was there, that he'd physically changed something in the way his brain worked. Whatever he did, it seemed to work. Duran appeared immobile and Finn hovered in a sea of sparkling molecules. He moved around the room a bit, decided everything was the way it should be, and then regained his human form.

He was just as naked as he'd been while sleeping.

As bare assed as he'd been while Lizzie lay beside him. Damn. And he hadn't even tried anything with her. Which was probably a good thing, because for the life of him—and he didn't know exactly why—he really didn't want to screw up what was probably the first real friendship he'd ever had with a woman.

"Excellent." Duran smiled.

It took him a moment to realize Duran wasn't commenting on his behavior with Liz. "So, I can go?"

Duran nodded. "Yes, Finn. Thank Nyria, you appear to have

regained your strength." He stepped close and touched Finn's shoulder. "I'm sorry if I sounded impatient. I've been worried you couldn't go with us, and I want you there as part of this team. Pick clothing to wear on board the ship—good boots that won't slip and warm clothes. It's cold in the level where the engine room is. Take water. The air is dry. I worry your human body will dehydrate quickly."

"Sounds lovely." He dressed, grabbed a small pack that fit around his waist, and stuffed a water bottle inside. "You're sure I can take this stuff with me?"

"Try it."

He checked the clock; still plenty of time. Finn quickly disassembled, moved across the room, and shifted back. The water bottle and pack were still in place, he was fully dressed, and he had absolutely no idea how that could be.

Duran stood there with his arms crossed over his broad chest, laughing softly. "Don't question it. Our greatest minds were unable to figure it out. It just happens."

"Were?" Finn added a Leatherman pocket tool and a small flashlight to the pack and glanced at Duran. "You mean they quit trying to understand the process?"

Duran turned away and stared out the window. The view from Finn's bedroom wasn't all that great—the bunkhouse for employees and the forest beyond, but it seemed to hold Duran's attention for a very long time. Finally he sighed softly and said, "Not by choice. Our best minds died on Nyria. Only fools like me were willing to go aboard the Gar ship."

Finn stepped up beside him. Put a hand on his shoulder and squeezed. "Not foolish, Duran. I imagine you were curious about another people. I would have done the same. I mean, look at me now. I'm getting ready to board an alien ship populated by a race of beings we know are out to get us. You had no idea what the Gar were really like. They lied to you, let you think their intentions were good. He squeezed Duran's shoulder again and stepped away. "Besides, in another hour or so, you'll have avenged your people's deaths. All the deaths, not only from Nyria, but those other worlds as well. Let's go."

Duran straightened and glanced over his shoulder at Finn. "You're right," he said. "Thank you."

Finn opened the door and Duran followed him out into the late-afternoon sunlight. They circled around the lodge and joined the crowd standing near the dream shack. Tara stood between Rodie and Bolt. Morgan knelt beside them, checking items in his pack.

Mac sat in an Adirondack chair up on the covered porch that circled the lodge, holding Zianne in his lap. She looked pale and wan, as if merely holding her head up was an effort, but Dink was there with the news crew and it was obvious she was doing her best to answer their questions.

Lizzie strode across the open area, a small dynamo of brains, beauty, and energy. She planted her feet in front of Finn and folded her arms across her chest. "You're going."

He nodded. "I am. And, Liz, thank you. That meant a lot to me, that you came by. That you stayed."

"It's going to mean a lot to me that you come back safely. Be careful, Finn." She tilted her head and looked up at him, and all he could think of was the fact her brown eyes actually twinkled, they were so filled with mischief. He liked that about Liz. Brilliant and funny, and a serious scientist, but she'd cared enough to spend some quality time with him. It was such a new feeling he felt like savoring it.

Then his inner jerk took over, he leaned close, tapped her lips with a fingertip, and whispered, "A kiss for luck?"

She grinned. "Don't push it, bud." But she stretched up on her toes and planted one on him, quick and hard with just a hint of tongue. "Be careful, Finn. Promise?"

"Yeah. I promise." He realized he was staring at her, smiling like an idiot, but she was grinning right back at him. "Keep an eye on Tara for me, will you?" He glanced at the Nyrian. She stood close to Duran, looking so tense he was afraid she'd snap. "She's right on the edge and worried sick about Duran. They've been together since Nyria was destroyed."

"Wow. Really?" Lizzie shot a quick glance their way. "How long ago was that?"

Finn just shook his head. "I don't know. Long before there were civilizations on Earth, because Mars was still a living world. They don't keep track of time the way we do. When you're immortal, I don't think time really matters."

"I disagree, Finn." Lizzie sent another quick glance at Tara and then focused on Finn. "I think when you're a slave, time does matter, no matter how you keep track of it."

He thought about that a moment. Thought of what Duran's and Tara's lives had been like for so terribly long. It was impossible to imagine. "You're probably right. But with any luck, the last Nyrian slave will be freed in the next hour or so."

Lizzie stared at him for what felt like forever. Then she quickly shifted her gaze. "I'll stay with Tara," she said. "But you and Duran damned well better come back safe." Before he could respond, she'd turned and walked away from him, but Finn was almost certain she'd had tears in her eyes. Lizzie? Tears? For him? Impossible, but wonderful. Absolutely wonderful.

He watched her cute little butt as she strode across the dry ground toward Kiera and the dream shack.

No doubt about it, Lizzie. I'm coming back.

She stopped, glanced his way, and frowned. Then she looked away and kept going forward. Finn wondered if she'd picked up his mental promise in spite of his shields.

He definitely planned to be careful, because he fully intended to spend a lot more time with Lizzie once this was all over with. With Lizzie, Tara, and Duran.

* * *

Kiera stood in the doorway to the dream shack, watching the activity. The news crew had been all over the place, taping stuff to use later. Right now they were interviewing Zianne and Mac. She'd love to know what they were saying, because even though she hardly knew Zianne, Kiera already felt connected to her.

Merely knowing her history and Mac's was like hearing the world's greatest love story.

To think of any man spending twenty years to rescue a woman he'd known for only a few months. Twenty years and sixty million dollars. Now that was love. Up until now, love was something she'd never believed in—at least, not until she joined the dream team.

Now it felt like it was all around her. She breathed it in, felt it in every word, every hug, every smile. She feared for Morgan, Rodie, and Finn every bit as much as she did for the Nyrians. All people she'd known for mere days, and yet knew better than the man she'd married or anyone she'd been involved with, male or female. All because of Mac.

He'd set one hell of an example.

Standing here, watching the activity outside the shack, she could have felt separate, apart from everyone, but she didn't. No, her job was important. They counted on her, and what she did, she did for love. Emotional love and physical, because damn it all, she'd discovered you really couldn't have one without the other.

And that alone was almost funny, the fact she'd gotten so intimate with so many guys in such a short time. She'd listed herself as a lesbian. Not bi, not heterosexual, just lesbian, and yet of all of them here, she was the only one to give corporeal bodies to nothing but men. Go figure.

Of course, watching Lizzie plant a kiss on Finnegan O'Toole had been a bit of a surprise. Liz was comfortably bi, which, as far as Kiera could tell, most of the team members were.

Except Cameron. She hadn't seen him with any guys yet, at least not beyond Nattoch, and that was just to learn about the Gar ship. Besides, that guy was so old and decrepit he hardly counted. No, Cam seemed perfectly happy with his two women, and she had to admit, Mir and Niah were hot. Very hot.

As were all the Nyrians. An entire race of people who gained strength from sexual energy. Cam wasn't kidding when he said the bennies for this job were way beyond cool. Kiera glanced at the brilliant blue sky and thought of the alien spaceship headed their way. They'd better do something to stop the Gar ship, and soon, because it would sure screw up a great six-month gig if the thing exploded too close to Earth.

Not funny, Pearce. No, not really anything to joke about. She glanced at her watch. Almost five. Teev and Sakel could show up anytime, soulstones in place, and then the only one of her guys she'd have to worry about was Tor.

Tor. Now there was a fascinating man . . . Nyrian. Whatever. Was she ever going to get past all these crazy adjustments in her life? Things that had once seemed impossible, now normal and natural in her new reality? She wasn't sure how she'd handle it if anything happened to Tor. He'd been her first, the one who'd taught her that men did have their good points.

The one she already cared way too much about. "Sheesh," she muttered. "First alien. First guy lover who made me want more. First really great kisser." The first climax she'd ever had during sex with a guy. And not just a simple orgasm, either. A damned showstopper! Smiling now, she turned around and went back inside the shack, back to the chair. She scrunched her butt down in the comfortable recliner and replaced the little mesh cap that hooked her directly to the array. Not that the Nyrians seemed to need the connection to get here.

They appeared able to find the team members now without the massive antennae. It almost seemed comical that Mac spent a fortune building the satellite array just to help rescue the Nyrians, and now they didn't need it. At least they didn't seem to need it. She'd never really asked.

No, when the guys showed up, it was all about sex and fantasy and turning those fantasies into reality. Talk about your dream job. She checked the dials, whistling under her breath. Settings all looked good, but she was going to worry about Tor until she finally had him back here, safe with his soulstone.

Safe with her.

"I'm here, Kiera."

"Shit!" She spun around and there he was, standing beside her, laughing softly. Kiera struggled to get out of the recliner. He grabbed her hand, lifted her out, and pulled her close. She practically melted against his broad chest, wrapped her arms around his waist, and pressed her cheek against him, soothed by the steady thumping of his heart.

His very human heart.

"I didn't expect to see you. Not until it's over. Is everything okay?"

"So far. I just wanted to make sure you had the antennae powered up. Xinot, Ian, Darc, Teev, and Sakel will be escaping in just a few minutes, but Xinot, Ian, and Darc have been providing energy for the ship entirely on their own for the past ten hours. Once they retrieve their soulstones, they'll be too exhausted to make the journey to Earth without full power from the array. And, they're going to need your fantasies."

"Should I call the others here to join me?"

Tor nodded, rubbing his chin against her hair. "That would help. We had no idea how much this would drain them. Until today, we've never attempted running the ship with just three of us. While we were in orbit, it was not as difficult. When the Gar decided to move the ship, they powered up more systems and it's taken everything the men could give. I'm especially worried about Xinot. His condition is poor." He cupped her chin in his palm, tilted her face to his, and kissed her.

"I must return. Tell Bolt they should come aboard within the next fifteen minutes or twenty. By then, only Nattoch, Arnec, and I will remain, but the Gar will know something is wrong when no one returns to the barracks. We have no idea how they'll react."

Kiera clutched his forearms and stared into those beautiful dark eyes. "You have your soulstone now, don't you? You haven't surrendered it to the Gar yet, because they still think you're in the barracks. How did you get out?"

"Yes, I have it, and it feels wonderful to be on your world and be whole. Arnec was able to help me get away, but I must hurry. Call any others who can help. We need their energy and the power of their fantasies now more than ever."

She stood on her toes and kissed him. His lips were full and warm, the kiss much too brief before he set her away from him. "I love you, Kiera. Never doubt my love for you."

Love? She pressed her fingers to her lips as he disassembled and the gorgeous dark-skinned man she'd been kissing turned into a column of energy, a swirling mass of blue and gold sparks of life.

"Be safe," she whispered.

But he was already gone.

Kiera stared at the empty space in the dream shack for a moment. It was starting. Now. She spun about and raced outside, raised her arms, and called for attention.

"Hey! Everyone! Come quickly." Kiera stood in front of the dream shack, waving her arms and practically jumping up and down to get their attention.

Finn glanced at Duran and nodded. The two of them turned and raced across the open area with the rest of the crowd on their heels. Mac followed behind with Zianne in his arms, but the news guys caught up to Finn before he reached Kiera. "What's up?"

"Tor was just here."

Dink stepped closer, into camera range. One of the guys who'd arrived earlier had a microphone that he held in front of Kiera. Another guy, the one who'd piloted the helicopter, held a camera braced against his shoulder.

Dink asked, "Who's Tor?"

Kiera flashed a quick glance at him, but it was obvious she was speaking to Mac and the rest of the team. "Tor's one of the Nyrians I brought down. Mac, he said that we should have five more Nyrians with their soulstones arriving in a few minutes. Teev and Sakel, my guys, have been in the barracks recharging, and they're fine, but Xinot, Ian, and Darc have been running the whole damned ship on their own for ten hours, and Tor said they're in rough shape. Especially Xinot, for some reason. He said the dishes have to be at full power and he needs energy from more than just me. And, Finn, you guys need to be ready to go as soon as they arrive."

Lizzie pushed through the crowd. "Ian, Xinot, and Darc are my guys. I'll help."

"Good." Kiera stepped aside. "There's probably room for one more to hook up to the array."

"I'm here." Cam stepped past Finn and headed straight for the drawer where the mesh caps were stored.

Lizzie turned and stopped him with a light touch to his arm. "Cam, they're all men. Can you . . . you know . . . fantasize about them?"

He cupped the side of her face in his palm, and Finn felt a funny little twinge that couldn't possibly be jealousy, could it?

"Liz, think about it. Finn, Rodie, and Morgan are leaving in a few minutes. Mac's busy with too many other things. Who else?" He leaned close and kissed her forehead. "Trust me. I've got a great imagination."

"I know you do." She gave him a sheepish look. "I'm sorry. I'm . . . well, shit." She slipped her cap on and scooted into the big chair beside Kiera. They were both skinny enough that they fit—just barely. Cam leaned over the back and draped an arm around each woman. Finn and Duran backed out of the shack and gave the cameraman room to film.

Dink stepped up behind Finn. "Can you explain what they're doing? They almost look like they're going into a trance."

"In a way, they are." Finn kept his voice low but spoke directly into the microphone. "You're aware how Mac discovered that Nyrians thrive on the energy generated by sexual fantasy, right? All of us are moderately telepathic with vivid imaginations. When we're hooked up to the array—see that mesh cap each of them is wearing?—those fantasies are broadcast as energy to the Nyrians on the Gar spaceship. The satellite antennae are programmed to automatically lock on to the ship. That link was established early on. Think of it as a tether between us and the ship. Once the Nyrians pick up the energy signal, they can follow it here."

"Do they look human when they arrive?" Dink was focused on Finn, but Finn couldn't take his eyes off the three teammates. They'd already slipped into fantasy, if the sexy smile on Kiera's face and the boner in Cam's pants were any indication. Liz had a little frown between her eyes, and he wondered what she was thinking, and why she looked so worried.

"Uh, no. Sorry." Finn shot an embarrassed grin at Dink. It was so easy to get lost in what was happening. "They first arrive as columns of energy. Usually blue and gold sparkles, though I don't know if everyone looks the same, or if the fact that three of these guys who are coming are pretty weak right now will change the color or intensity of their appearance in the energy form. You'll get plenty of warning when they arrive. They're hard to miss. You should be able to get film of them turning."

"Oh, no!"

"Liz? What's the matter?" Finn heard her cry and was beside her in a heartbeat. He took her hand and she clutched at his fingers. "Xinot? You can make it. You can!"

Her eyes were closed and she was locked in her fantasy, but somehow she'd connected with her guys. That had to be it. Finn squeezed her hands, amazed that neither Cam nor Kiera seemed to notice Liz's distress. Holding on to her, he slipped into her thoughts, and it was like stepping out onto the deck of a small ship in a massive storm at sea.

Buffeted by wind and stinging needles that could have been rain but obviously weren't. Needles that seemed to slice through his skin, leaving burning trails in their wake.

It took mere seconds for Finn to realize he'd not gone into Lizzie's mind. Somehow, he'd ended up in Xinot's, and the man was in agony. Finn reached for him, holding tightly to Liz as he tried to strengthen the connection with Xinot. He'd never met the guy before, only knew of him from what Lizzie had said, but he sensed Xinot's desperation, his unwillingness to surrender.

Finn tightened the connection, narrowed it even more.

He was vaguely aware of energy streaming into the shack, of soft cries of pain and the sound of bodies falling to the floor, but still he held on to the one who'd not yet completed the crossing. *Xinot. Hang on, man. I need you to hold tight and follow the others.*

I'm injured. A guard fired just as I prepared to cross over. I did not think it would affect a human body, but it did. I managed to switch over but my strength is failing—still caught in stasis. Can't complete the journey.

You damned well will complete this journey. What do you need?

I don't know. I don't know!

Finn sensed Lizzie joining his link to Xinot and the surge in power was almost tactile. A moment later, Cam formed a third point in their connection, and then Kiera was there, lending her surprisingly strong mental acuity, sharpening the focus with that brilliant mind of hers.

Liz's telepathic voice was strong and clear. *Xinot? Are you there? I can feel you. We have you. Just ride us home.*

I'm coming. I feel it. Hold me, Lizzie. Hold me close.

Finn felt an extra surge as Lizzie's mind went into overdrive and she replayed the fantasy that he assumed had originally given Xinot his corporeal form.

It was Lizzie, but not the same Lizzie Finn thought he knew. No, this woman was dressed in a short, skintight, black leather skirt with matching thigh-high leather boots and stiletto heels. Her torso was encased in a red silk bustier that cupped her bare breasts and held them high and proud.

She held a whip in her right hand and those fuzzy handcuffs she'd mentioned dangled from her left, only it wasn't anything like the hand Finn was holding with its neatly trimmed, unpainted nails. No, the hand in her fantasy had long fingers tipped with deadly looking nails painted the same bloodred as her bustier.

And her hair, always such a neat brown cap, spilled around her shoulders in wild disarray. Finn latched on to her fantasy and felt their energy output soar, felt the connection between the four of them and Xinot strengthen.

Cam was there, naked and stretched out across a huge bed, his hands and feet tied at all four posts. His cock stood tall and thick, and Finn knew that this was Cam's addition to the fantasy, that he saw himself at Liz's mercy.

Kiera slipped into the image, standing beside Liz, wearing a red leather thong that displayed her perfect body and left nothing to the imagination. A thin leather strip cut between her legs, pulled up tight with a tiny slit at the front allowing her clit to peek through. The perfect globes of her buttocks glistened, and her chocolate skin looked as if it had been oiled.

Her breasts were cupped in a matching red leather push-up bra that left her dark nipples bare and showcased the dark sheen of her skin. She crawled across Cam, turned, and took his cock in her mouth while he attacked her clit with his tongue.

Suddenly, another man joined them. Naked, beautiful, his skin the same smooth porcelain as Cam's woman Niah. His dark blond hair hung in blood-soaked tangles about his face. More blood ran from a deep slash across his chest.

Lizzie screamed. Finn pulled free of the fantasy just in time to catch Xinot as the naked Nyrian tumbled out of space in human form and into Finn's arms.

Blood flowed freely from his wounds, garish stains against fair skin and blond hair, but Finn managed to catch him and slowly lower him to the floor. Someone handed him some clean towels. With the camera going, Finn covered the man's groin with one, pressed another against the deep slash in his chest, and held a third against the wound to his scalp.

"Bolt?" Finn raised his head, looking for the man. Where the hell was he? "Can you help him? Did the others make it?"

Dink answered. "Five guys showed up. How many did you expect?"

"Five," Cam said. "Are the others okay?"

"They appear to be. A couple of them look wiped out, but they're in better shape than this poor guy. Kiera's with them. What do you think happened to him?" Dink turned to the cameraman. "Did you get that? Good lord, he just tumbled out of nothing, a fully formed human. The others were sparkly, but not this guy."

Finn folded the towel on Xinot's chest. It was already soaking through. "I think he just about burned out getting here.

Xinot, hang on, buddy. Bolt?" What was taking him so long? Xinot needed help, and they needed to hurry. Hadn't Tor said that as soon as these guys showed up, he and the others had to head to the ship? He had no idea how long it was going to take them.

A woman shoved through the small crowd in the doorway. Fair and slender, and Finn knew he'd met her but . . .

"Niah? Can you help Xinot?" Cam grabbed her arm and pulled her farther into the room. "That's why I'm here." Niah spread a blanket on the floor. "Bolt has to leave for the Gar ship. He can't heal Xinot now."

Finn helped Cam lift the unconscious Nyrian and laid him on the clean surface. The moment Xinot was in position, Niah spun into energy and slipped inside the man.

Finn heard a sharp gasp and glanced up at the cameraman. "She'll heal him from inside," he said, feeling like a narrator in a documentary, which, in many ways, this newscast might be. "In energy form, she's capable of moving at the speed of light. It shouldn't take too long. Watch this." He pointed at the pool of blood that had spilled beside Xinot. As the camera recorded, the blood appeared to shrink back into his chest wound, which was already closing.

Duran knelt beside Dink, and stared at Xinot. "This changes things. We didn't think the Gar weapons could harm human flesh." He reached across Xinot and grabbed Finn's arm. "We have to go. Now. I just heard from Bane, and the attack against the fence on the far side of the plateau has begun. We can't risk waiting any longer. If they damage the satellite array, it could affect our ability to get to the ship."

Shit. Finn leapt to his feet. "What about getting back to Earth?" He thought that seemed pretty important.

"We'll worry about that later." Duran laughed. "You said you wanted an adventure, didn't you?"

Bolt crowded into the small shack with Morgan and Rodie.

The cameraman stepped back out of the way, along with Dink and the other reporter with the mic, though it was obvious they really didn't have a clue what was coming next.

Bolt took Rodie's hand in his left and Morgan's in his right. Finn clasped Morgan's right hand and held on to Duran, who held Rodie's. "Rodie, you and Morgan are going to meld with me. You don't have to do a thing—I'll grab you as soon as you disassemble. Finn, you're going with Duran. We'll head straight to the service bay on the engine room level. The air will be thin and it smells terrible. If you feel like puking, go ahead. That's partially why I had you pack water."

Morgan grunted. "Now he tells us."

Duran glanced at Finn. "Are you ready?"

Finn's heart pounded in his chest and his lungs tightened until he couldn't breathe at all. Nerves. He knew it was all nerves, but damn it, he had a right to be nervous. Sucking in a deep breath, he forced his lungs to expand. "Hell, yes. Let's go!"

He glanced at Morgan and winked. Rodie grinned and they all disassembled at once. The moment he lost his corporeal body, Finn felt a slight suction and knew he was caught in Duran's energy. Blue and gold motes of light sparkled and swirled all around him, and Finn imagined how they must look to everyone watching.

He thought of the first time he saw the energy spiraling and knew it was a Nyrian. Never in his wildest dreams had he imagined being a physical part of anything like this. The cameraman, the reporter, Dink and Cam, Lizzie and Kiera, Mac holding Zianne; all of them appeared as part of a still-life tableau, all focused on the spot where energy that had been five human figures now spun madly. The five of them flashed upward, spiraling higher and higher until the earth was a spinning blue marble beneath them. There was no sense of movement, no sensation of the atmosphere they immediately left behind.

The dark stillness of space gave way to the massive Gar ship, and they were through and inside before Finn had time to consider the fact he should be utterly terrified.

No, it was all too amazing, too unbelievable. A movie in three dimensions, a fantasy after smoking some really good weed. This could not be happening, could not be real.

You're free of me, Finn. Take your human shape, as will I.

Okay. Just hoping we can breathe in here.

That would be nice, don't you think? Only Rodie.

Let me go first, he said. *Better if just one of us keels over than all three.*

Before any of the others had time to respond, Finn reassembled his body. The stench hit him first, a smell worse than rotting meat, but he sucked in a deep breath and decided there was enough oxygen buried within the stench that he could breathe without passing out.

Puking might be another matter. He glanced at the swirling energy and nodded, hoping they'd see he was okay. The area they'd landed in was dark and filled with what looked like containers of some sort, marked with unknown symbols and signs.

"Shit. What died in here?" Morgan shook his head and grabbed Rodie's arm as she stumbled into her human form.

"Maybe it's the latest in Gar perfume," Finn said. "Eau de roadkill."

"Oh. Smells bad." She covered her nose with one hand and clung to Morgan, staring around them at the odd shapes and unknown machinery. "That's just gross, Finn. Yuck. What now?"

Duran reformed, and then Bolt stood beside him. "There is a long hallway that leads to the engine room. Right now, Bolt and I plus the three powering the ship are the only Nyrians on board. I've communicated with Nattoch. The Gar know there's a problem, but they have no idea what it is. Nattoch says Arnec managed to leave some form of residual energy in the barracks. No one realizes the room is empty. We have but a short time before the Gar figure out they've been duped. Bolt will go to the engine room and meet with the others. He'll help them shut down and escape. It's our job to rescue all the soulstones. Ours and Zianne's."

"You're certain they won't have separated hers from the rest of them? Destroyed it, somehow?" Morgan checked the buckle on the small pack around his waist.

"The Gar have no way of knowing which stones belong to any of us. Our soulstones glow so brightly, their light blinds the filthy creatures. They fear them, even as they hold them hostage."

"I sure hope you're right. We know the Gar are armed with stunners that can screw up your energy fields." Morgan glanced at Finn. "And from the look of the guy you brought in, they've got other weapons as well, because he had a pretty good slice across his chest. How did that happen?"

"Xinot was the last to pick up his stone. He was exhausted after the ten-hour shift with just the three of them," Bolt said. "The Gar who was guarding the stones became suspicious and fired his stunner, but Xinot tried to shift to his human form, hoping the confusion would give him time to escape."

He glanced away and then turned and looked directly at Morgan. "We did not know until Xinot returned wounded that the standard Gar weapon would damage human flesh. You will have to be very careful to avoid them."

"Great." Rodie rolled her eyes. "I guess we don't just waltz right in like we planned."

"I don't like this, Rodie." Morgan glared at her. "It's too dangerous."

"I don't like it either, Morgan." She met his glare with one of her own, planted her hands on her hips and growled, "So I suggest we get our butts in gear and go rescue the guys in the engine room, grab the stones, and get the hell off this stinking spaceship before something dangerous happens."

"Something dangerous? Like being here is safe?" It wasn't at all funny. Really. Except Rodie looked so damned outraged, Finn had to bite his lip to keep from laughing. He glanced at Morgan. Morgan made eye contact and his lips twitched. Then Rodie turned and saw both of them struggling to maintain. She lost it.

It took them forever to stop giggling. Duran and Bolt stared at the three of them as if they were nuts. Maybe they were, but the laughter settled whatever fear had gripped them—at least it did for Finn.

They were here to do a job and it was time to get it done.

Rodie muttered, "Well, it really does stink."

Finn snorted and refused to look at Morgan, who was paying a lot of attention to the door in front of them. Duran shot a confused look at Bolt. "It must be a human response we've not learned yet."

Frowning, Bolt nodded seriously, which almost set Finn off again, but he took a deep breath, held it a moment, and got control. Yeah, he wanted to say, it's definitely a human response to blind terror. When in doubt, get the giggles.

Bolt shifted to his energy form and went on ahead. A moment later, with Duran in the lead, the rest of them headed through the doorway and down the long hallway that would take them to the soulstones—and the Gar.

9

Dink stared at the empty spot in the dream shack where three humans and two Nyrians had been standing. Unbelievable. He glanced over his shoulder at Nick Shaw, the young helicopter pilot doing double-duty by toting the camera gear, and figured Nick looked just as stunned. "Did you get that?"

"I think so. Where'd they go?"

"I imagine they're on the Gar ship by now." Zianne glanced at Mac and sighed. "It's begun, gentlemen. In their energy form, they will travel at light speed. It's how I was able to go back in time to find Mac, so that he would have the next twenty years to develop the technology and make enough money to build this array."

"You couldn't go forward, see how this all pans out?" Dink stepped aside so Carl Waters, the one hanging on to the mic, could hold it closer to Zianne. "That would sure ease a lot of tension." He laughed. Zianne merely smiled.

"True, but you cannot go into a time that has not happened. You can only see that which has passed. We won't know how everything is going until they're back. I'm sorry, Dink, but we're into real time while they deal with the Gar."

"Xinot? Are you all right?" Liz's question tugged Dink away from Zianne. The dream shack was such a small building and just the few of them filled it—how the hell could he have lost track of an injured man being healed from the inside out?

After a while, maybe the brain just refused to process any more unbelievable stuff. That had to be it. Dink focused on the man lying on the floor. Lizzie knelt beside him and the Nyrian woman who'd disappeared *inside* the injured alien was now sitting next to him, holding his hand. His eyes were open, his color finally returning to what Dink assumed was his normal fair complexion.

Like the other aliens, this guy was absolutely beautiful. He certainly appealed to Dink's appreciation of the male form. Almost angelic with thick waves of dark blond hair curling around his face, and eyes such a brilliant blue he looked as if he wore fake contacts. Lizzie was helping him to sit up, and he was smiling at her while leaning against the one who had healed him.

"I am well now. Thank you, Niah." He nodded formally to the Nyrian. She leaned over and kissed him, brushed his hair back from his face in a tender, almost motherly gesture, and then quickly stood.

"I'm going to take Ian, Darc, Teev, and Sakel to the lodge with me," she said. "They need food, time to adjust, to rest in case we're needed later." Teev and Sakel each kissed Kiera and followed Niah and the other two as they left the shack.

The door hadn't had time to close when gunshots echoed across the plateau. Dink stared at Mac. "What's going on?"

Zianne closed her eyes for a moment, and then, if anything, looked even more pale than she'd been. "The ones on the back side of the plateau have torn through the fence, rushed the guards, and fired upon them. Your men are returning gunfire, but the Nyrians are not armed. They've shifted and will do what mischief they can to slow the attack, but they're outnumbered."

"Shit. Kiera?" Mac shifted Zianne in his arms. "I need to leave Zianne here with you. The shack's like a bunker. Lock the door behind us. You should be safe and we need to hang on to the connection here with the ship."

Lizzie helped Xinot to his feet. "I'm taking Xinot to my cabin. He needs to get his strength back. Kiera? Call me if you need me. I'll keep my phone handy." She and Xinot moved aside as Mac carried Zianne to the recliner.

"Sounds good, Liz." Kiera stood as Mac settled Zianne into the comfortable chair and kissed her soundly. Dink made sure the camera caught all of it before following Mac outside. "Mac, I can't believe they're attacking in broad daylight. I was sure you'd have plenty of time before they rushed the site."

"I know." Mac continued on toward the lodge where Meg waited on the porch. "Meg? I want you to get all the Nyrians who aren't working with Ralph in here; take them into the basement. Make sure you've got plenty of food with you. There's water and rations stored down there along with plenty of bedding and supplies."

"My chicken's a lot better than your rations, Mac Dugan." Meg was already signaling to the women around her, gathering them together. Many of them looked totally out of it, as if they'd had one too many shocks in too short a time. Niah and the four men stood off to one side.

Mir walked in. She touched Mac's arm. "I'll help," she said. "Tara will stay in the dream shack with Zianne and Kiera, in case someone needs to share energy with Zianne." She raised her voice. "All the rest of you, let's help Meg carry what we need and get below. We'll be safe here until we're needed."

Niah followed the group of frightened women, and the few men who'd just arrived from the ship, across the open area, helping to herd them up to the porch. "There are quite a few of us. Will we fit in your safe room?"

Meg opened the door and held it wide. "Plenty of room. We'll be fine, and there's a computer down there so we can get online and follow what's happening."

Niah paused between Mac and Dink. "The guys will be fine once they've had time to rest a bit and adjust. As far as the women, if you need our help, don't hesitate to ask. Not all of us are frightened. Some of us are truly angry, and we have many ways of dealing with stupid men who tend to underestimate our abilities. And remember, Mac. I can heal humans as well as Nyrians. So can Mir."

She had such a big smile on her face, Dink figured she wished she was one of the guys on the front lines.

"I do," she said. Then she winked at him and followed the others into the lodge.

Mac watched her go with a stupid grin on his face.

"What are you laughing at?" Dink realized he was smiling as well, which was really stupid with the sound of gunfire escalating and the potential for some real danger way too close.

Mac shook his head as he headed back down the stairs. "Just thinking how much these people amaze me. I have yet to meet a stupid or cowardly Nyrian."

"They've lived a long time. Long enough to get smart."

"Ya think?" Mac stopped in front of the helicopter. "Can you guys fly over, take a look, maybe see if you can get any idea what their plans are?"

"Works for me. What about you? Carl? You stay with Mac. Use the handheld camera for any video you think we can use. It records sound. The quality's not as good, but it's okay. We'll worry about editing later. I'll go up with Nick."

"I'm calling General Adams and updating him," Mac said. "Can you broadcast live from the chopper? Have you aired enough to at least have people appreciating the fact that the Nyrians are the good guys?"

"Carl?" Dink turned to the other reporter. Carl stood a few feet away with his cell phone to his ear. "You get any feedback yet on our earlier reports?"

The man nodded, held up a finger for time, and continued talking a moment longer. Then he tapped the phone off. "They're coming around, at least from what our man-on-the-street reporters are hearing. The boss says our phone system's crashed twice now due to incoming calls, but they're mostly on our side, wondering who's going to stop the bad aliens. Showing the guys turning into sparkles and leaving for the ship definitely got everyone's attention. It's a good visual, all those pretty sparks. Reminds people of the old *Star Trek* movies."

Dink just shook his head. "I'll admit to hearing, 'beam me up, Scotty,' in my head whenever I see them, but that's a good thing. It's a positive connection for viewers, something that actually makes sense."

"Unlike the rest of what we're seeing?" Carl grabbed a small video camera out of his pack.

"Exactly." Dink paused before climbing into the helicopter as Mac glanced at his cell phone and cursed.

"It's been set to vibrate so it wouldn't interrupt your broadcast. Looks like the general's been trying to reach me."

Mac tapped to reply and held the phone to his ear. Dink rubbed the back of his neck, only now aware of the tension tightening his muscles, of the adrenaline coursing through his body. He hadn't felt this jacked up since Afghanistan. No, he'd never felt this jacked. This was way bigger than anything the Middle East could throw at them.

Mac turned his back while he carried on his conversation. Dink glanced at the reporter. "Carl, we'll be doing a live feed from the chopper." The pilot snorted in disbelief. Dink just laughed it off. The guy didn't know Dink any more than Dink knew him. "Don't worry," he said. "I'm not just another pretty face."

Nick flushed beet red. "I, uh . . ."

"Relax. I'm teasing you." The last thing he needed was a pilot who thought he was an idiot, especially with the escalating sounds of fighting coming from the plateau. "Look, Nick, I've handled plenty of cameras, and I've done it with people shooting at me in countries all over the world. Don't worry about anything but the chopper. You need to fly. And keep flying. I prefer not to get shot down. That would look really bad on your résumé, not to mention it would totally ruin my day."

"Uh, sure thing, Mr. Dinkemann. Nils." The kid was a good cameraman and one hell of a pilot from what Dink could tell, but he was stumbling all over because of Dink's fame. A little hero worship was fine, but not when it got in the way of performance.

"Nick, at this point, I think you can just call me Dink. There's got to be a rule somewhere that when you're getting shot at, the formal crap gets dropped."

"Yes, sir." The minute he said it, Nick blushed again, Dink laughed. A huge explosion rocked the ground.

"Shit! What the . . ."

Flames rocketed skyward from the far end of the plateau, followed by a thick cloud of black smoke. Dink heard Mac yelling into his phone, but Nick had lost all his earlier hesitancy. He'd already jumped into the chopper and was firing up the engine. The rotor began turning almost immediately as he prepared for takeoff. Dink raced around to the far side and buckled himself into the passenger's seat.

It took just over a minute to get the bird off the ground, but then they were in the air and flying over the remnants of one of the huge satellite dishes, now a crumpled mass of twisted metal. The ground around the base was blackened, but with nothing but dirt and rocks to burn, the fire had gone out. Dink kept the camera going as Nick swooped low over the tangled wreckage.

Then he took a pass out over the fence and down the side of the plateau. Dink spotted half a dozen men hunkered down behind a natural wall of what had to be part of the old lava flow that had created the plateau many thousands of years ago.

One of them stood and fired a shot at the helicopter, but he was using a handgun and didn't have the range. Nick was already taking evasive measures and the bullet missed. He circled the chopper back around to the top of the plateau.

As they flew over the fence, Dink spotted a huge section that had been ripped out. A small tractor lay on its side just over the edge of a short drop, trailing about twenty feet of chain link fencing behind it.

The chopper swept on around so Dink could film the damage and then headed back over DEO-MAP property. Mac's security guards were huddled behind a large group of boulders not far from the blast. Dink pointed to them. Nick set the chopper down nearby, but far enough back from the plateau's edge for some protection from the men on the hillside below. They both got out and Dink handed the camera off to Nick as they ducked beneath the spinning blades.

"Are you guys okay?" Dink bent low behind the rocks, furious that the jerks on the hillside below didn't appear to have a problem firing at unarmed men.

"Yeah. No one's been hit, but we're all a little pissed. Where the hell's the sheriff?" Ralph popped up for a quick look over the rock and then slid back down behind it. "We're under attack here. They tore out a section of the fence and blew one of the dishes. We thought we'd have help by now. What's happening?"

"When I left, Mac was on the phone with someone from the Pentagon. As far as the sheriff showing up with help, Mac said not to hold your breath. The guy running your resident domestic terrorist group has one of the local county supervisors in his pocket. The board has openly declared that they're not a problem."

"Like we are?" Ralph leaned over and spit. "I'd like to see someone from the board of supervisors down here dodging bullets and then see what the sons a' bitches have to say. If not for these guys"—he nodded at the Nyrians who'd held on to their human form—"I think a couple of us might've been shot. Or worse."

"You guys aren't armed, are you?" Dink spoke to the men, well aware of the camera Nick focused on their conversation.

Bane shook his head. His face was smudged with dirt, but he looked as if he was having a great time. "They don't cope well with Nyrians disassembling in front of them. We've been trying to keep them confused and uncertain of our number."

"How'd they get in with the tractor, pull so much fencing out? It's going to be hard to protect an opening that wide."

"They used a diversion," Ralph said. "These boys weren't familiar with dirty tricks. They are now." He laughed. "They made the bastard pay for that piece of fence, though."

"How?" Dink turned to Bane.

"We disassembled and a few of us swarmed the one driving the tractor. We got him inside and out. He was so busy swatting bugs he thought were crawling on him, and reacting to the sensual rush inside, that he totally freaked out." Bane grinned at the other Nyrians. "We were just discussing trying a similar approach with the ones who are armed."

Dink directed Nick to film Bane. "Where does a Nyrian get a totally human phrase like *freaked out?*" he asked. "And when you say *sensual rush,* what are you referring to?"

Jesat nudged Bane. "We could show him?"

"Not now." Bane laughed. Obviously, the man was thoroughly enjoying himself.

Dink waited while Nick kept the camera on the Nyrians. "Language, first. How do you know our slang?"

Jesat shrugged. "The same way we know any of your language, or how to behave in your society, how to care for our human bodies. How to be human. We take information from the minds of those around us. In essence, we are all a combination of a lot of bits and pieces of information from the humans we've been near, but those insights blend with our individual personalities." He shrugged. "We do have our own distinct personalities. Take Bane, for instance."

"Yes," Aza said, nudging Jesat. "Please, take Bane."

Dink laughed. Jesat just shook his head. "See what I mean? Bane has always been bossy, and Aza's just a smartass. No matter how much we absorb from other humans, our basic nature is still who and what we are."

"Exactly," Bane said. "I will always take charge, and Aza will do his best to screw things up. We are who we are."

Aza jabbed him in the ribs with his elbow. "You will pay for that, you realize?"

Bane merely threw his arm around Aza's shoulders, emphasizing their friendship and everything Jesat had said. Dink had the feeling these guys had shared the same conversation before, no matter their physical form.

"Okay," he said. "That makes perfect sense. I think. Now explain what you meant by going inside the . . ." He paused, frowning. Should he call them terrorists? Is that what Bartholomew Roberts's army was? "I guess I would call the guy driving the tractor a domestic terrorist. What did you do to him?"

The others deferred to the big blond Nyrian this time. Dake. Another gorgeous guy. Dink hoped Nick got the camera on him in time to catch him rolling his eyes. "Nothing bad," he said. "At least we didn't hurt him. I disassembled and went inside him, in much the same way we heal from within. However,

I went directly to the pleasure center in his brain and the eroge-nous zones of his body."

"And how does that affect someone?"

"Well..." Dake glanced at Bane and sort of checked him out. "I wouldn't complain if he chose to give me the same expe-rience. Imagine your body reacting to sexual stimulation that affected all your erogenous zones—both mental and physical—at once."

"While at the same time, Ankar, Jesat, and I were buzzing around on his skin, inside his clothing." Aza steepled his fin-gers, laughing softly. "He had little bugs crawling all over his body with concentrations on his nipples, testicles, and penis, while Dake was doing the same thing from the inside."

Dink bit back a grin. He really needed to keep this on a pro-fessional level, but the visual Aza was painting didn't help. "How did he react?"

Nick slowly panned the five Nyrians as they looked at one another and grinned. Dink figured the women were going to love this shot. Women and any men with the same sexual predilection as Dink. Five self-assured, cocky, drop-dead gor-geous guys discussing how they'd sexually stimulated a man in-side and out. Dink was hard as a rock inside his jeans, his cock pressing against the zipper so fiercely that the pleasure verged on pain. Not very professional, but totally unavoidable . . . and enjoyable.

"He, uh..." Dake finally grinned directly into the camera, and, as if he were a professor addressing a classroom, said, "He experienced a profound sexual event which affected his atten-tion and caused him to drive off the edge of the trail into a gully. He was not injured, but his vehicle will never be the same."

"Or his dick." Aza doubled over, laughing. Bane merely sighed and thumped him on the head.

Then he turned to Dink, totally ignoring the camera aimed

at him. "What's happening with the rescue?" He wiped sweat off his forehead, and if Dink hadn't known better, he would have tagged him as just another security guard. A very large, good-looking security guard. "Have they recovered the rest of the soulstones? Are Nattoch and the others safe yet?"

"Not yet." Dink checked his watch. It was almost five thirty. "They left around twenty minutes ago, a bit later than planned, but when the most recent group got away from the ship, one of them arrived badly injured."

"Who was it?" Aza's jokester attitude disappeared entirely.

"A guy named Xinot. He'd taken human form when a Gar guard targeted him. He didn't think the weapon could hurt him in that form, but he was wrong, and he was shot during their escape. That changed a lot of the team's plans, since it means the weapons that can neutralize your energy field can also damage human flesh, plus the Gar are aware now that something's going on. Whatever plan Finn and the others had will have to be adjusted accordingly. They did say it might take them longer, knowing that the Gar have weapons that can stop them, but they're smart and determined."

Aza wrapped his fingers around Dink's wrist. "Is Xinot okay? We are good friends." He glanced at Bane. "He's Bane's brother."

Dink looked at Bane. The man hadn't said a word, but he nodded at Aza. "I'm in contact with him now," Bane said. "He was injured but he's healing."

"I forget how well you guys can communicate," Dink said. "Don't worry. He's fine. Niah healed his injuries, and Liz has taken him with her to rest at her cabin."

Aza nodded and wrapped an arm around Bane's shoulders. "Niah is one of our best healers. We don't need to worry about him if she's the one to repair his injuries. I'm glad she was there."

"What about these jerks?" Ralph waved a hand toward the

battered fence. "We can't continue to hold them. There aren't enough of us."

Dink wished he had an answer for the guy. "Ralph, I just don't know. Mac had your wife take the Nyrians who arrived earlier into the safe room beneath the lodge. They've got plenty of food down there and the place is fireproof. I think the main thing, for now, is to try and hold these guys off until the rescue is complete. You and your guards are armed."

He grinned at the Nyrians. "You guys don't need guns. After the rescue, who knows? Mac's in touch with people at the Pentagon as well as the Department of Defense. I think they'll come around, once they have all the facts."

"I'm glad Mac thought to have the women take shelter," Ralph said. "I was there when he had it built. That thing's a totally reinforced bomb shelter. They'll be safe in there, and Meg's like a mother hen when she's got someone to watch over."

"Well, she's got a room full of totally stressed-out Nyrian women and four guys who just escaped from the Gar. I think they've had all they can take for now."

Bane agreed. "It's been especially difficult for our women. They're brave and willing to fight to protect those they love, but we've all been beaten down for so long. It's hard to remember what we're fighting for."

"Your freedom, Bane." Dink stood but with the camera still running. "In just a very short time, this should all be over, and you and yours will be free."

Nodding slowly, he tilted his chin and gazed up at Dink. "I hope you're right. My only fear is that we will trade one captor for another." He turned his head and looked in the direction of the small army waiting on the hillside below. "What if the people of your world are more like them?" Then he smiled. "We're all hoping they're like Mac, like you and the others in the dream team. Like Ralph and Meg. You don't see us as aliens.

You don't fear us. You've shown us nothing but kindness." His smile was sad and somewhat pensive. "It's been a long time since we've known kindness, since we've had any chance at freedom. Please forgive us if we find it difficult to trust until we know for sure that freedom is ours to hold."

Duran held up his hand. Finn pressed close against the wall, running his fingers over the slick surface. It felt cool, though not quite as cold as the air around them. Duran hadn't been kidding when he'd told them to wear warm clothes.

There was no sense of air movement, at least not at this level. He couldn't even guess what it was like in the upper, more populated levels of the ship. He was vaguely aware of sound—a distant rumble that was all around them, and could only be the engines that were powered by the Nyrians. He wondered if that sound would stop when they left the engine room.

When the ship began to die.

He just hoped he was off it when that happened. Hoped all of them—and the soulstones—were far away when the thing imploded. Probably not a good idea to think of that now. He knew the Gar were horrible, that they'd killed and would kill again, but the idea of wiping out an entire civilization bothered him on a level he couldn't define. He'd damned well better get over it.

Finn studied the part of the ship where they'd paused. The overhead was softly illuminated, more than sufficient to light their way. The surface under their feet was rough, which meant his boots didn't slide at all, but he still wasn't sure what the interior of the ship was made of. At first he'd assumed it was some kind of metal, but it felt almost like plastic. He'd love to take a piece of it home with him and stick it under a microscope.

Hell, here they were on an alien spaceship and no one was getting samples of anything. At least Rodie had taken her little camera out and hung it around her neck, so he figured she was getting some movies of them as they got closer to the soulstones.

They waited while Duran peered around the corner before slipping back into the shadows beside the three of them. "There's a door up ahead," he said. "It opens to an elevator that leads to the guards' barracks on the next level. We've been trying to figure out a way to disable the lift to prevent more Gar from coming down should there be a cry for help. They have a fairly sophisticated intercom system built into their uniforms that our energy doesn't affect, so we can't interfere with their transmissions, but the elevator is purely mechanical."

Now that sounded like something Finn could sink his teeth into. "Does it have an access panel? A place where you can get in to the machinery to repair things?" He dug into his little fanny pack while he questioned Duran. Found the water bottle and realized he was thirsty, so he took a drink before putting it back. There it was. Just what he was looking for.

"I'm not sure," Duran said. "It's just ahead, but we'll have to be very careful. The entrance to the elevator is close to the station where the soulstones are guarded."

"Do you two mind waiting here for a couple of minutes?" Finn glanced to his left at Rodie. She shrugged. Morgan shook his head. "Good." Whispering, Finn said, "Duran, I want you to show me where it is."

Rodie stayed really still, but she didn't seem at all frightened. Mostly pissed off about the stench, if her hand over her nose meant anything. "What are you going to do?"

It was hard to understand her, whispering through her fingers like that, but Finn grinned and held up his favorite grownup toy—a Leatherman multitool. It looked like a little pair of needle nose pliers, until he started flipping different tools out of the handles. "Remember the night we all met, and Mac asked about our background? When I said I can fix anything that breaks, I meant it. As long as I have this baby."

"Well, we certainly don't want you fixing their elevator now, do we?" Morgan's eyes never quit moving as he scanned the hallway in both directions, but there was no missing the typical Morgan Black sarcasm.

Luckily, Finn realized he was immune to it by now. Besides, he'd decided he liked the guy in spite of the bad-boy attitude. "You're right, Morgan. But if I can fix anything, I can also take anything apart." He winked. Morgan just shook his head. "Duran? You ready?"

Duran gave a quick jerk of his head and then slipped around the corner. Finn followed. This hallway was a little wider than the one they'd just left. The light was brighter, but the stench was, if anything, worse. He wondered if it was the natural body odor of the Gar, or was it the accumulated stink from centuries living in an enclosed system?

He no longer felt like throwing up, but neither did he want to think of what he was drawing deep into his lungs. It wasn't easy to breathe—the air was thin, as if he were high in the mountains, but it lacked that pure mountain air scent.

Duran paused in front of a large set of double doors. These were definitely some sort of metal, similar to titanium, if Finn's guess was right. They looked like doors to an elevator you might find in any high-tech office building. He ran his fingers along both sides and then got down on his knees to check along the floor line. There! He couldn't actually see the panel, but he could feel the seam where two pieces of metal were perfectly joined.

Now, if he could just get it open. Finn used the razor-sharp blade of his knife to run along the edge. He applied just a bit of pressure, and the blade slipped into the invisible seam. It took just a bit of prying. The cover popped off.

Duran gasped but Finn caught the metal plate before it hit

the ground. He heard Duran's sigh of relief, but he knelt there a moment, holding on to the plate, much too aware of his thundering heart and trembling hands.

Then he heard a rumble, above and beyond the pounding of his heart or the normal sounds of the ship. A sound vibrating through the walls, coming closer.

Coming from the elevator.

"Shit. Someone's coming."

Duran grabbed Finn's arm and dragged him to his feet. Clutching the small access panel to his chest, Finn raced after the Nyrian, back to their hiding spot down the hall and around the corner.

Rodie glanced up, wide-eyed, as he and Duran slid to a stop and pressed back against the wall, both of them gasping for air in the putrid atmosphere. "What's wrong?"

It took Finn a while to catch his breath. "Someone's coming down the elevator. I got the panel open, but haven't had a chance to look inside." He held up the metal cover.

"Won't they notice it's missing?" Rodie hung on to Morgan's hand, but she wasn't freaking out. That was a good thing.

"I don't know." Finn held a finger to his lips. He'd heard the solid thud as the elevator stopped. Now a soft swish as doors opened. Voices? Must be the Gar talking, but they sounded almost like birds chirping. Actually, he thought of ravens with the combination of high tones, some lower sounds, even the loud clicking he'd heard the big birds make. The voices disappeared in the distance, which meant they'd probably joined the other guards.

He hoped it was just a shift change, that they were relieving the guards on duty now and those guards would leave. The idea of even more Gar to deal with made him very nervous.

10

Rodie hated this, being stuck in a long, fairly well-lit corridor without any kind of cover, waiting in plain sight of anyone who might come by, knowing they still had the hardest part of the mission ahead of them. It didn't help, breathing air that stank to high heaven. What the hell was that smell? She raised her head like a dog sniffing the breeze. The ship reeked of carrion, that sickly sweet yet acrid stench of death and rotting meat.

She couldn't get past the thought this was like being trapped in a box with roadkill. *Think about something else. Anything else.* She curled her fingers against the slick wall, and her nails caught on something that felt like an indentation of some sort. Slowly turning, Rodie ran her fingers over the area that was just a little bit lower than a door handle would be.

There wasn't really anything to grab hold of, but she tried pushing along one edge. A curved ring popped out of the wall. Tugging slightly, she gasped when the entire section of wall slid to one side.

"Oh, shit." The stench just about knocked her over.

"What the hell is that?" Morgan was looking over her shoulder, but the room was icy cold and very dark, and from their spot here in the doorway, there was nothing to see.

"No idea." Rodie swept her hand over the wall inside the door, looking for a light switch. Nothing but smooth, cold wall.

Morgan stepped back. He whispered something to Duran and then she caught the slight whisper of Duran's reply. Morgan draped an arm over her shoulder. "He says the light will go on automatically once you step over the threshold."

"Okay." Rodie pressed the on button for the little video camera she'd strung around her neck, covered her nose and mouth with the sleeve of her jacket to cut the worst of the stench, and stepped into the room with the digital camera recording.

The lights went on, and thank goodness Morgan's hand covered her mouth, though it was barely in time to catch her scream. She could hardly hear him whispering rapidly to the others over the roaring in her ears, and the gorge rose in her throat until she was swallowing repeatedly to keep from puking all over the floor.

Slowly she peeled his fingers away from her mouth. She turned and looked at him, and she knew her eyes were probably bugging out of her face, but she wasn't going to scream. She absolutely was not going to make a sound.

Morgan stared back at her with the same shocked expression that she felt. They nodded to one another, and she finally forced herself to turn around, to see exactly what she'd discovered.

The room was massive. Absolutely huge, and filled with bodies hanging for as far as the eye could see. Row upon row of gutted bodies of alien beings, hanging from overhead hooks like slabs of meat in a butcher's locker. Not Gar and obviously not Nyrians, these were still humanoid enough that she knew they had to have been sentient beings from some civilized world.

"Holy fucking shit."

Rodie looked over her shoulder at Finn and Duran standing directly behind Morgan. Finn was staring at the bodies with an expression of absolute horror on his face. Duran just looked . . . bored? As if this wasn't anything awful or even interesting?

"It's a fucking meat locker," Morgan said. "Duran? Who were these people? There are . . . good lord, there must be thousands of bodies in here."

"I have no idea." Duran shrugged as he looked down the long rows. "This is one of their storage facilities. There are many of them about the ship, usually segregated by species according to quality. This locker is a long way from the kitchens, so I imagine this species isn't top quality. You know. Not as good to eat."

Rodie's shocked gasp seemed to surprise Duran. He frowned and actually focused on her expression. Didn't he get it? Didn't he understand just how disgusting this was? How wrong?

Duran nodded, and she realized he'd been reading her thoughts. "It is wrong by human standards, but I believe I've told you, the Gar are carnivores. This is their food. Sentience in another species doesn't preclude the Gar from eating them. When a species is consumable, they are slaughtered like your cattle and removed from the planet for storage aboard the ship before the other resources are mined."

"But these were people. Not human, but still sentient people. They had families. Oh, God. Some of them look like children." Rodie had gotten past the nausea and her initial shock enough to remember her camera. She held it out from her chest but left the cord around her neck, filming as she walked over to the closest row of bodies. "Look. This one is still wearing clothing." She focused the camera on tattered pants covered in thick maroon stains. Blood? She didn't know. Didn't really want to know, though this one, like all the others, had been eviscerated and the internal organs removed.

Speaking to the camera, she described what she was filming. "The creature is bipedal, about five feet tall with four toes on each foot and three fingers on each hand plus what appears to be an opposing thumb. It's hard to tell because the hands are clenched, but there are metal rings on some of the fingers. Jewelry of some kind. From the musculature, I'm guessing this one's male."

She kept up her running commentary as she filmed the entire body before moving on to the next, a child this time by its smaller size and softer facial features. Her hands shook so much, she hoped it didn't screw up the images she was trying to capture. The one beside it had two sets of breasts. Female, though like all the others, the chest had been split open, the body eviscerated, which somehow made the sagging breasts—two on either side of the open chest cavity—a horrible parody of the female body.

She wondered if this one had been the child's mother. Had she been forced to see her baby slaughtered? The female's facial features were frozen in a rictus of agony. Rodie stared at the face, wondering if this one—if any of them—had been killed before the Gar gutted her. Some of the bodies were nude. She filmed them from all sides and angles, in case scientists might be interested in the differences between the men and women.

She couldn't get the image of the breasts out of her mind, of the child hanging beside the female. The gorge was rising in her throat again and she had to stop and close her eyes. Look away from so much carnage.

"Over here, Rodie."

She glanced up as Finn gestured to a row of different-looking creatures. Some had four and others had six legs, but these bodies had all been skinned. There were tufts of dark fur near oddly shaped hooves, but they looked more like animals, not sentient beings. They hung in long rows that disappeared into shadows.

"This is what they had planned for Earth." Morgan didn't strike Rodie as a man easily shaken by much of anything, but he looked as pale as she felt and his voice cracked on the words. Rage? He didn't look afraid. No, he looked totally pissed off.

He glanced at her camera. "Are you getting all of this?"

"I am. As much as I can. It's just a cheap little camera, but it's good for about two hours. I hope Dink can use it for his newscast."

"It's better than nothing. I'm glad you thought to bring it." He brushed a hand over her hair. "You were right when you said you had different skills we would need. You think of stuff ahead of time."

"It's a girl thing," she said, though her smile was forced. "We're smaller. We have to be smarter and faster. And better prepared."

Morgan nodded and glanced at the door. Duran had slipped back outside. "The world needs to know what the Gar are capable of. Dink said there's a lot of sympathy for the poor aliens coming to Earth. Damned fools. C'mon. We need to get out of here before someone comes by."

"Good idea." Finn stared at the body closest to him, what looked like a young male. "I don't want to end up on the menu."

Rodie felt absolutely numb. This was so much worse than anything she'd expected to see on this mission. These weren't just slabs of meat hanging in a freezer. They were the bodies of people—many of them children—obviously sentient beings who had lived on another planet somewhere.

A planet that had been their home.

Possibly a world like Earth, with forests and mountains, with a sun overhead and atmosphere they could breathe. Now they were nothing more than slabs of meat for a stronger race.

She turned away, flipped the camera off, slipped the cord over her neck, and stuck the camera in her pack. She was not going to cry. Not now. She'd do that later, when they were home safe and she had the time to mourn a people gone forever.

Home safe. Morgan was wrong. She hadn't really thought this through, hadn't considered the danger. Now it felt all too real, what they were doing. What they were hoping to prevent.

Morgan and Finn followed her out of the freezer.

Morgan carefully shut the door behind them, but it didn't make the stench go away. Or the horror.

Finn leaned against the wall, fighting a combination of nausea and blinding rage. He would never forget what he'd just seen. Never forget all those individuals hanging in long rows, each face totally unique. Not human. Not even close to human, but they were obviously people.

Any guilt he'd felt about destroying the Gar ship and all the people aboard was gone. They were murderers. He had faces of their victims now. Males, females, and from the size of many of the bodies hanging in the freezer, children. Many, many children.

The women had four breasts, which meant they probably had larger families. That would account for all the children. God but he didn't want to be sick. Not here. Not now.

His heart pounded against his chest and he felt the anger flowing off Morgan and Rodie. All of them in this together. The sense from Duran was not so strong, but he'd lived with this for thousands of years. Did one become numb to so much death?

He must have. All of the Nyrians must have, or they wouldn't have survived this long. Of course, they fed off energy, not meat. They wouldn't have been involved in the actual preparation of bodies. He tried to imagine what it was like for the Gar who killed the various inhabitants of different planets. Did they see other species as equals? Probably not. They only saw the Nyrians as a source of energy, not as a sentient race.

He leaned his head against the wall and concentrated on calming down. On controlling the rush of adrenaline that had his muscles twitching and the blood rushing through his veins. He needed to find his center and hold on to it or he'd not be steady enough to work on the elevator controls.

Then he needed to finish this mission. Find the soulstones and blow this goddamned ship to smithereens.

He felt as if they'd been holding their position here for forever. A lifetime had passed since he'd walked into that damned meat locker. Something inherently central to who and what he was had been forever changed. Could anyone see something that horrible and not change?

Then Finn heard that odd clattering sound again, heard the door to the elevator open, then close, and the deep hum as the machinery kicked on. He pushed himself away from the wall.

Duran caught his arm. "Wait. Let me see what's happening in the engine room. The walls are blocked so we can't communicate through them." He disassembled for no more than a few seconds of swirling energy and sparkling lights before reappearing. "Bolt says they're just waiting for our word. They intend to power the ship until the last minute to give us more time to escape. As soon as we've got the guards near the vault under control, they'll shut down and meet us to collect their soulstones. Then we're all going to disassemble and get off of here as quickly as we can. They figure fifteen, maybe twenty minutes before the systems begin to destabilize."

Morgan grunted. "It can't be soon enough for me."

"Me, either." Rodie still looked slightly nauseous, and her skin was way too pale, but she didn't appear to be at all afraid. If anything, Finn thought she sounded even more determined.

"I definitely agree. Okay, I'm ready to take another shot at the elevator controls." Finn glanced at Duran for confirmation.

He nodded. "I think we should all go this time. We'll be that much closer to the guards, but still out of sight of their post. Remember, they're fresh. They'll be more alert."

"Great," Rodie muttered. "Just what we need."

Morgan leaned close and kissed her. "You can handle 'em," he said. "Hey, Duran? Do the Gar have sexual fantasies?"

Duran gave him a disgusted look. "Nothing we get a charge from, that's for sure. Humans are the best we've ever found."

"As it should be." Morgan glanced at Finn. *We need to get her thinking of something else.*

I agree. Finn nodded. He followed Duran around the corner and along the broad hallway with Rodie and Morgan close behind. Morgan's voice in his mind had been clear as glass. Their ability to communicate telepathically was growing stronger.

Finn moved ahead of Duran and knelt before the small opening beside the elevator doors. Nothing looked familiar, but that hadn't stopped him before. "Duran? Is this electrically charged? Am I going up in a cloud of smoke if I touch anything?"

"It's a form of power similar to your electricity. Avoid the yellow wires. I think everything else is safe."

"I hope you're right." The wiring was obviously old, covered in some sort of fabric that had scorch marks where wires rubbed against each other. This ship was ancient, and if what Duran and Bolt had said was true, it hadn't been properly maintained for a long, long time.

Parts inside the panel looked worn and discolored, but he carefully clipped all the wires he could get to, pulled out what looked like a small motherboard, and stuck it in his fanny pack to show Mac. Then he carefully replaced the cover plate he'd removed and tapped it with the side of his hand until it slid into place.

"Do you think you've got it stopped?" Rodie stared at Finn, obviously expecting an answer.

"I don't know." He grinned and stood. "Hell, I don't even

know if that controls the elevator, but I know I must have screwed up something."

The lights overhead blinked, flickered some more, and then dimmed to a fraction of what they'd been moments earlier. Finn glanced along the hallway in both directions. It was noticeably darker. He nudged Duran. "Is that normal?"

Duran shook his head. "No. We'd better get moving before the guards decide to check on the lights."

They raced along the corridor until Duran held up his hand. They all stopped as he slowly moved a few inches farther so that he could look around the corner, then flattened himself back beside Morgan. "The guards are both focused on the control panel at their station. They're not looking this way at all. Do you think you can overpower them?"

"Hell, man." Morgan looked as if he were grinding his teeth. "We haven't even seen them yet. I have no idea what they look like, how big they are. How the hell can I say we'd be able to overpower them?"

A visual popped into Finn's mind, and from the surprised looks on both Morgan's and Rodie's faces, he figured Duran was sharing the same image with each of them. The guards were exactly as Cam had sketched them—pale skin, bulbous heads, big eyes, flat faces, with slits for nostrils. They wore dark gray uniforms, but their bodies lacked the mass of humans—long thin arms and legs, narrow shoulders, and slim bodies. From the size of the elevator doors, Finn judged them to be taller than humans with longer reach, but hopefully not as strong.

Morgan leaned down and planted a big kiss on Rodie. "Try not to get shot, okay?" Then he pushed away from the wall and walked down the corridor toward the guards as if he owned the place.

Finn shot a quick look at Rodie, shrugged, and followed Morgan. The two guards appeared to be totally focused on the counter in front of them. They were definitely tall, but not as large as Finn had thought, and so thin they looked as if they were little more than skin over bones.

Morgan walked right up to the closest and tapped him on the shoulder.

Finn picked up his pace as the first Gar jerked around, stared at Morgan, and let out a blood-curdling screech. Morgan hauled back his right arm and landed an undercut just below what should have been the alien's jaw.

The screech cut off; the Gar swayed for a moment and then went down. Finn planted his hand on the flat surface, vaulted over the counter, and slammed his feet into the chest of the second guard. This one was reaching for what had to be a weapon, but Finn grabbed the thing out of its hand as they both went down, and landed a solid punch to its nose. At least where he thought its nose should be. The creature went limp beneath him.

"Damn." He shoved the Gar's weapon into his fanny pack, straightened, and looked at Duran. "I didn't bring anything to tie them with."

"I did." Rodie pulled a handful of cable ties out of her pack, the kind riot police used to restrain prisoners. It took them only a moment to restrain both Gar and drag them back behind the counter.

Finn took another look. The two were either dead or unconscious. Hard to tell. He glanced Duran's way. "Duran? Will there be other guards on this level?"

"Two at the most. Near the barracks." He jerked his head in the direction they'd just come. "If they come, they'll be using that corridor."

"Okay," Finn said. He glanced that way, just in case. "Where are the soulstones?"

Duran pointed toward a large set of doors beyond the counter. Tightly closed doors.

Rodie found the first Gar's weapon lying on the floor where

it had fallen. She stood in front of the unconscious prisoners and pointed the thing at the two of them.

"You sure you're pointing the right end?" Finn stopped to give her a hug.

"Funny boy. I am. And if either of these guys move, I'm sure I can figure out how to use it."

Duran stood in front of the double doors. "These are always open when we change shifts. I've never seen them closed before." He ran his hands over the smooth panels, growing more agitated as seconds passed. "Finn? Do you see any kind of switch over there that might open them?"

Finn was already going over the panel the Gar had been working on. Buttons and gauges were labeled with totally unfamiliar symbols. "Do you have any idea what these mean?"

Duran ran back to the panel and stared at the dozens of different blinking lights and moving dials, at gauges and buttons that were all beginning to blink in what didn't look like a normal pattern. "No. We were never allowed to see any of this."

Finn looked for a pattern but couldn't see anything at all familiar, nothing that looked like it would open what was essentially a vault for the soulstones. He grabbed his Leatherman's tool out of his pack and raced back to the doors.

Running his hands over the smooth surface, he felt a slight vibration near the center. Once again he used the edge of his blade to find a seam, and with the slightest pressure, popped off a metal cap that was hardly larger than his hand.

The dial inside was familiar enough that it sent a chill along his spine. "It almost looks like a combination lock, but I don't recognize the symbols on it." He took a quick look at the Gar, who were still lying on the floor. "They're not going to be much help. Duran, have you ever seen them open this thing?"

He shook his head. "It was always open during the shift change. We went in, got our soulstones, and came out again."

"I imagine it's locked after they had their run-in with the last group. I wonder if it's set on a timer?" Morgan stared at the dial a moment and then walked back over to the panel. "If the shifts always change at the same time, that would make sense. Duran, what time is it here on the ship? Can you tell me if any of these dials are timekeeping devices?"

Duran pointed to a readout. "This is the clock that denotes shift changes. There's not another shift for over eight hours."

Finn joined Morgan and Duran, staring at the console. "Okay, then maybe we need to reset it."

"And you plan to do that how?" Morgan raised an eyebrow.

Finn rubbed his knuckles against his chest. "I have no fucking idea, Morgan. You got any suggestions?"

"Actually"—Rodie shoved Finn aside—"I think I do."

Finn stood back and watched Rodie work the controls as if she actually knew what she was doing.

She glanced up. "I can program my microwave. No reason I can't do this. Duran? Can you tell me when I get to the time it is right now?" She was slowly spinning a dial that moved symbols across a small screen.

Duran leaned over her shoulder. "Here." He pointed at a symbol. "Line this one up with the red line."

Rodie lined the symbol up the way Duran had instructed. The lights on the console began blinking in a strange almost rhythmic sequence. Finn heard a series of clicks and looked up, expecting to see more Gar coming along the corridor.

The door to the vault slid open and a brilliant glow spilled out. Duran did a fist pump and whispered a soft, "Yes!"

Lights up and down the corridor suddenly flashed. A mind-numbing shriek filled the air. Rodie covered her ears and shouted, "What the hell happened?"

"I don't know," Finn yelled, "but the door's open. Duran? Get the others. We're going for the soulstones."

Duran nodded and flashed out of sight. Rodie, Finn, and Morgan raced for the vault. Finn went straight to the source of the light, but it was so bright he couldn't tell where the individual stones were.

"Which one's Zianne's soulstone?" Rodie leaned over the light, squinting against the blinding brilliance.

The moment she said Zianne's name, the glow softened until the stones were each visible on their own. One glowed brighter. Working on pure instinct, Rodie reached in, grabbed it, and stuck the brilliant egg-sized diamond in her pack as the Nyrians flashed just outside the vault. Still in their energy form, they flowed over the tray of diamonds, absorbing their soulstones into their glowing bodies. Then Duran and Nattoch, Tor, Arnec, and Bolt regained their human forms.

Bolt grabbed Rodie in a tight hug. Tears sparkled in Rodie's eyes as she hugged him back.

"Someone's coming!" Morgan grabbed the door to the vault and began shoving it closed.

"No!" Bolt reached out to stop him and caught the door just before it slammed shut. "If you close it, we're trapped. We can't get out of the vault. It's lined with a material that won't allow us to pass, even in energy form."

"Shit." Finn glanced out through the tiny sliver. "There are at least two Gar out there. Right now they're checking the ones we knocked out, but they're going to figure out where we are before too long."

The chattering, clicking, and chirping got louder. One guard stayed with the two unconscious Gar. The other raced down the corridor.

"He's going to the engine room." Nattoch kept his voice low. "We need to go now, while there's only one."

Finn glanced over his shoulder. Rodie had one of the Gar weapons in her hand. He grabbed the one he'd confiscated and tested the weight.

Morgan whispered, "I'm going to open the door. Finn, you aim for the guy standing. Rodie? Shoot anyone else who shows up. Duran? Can we get out of the ship from here, or do we need to head for the service bay? We have to get the hell out of here before this thing blows."

"We can go from here, once we're outside of the vault."

"Good." Morgan grabbed the edge of the door, but he glanced up and Finn caught the challenge in his eyes.

He answered. *Hell, yes, we're going to make it.*

Morgan hauled back on the door. It slid quietly along an invisible track, but the Gar kneeling by his downed comrades jerked around and raised his weapon.

Finn pointed his and pressed what felt like a trigger. A blast of energy caught the guard in the chest, spun him around, and he dropped without a sound. Morgan scooped up the weapon he dropped and shoved it in his pocket. "Disassemble now. Hurry!"

Finn went for the mental switch and felt his body change. Rodie, Morgan, and the Nyrians dissolved at the same time. Finn sensed the swell of energy and the change in pressure as Duran began to pull him within his own mass of molecules for the return to Earth.

But the one guard who'd raced for the engine room was back. How had he moved so quickly? His arm was already raised. The flash of light from the end of his weapon meant he'd pulled the trigger.

The energy blast from the guard's weapon moved much slower than Finn's molecules, but faster than human eyes could follow. The familiar sensation of being sucked inside Duran's energy washed over him just as the brilliant beam made contact.

Pain exploded. Pain unlike anything he'd ever felt before. Finn heard Nattoch's scream and Rodie's cry of agony.

Deep within his own pain, Finn experienced a horrible sense of loss. They'd failed. So damned close, but they were just a fraction of a second too slow. The ship would explode and the Gar would die, but no one would know of the thousands of beings the Gar had murdered.

He and Rodie and Morgan would die. Zianne's soulstone would be lost, as would the five Nyrians he'd come to know as friends. More than friends. He thought of Duran, a man he already loved. And Tara. Tara would mourn Duran for eternity.

Would she mourn Finn as well?

The pain had become a steady, fiery agony, more than he imagined any person could endure for long. He hoped he'd not be caught in an eternity of pain, trapped in this undying form, forever interacting with the force of the Gar projectile.

He barely had time to think about the miserable consequences of never-ending agony. Then everything disappeared, leaving only darkness. And pain. Unrelenting pain.

Mac showed Carl the underground bunker and turned the man loose to interview the Nyrian women who'd taken shelter with Meg, along with the four guys Niah had brought over. Then he got back on the phone with General Adams.

"You're telling me there's no help coming? I've got an idiot out here with a heavily armed, quasi-military force that's growing by the minute, attacking my few rent-a-cops and it's okay for him to shoot my people? What kind of fucking stupidity is that? I've got unarmed women here. Scientists working on an extremely sensitive project, and you're saying we're on our own?"

He listened to the general's half-assed excuses as long as he could. "Yeah, well you can tell your congressmen that while they argue over protocol and whether or not we should welcome these bastards with parades and diplomats, I've got three of my people on board that spaceship, doing their best to rescue the last of the Nyrians before they blow the damned ship to bits. Yes. You heard me. They're on board now. No, General Adams, I am not going to tell you how they got there, but I will tell you that you'd better hope like hell they succeed, or you can bend over and kiss your ass good-bye."

He really wanted to throw the effing phone against the wall, but managed instead to shut it off and pocket the thing before he stalked across the room to where Carl was talking with Meg Bartlett and Cam's Mir.

"Mir? Where's Cam? I thought he was down here with you."

She seemed startled by Mac's question. "No. He's in his cabin, painting."

"Now? What's he working on?" Mir shrugged and focused again on Carl. Mac rubbed a muscle in the back of his neck that felt like a steel spike running straight from his shoulders to his skull. It was all going to shit. Politicians were busy debating parades and protocol while the entire world was at risk. He could feel the whole project falling apart around him, and he really needed to get outside and see what was going on at the fence.

And Zianne. He should be there with her now. He didn't want her to die alone, and damn it all to hell, but he couldn't allow himself to think like that. She wasn't going to die. He wouldn't let her.

"Carl? Do you want to continue with the Nyrian's stories here?" There was too much going on. He really needed to be in three places at once.

"I do, Mac. What they have to say is important. The women have a totally different perspective than the men and I think it's one our viewers need to hear. And I want to find out what it was like on the ship for the four guys who just arrived. A couple of them look pretty rough." Carl held up his small camera. "I'm getting good visuals and the sound is excellent. We'll be fine."

"Thanks. Meg? If you have any problems, hit the alert button and it'll buzz my phone. And someone needs to secure the door behind me when I leave."

Meg nodded and sent Satza to lock the door. Mac raced up

the stairs, checked to make certain Satza locked the door securely, and started across the open area to the dream shack.

Cam's voice popped into his head, so clear it was as if the artist was standing beside him. *Mac? If you're available, I think you need to come to my cabin. Now.*

On my way.

Now what was going on? He reached the top step at Cameron's and everything suddenly spun out of focus. Grabbing the post supporting the porch overhang, he clung to it for a moment, struggling for balance. What the hell was that all about?

Of course, he'd not slept now for over thirty-six hours. Maybe that had something to do with it. Damn, he was such an idiot not to have gotten some rest when the chance was there, but he sucked it up and knocked on Cam's door.

"It's unlocked. C'mon in."

He stepped into absolute chaos. Cam was wearing nothing but a pair of ripped-off sweats. Paint-spattered and worn, they hung low on his hips. His arms and chest, even his face and hair, were speckled and smeared with paint, yet it had been just a short time since Mac had last seen him.

"What the hell happened to you?"

Cam turned to him. His eyes stared out of dark hollows, his normally youthful face was gaunt, and he looked as if the demons of all hells haunted him. "I don't know, Mac. You need to look at these." He swept his arm around the room, and Mac saw at least half a dozen paintings, rough splashes of color that somehow still told a story.

A story as it was occurring now? But how? He walked from canvas to canvas, unable to accept exactly what he appeared to see. "Is this what's happening on board the ship? What Morgan and the others are seeing right now? Where are you getting the images? How the hell have you had time to paint these? They just left, not twenty minutes ago."

Cam nodded. "I'm not sure, but, yeah, I think this is what's happening now. The images won't leave me alone until I paint them. See this? I think this is the service bay where Duran said they'd be arriving. And here's the guard on duty, and the vault where they keep the soulstones."

"What the hell's this?"

Cam shook his head and stared at the painting. "I thought at first it was row after row of hanging uniforms, but then I realized Rodie was filming them, that she looked like she wanted to either cry or throw up. I think they're bodies, Mac. They look almost human but not quite, but look at this." He pointed to a dark slash on one that had more detail than the others.

"Holy hell. It's been gutted." He focused on some dark lines that appeared to pierce the bodies. "Are those meat hooks? Damn it, Cam. How are you getting these images? From Rodie, or Finn, maybe? Are they telepathically that strong?"

"I don't know, Mac. I don't think it's any of our guys. See? If one of them were sending me the image, they wouldn't be in the view I'm getting. But all of them are in this first one. Someone else has to be giving these images to me."

His entire body was trembling as he walked over to the painting he was working on. "This is what made me call you. All I'm seeing is darkness and the sparkles of energy you see when they disassemble, but the colors are all wrong. No blues or golds—just muddy dark greens, some gray. It's not right. And see this?" He pointed to some shapes on one side of the canvas. "Same shapes as you see in the service bay when they first arrived. Mac, I think they're trapped there. Something has happened and they can't get out. They can't get back to Earth, but they're all there, including the three guys who were powering the ship."

He gazed at Mac with haunted eyes. "That means the ship is without power. It's already degrading."

11

Dink slid to one side and made room for Bane and Ralph as the last two slipped back under the rocky overhang where all but Jesat and Aza had taken cover. Those two still covered the northern edge, where they'd managed to rout a small attack from that side of the plateau entirely by themselves.

Dink hadn't gotten all the details from Bane, but he seemed quite pleased with the Nyrians' efforts, something that included crawling over and inside more of Roberts's men.

So far, that seemed to be the best defense they had.

Dink had just returned to this spot as well, after going out with Dake to check along the perimeter to the east and north of their current location. All of them had spread out to check the fence line, hoping to see where the next attack might come. Now they'd returned to compare notes.

By taking part in reconnaissance, Dink had gone well beyond his job of reporting the news, but there was too much at stake here to pretend he was merely an uninvolved observer. He glanced at Nick. The kid had remained behind, staying under cover and recording what he could with the video cam. It was obvious he was anxious to be part of the action, but he'd been taught his role as a reporter well. He was unwilling to cross the line between reporting the story and becoming the story. So far he'd done an excellent job of maintaining enough distance to do the job.

Dink had to admit he'd stomped all over the damned line, and he reported to Ralph from the position of soldier, not newsman. "Dake and I didn't see anything on the northeast point. It looks like they've abandoned the site where they were mobilizing earlier. Any idea what's going on? They've been awfully quiet."

"No good, that's for sure." Ralph took his ball cap off and rubbed his head. Gray hair stuck up in all directions, but he slapped his cap back down, glanced at Bane, and shook his head. "We could see the road below the plateau. It looks like there are more arriving all the time, maybe close to fifty men in full battle gear now, more trucks coming up from the main road. That damned Roberts is at the bottom of the hill, directing people around to the north side of the plateau, but Jesat and Aza are covering that area for us. What bothers me is that we're so shorthanded. We haven't got a prayer of stopping a full-on attack, and we don't have anyone covering the front gate."

One of the younger security guards interrupted. "Mac said that's alarmed. Not that an alarm will stop anyone, but at least we'll know if the gate or perimeter are breached."

"True," Ralph said. He gazed at the azure blue sky overhead. "But knowing about it and doing something to stop it are not the same thing, and the gate isn't far from headquarters. I wish I knew how long we needed."

Dink checked his watch. "I expected the rescue team back by now. They've been gone for almost forty-five minutes." It was almost six. The sun had slipped behind the big mountain in the west and it would be setting within the hour, but there'd be plenty of light to see by for at least an hour beyond that.

Hopefully Roberts wouldn't attack until full dark, and by then, everyone should be home safely. Then he wondered if they'd see the Gar ship explode if it wasn't dark yet. Wondered if it was even visible from this side of the planet.

Ankar leaned over and touched Dink's shoulder to get his attention. "What is it with Roberts? Why does he fight Mac?"

"It goes back twenty years for us," Dink said. "In the beginning, Mac saw them as a bunch of religious nuts against the science this site represented. Then one of Mac's team members did some deeper research and traced Bart Roberts back to 1992 when Mac, Zianne, and I were attacked by a couple of men trying to scare Mac away from a legal investigation. It was a rough fight and Zianne managed to trip one guy and send him sailing off a third-floor balcony. I got stabbed in the gut—would have died if not for Zianne healing me—but first she went into her energy form and dragged the guy off of me and dumped him off the balcony, too. Both men died from their injuries."

He glanced at Nick to see how the kid was taking this. Ethically, Dink was much too close to this story to be the one covering it, but that was exactly why Mac had asked him to come.

"The whole scene was chaos. We'd walked into Mac's apartment without knowing the men were waiting for us. At the time, we didn't know Zianne was Nyrian." He laughed softly, fully aware that by then he'd been a little in love with her himself.

"I didn't see her change. By then I was unconscious from loss of blood. According to Mac, I'd almost bled out by the time Zianne went inside me and healed the injuries.

"When the police came, we told them we'd been attacked though we weren't certain why. Mac did tell them about the ongoing investigation and what his suspicions were, and he was eventually proved correct. Zianne and I were treated as innocent bystanders. What we didn't know until very recently is that Bart Roberts's brother was one of those guys Zianne killed, and Bart was there. He saw it happen, saw her change. He's been out for revenge ever since, but he's also built up a powerful hatred of aliens and he's dragged a lot of crackpots along with him. He knows that what he witnessed wasn't possible for a human. That's blossomed into a rabid case of xenophobia, with Mac at the center."

"I can sort of understand Roberts's issues," Nick said. "But how does he get all these other guys to come out here, armed to the teeth?"

"He's very charismatic." Dink had known his kind before and often wondered how many of them teetered on the brink of insanity. "I think he's drawn people to him by manipulating their fears while building on the need to protect the world from the evil aliens." He lightly punched Bane's shoulder. "That's your cue, evil alien."

"It's sad, really." Bane rubbed his hand across his forehead. He'd told Dink earlier that sweat was a new experience for Nyrians, one he wasn't overly fond of. "If anyone's evil, it's the Gar. How can we make people like Roberts understand how badly misplaced his actions and his hatred are?"

"I don't know if you can. I just wish we could convince the local law enforcement that we're being attacked by nuts." Dink looked over the top of the rock. Still no sign of movement.

"I wonder how long we'll need to keep this area secure," Bane said. "We can't hold them off indefinitely. Bullets will kill even Nyrians if we're shot while in human form."

Ralph nudged Dake's arm. "Now, if this was one of Meg's romance books, you could heal just by switching to another form. How come that doesn't work?"

Dake just shook his head and grinned at Bane. "I think I'd like those books Ralph's wife reads." He focused on Ralph then, frustration evident in the tension that seemed to wrap around his big frame. "We can keep ourselves alive that way, but whatever state the body is in when we shift, that's what we get when we return to it. If we disassemble and then go to a place where our healers are and retake our corporeal form, and if they can fix the damage before the human body dies, then we're okay. Or we can try to create a whole new body. For that we need a heavy charge of energy. Our energy form is immortal, but honestly? I'd rather not get shot in the first place. It hurts."

"Good point." Ralph chuckled and the guys went on talking about various ways to stop the attack that was obviously coming, and coming soon.

Dink tapped Nick's arm and the two of them moved away from the others. "Nick, I'm thinking it might be a good idea for you to take the chopper, fly out over the front entrance, check out the gate, and make sure no one is doing anything at that end of the property. If you see any mischief, let Mac know immediately and then get back here, but be careful. If they're with this group, they could be armed as well."

The kid gave him an odd look. "We're told to cover the news, not be the news. Are you sure that . . ."

He looked so damned sure of himself. Dink tried to remember if he'd ever been that young, that innocent. And then he thought of that time in his life with Mac and Zianne and realized he'd been even more naïve.

"No, Nick, I'm not sure of anything right now. You just heard my story, so you know it's already personal. Plus, I believe what happens here tonight has greater implications than anything I've covered in my entire career. We're not talking about a skirmish between neighbors or even a war that impacts countries. This is something that could have an effect on our entire world. I'm not a reporter talking to you right now. I'm a man concerned about people I love and the world I'd like to grow old on."

Nick turned away and stared at the chopper. Dink imagined he could see the wheels in the kid's brain spinning as he quickly thought through what Dink had asked him to do.

The helicopter sat in shadows in a clear area between an intact section of fence and the first row of the big satellite dishes. After a moment, Nick appeared to reach a decision. He smiled at Dink and shrugged. "I'll be back in a few minutes. I've got an extra camera on board, though it's not set up for a live feed right now. Should I get film?"

"Definitely. Thanks, Nick. Be careful." He took the camera the kid handed to him. "Anyone takes a shot at you, get the hell out of there. I don't want you hurt."

He watched Nick race across the open area and climb into the cockpit. Held his breath when a couple of guys popped up from behind rocks and aimed at the small craft, but a warning shot from Ralph had them ducking behind cover without firing their weapons.

Bane frowned and then grabbed Ralph's arm. "They're coming up the hillside from the north. Jesat says it's a larger group than the last, at least twenty men, heavily armed, moving through thick undergrowth. He wants to know if they should stop them."

"Can they do the same thing they did earlier? Buzz them with energy?"

"There are more men this time, and they can only affect two at a time, but they can move among them quickly and confuse them." Bane looked like he wished he were there with them. "I'll tell them to go for it."

"No deaths. Mac doesn't want to have to explain anyone killed by aliens." Ralph slumped against the rock. "You guys have to be the good guys here, which you are until you start killing off humans."

"Gotcha. And, Ralph?" Bane planted a firm hand on the older man's shoulder. "For what it's worth, we're not killers. None of us would ever take a life without serious provocation."

"I know that, Bane. You're good people. All of you, but

what these jackasses are doing is damned provocative. I'm ready to kill off a couple of the bastards myself."

Minutes slowly ticked by. Dink kept watch on the area where the fence had been torn out, but as the shadows deepened, it was getting harder to tell the difference between shrubbery and men in camo gear. He listened to the distant rumble of the chopper and knew that Nick hovered over the front gate, but then the sound moved farther away and he could no longer hear it.

What the hell was the kid doing?

Gunfire erupted on the north edge of the plateau. Then silence, followed by screams and terrified shouts. Dink glanced at Bane, but he was staring toward the noise and smiling, so it appeared the Nyrians were doing okay.

Movement caught his eye. Dink slipped around the edge of the boulders with his video camera. Those were definitely men, not bushes moving through the gap in the fencing. He tapped Bane's shoulder and pointed them out, then turned as he heard the echo of gunfire coming from somewhere across the plateau. He listened a moment before pinpointing the sound—down near the front gate. So much for the religious protestors. He hoped like hell Nick was safe and moving out of danger.

Then he checked his cell phone, but there was no word from Mac, which meant the team wasn't back from the Gar ship. What the hell could have gone wrong? Crouching down behind boulders and brush, Dink turned on the camera. Softly he began to describe what was happening here, now, at the edge of the DEO-MAP site, tying everything he knew into his story. One he hoped like hell would have a happy ending.

Liz held on to Xinot's arm as she walked with him to her cabin. He was white as a ghost and really shaky, but at least the ugly wound on his chest was healed—thanks to Niah—and he was no longer bleeding. He'd arrived naked, but at some point had added a pair of those loose pants the Nyrian men seemed to favor. She wondered if it was a style choice or just easy to imagine and create when they took on a corporeal body. No matter. The way they hung from his lean hips and clung to his muscular buttocks looked so damned sexy it was all she could do to keep her mind out of the gutter.

They paused at her door and she reached around Xinot to open it, but he covered her hand in his and looked into her eyes. Damn, but his were so blue they seemed to look right through her, and it was hard to remember that this body was nothing more than something he'd constructed out of her memories.

Except she'd never known anyone who looked this hot.

"Lizzie? Please don't guard your thoughts around me." He brushed a hand over her hair. "I can't learn if I can't read you."

"I'm sorry. I don't mean to. I'm human, remember? I'm new at this telepathy thing. I don't always realize I'm blocking."

He smiled, nodded once, and pushed the door open. They walked into the cabin together. This was the first time she'd ever been alone with Xinot. He'd always come with either Ian or Darc. Once with Arnec, but Arnec was still on the Gar ship. She worried about him. About all of them. Especially Finn. Definitely Finn.

"Tor is there as well." Xinot stared out the front window for a moment, as if he might actually see the alien star cruiser. "I've been trying to connect with him." He turned away from the window, walked directly into the bedroom, and sat on the edge of her bed.

Feeling a little awkward in her own cabin, Lizzie followed and sat down beside him. She folded her hands in her lap to keep from stroking his smooth skin. "Are you and Tor close?"

Xinot put his arm around her shoulders and hugged her. She leaned against him, close enough to feel his soft sigh. "Both Tor and Bane are my brothers. We've been together all this time, ever since we so foolishly went aboard the Gar vessel against our parents' wishes. We saw our world destroyed, knew our mother, father, and sisters were gone. Now Bane is out fighting crazy humans and Tor is still aboard the Gar vessel. I worry for both of them, for their safety."

"They'll be all right." Lizzie brushed the thick hair back from his eyes. "I refuse to believe the mission will go wrong. You just have to have faith in whatever power watches over us."

Xinot turned and wrapped both arms around her. "I have felt Nyria close tonight. When Niah healed me, our goddess was there. When I was falling through space without any sense of direction, she guided me to you and your wonderful imagination."

He kissed her, his lips warm and surprisingly soft, moving slowly over hers until Lizzie felt as if he'd drawn part of her into himself. "I need your strength, Lizzie. When we made love, I felt so powerful that nothing could stop me. Love me now. I will need your strength tonight, because my brothers will need mine."

She flashed for a moment on what was happening right now—that Rodie, Morgan, and Finn were on the Gar ship and she had no idea how they were doing, that there were men trying to break through the perimeter fencing here to damage the DEO-MAP site, and Zianne was in the dream shack, growing weaker by the minute.

And Liz was here with a man she hardly knew, an alien who was learning how to survive on her world by picking information out of her brain, and this—how much she needed him, how much her body craved his touch—was probably the last thing she should be thinking of right now, but it was the only thing she wanted.

Xinot was looking at her with those sapphire blue eyes and her heart was pounding like an out-of-control metronome. He traced the line of her chin with his fingertips, then followed that line with his lips and tongue, and she reveled in his open fascination with her, his blatant curiosity.

So far, with each encounter she'd had with any of the Nyrians, she'd been the one to take the lead.

For now, she turned herself over to Xinot, knowing full well she'd take charge at some point. Finn thought she was kidding with the whips and cuffs. Someday she'd have to show him there was more than a bit of the dominatrix in sweet little Lizzie.

She wondered how Xinot was going to react when she turned his explorations back on him. The sound of his name rolled through her mind. The way he pronounced it sounded almost French. *Zino* with a very soft *z*, long *i*, and silent *t*. She whispered his name and felt his lips curve against her cheek. Then he was slowly tugging her cotton shirt free of her pants, peeling the soft fabric across her ribs, over her head, off her arms. Tugging at her sweats until she kicked them off along with her panties.

She stretched, loving the feel of the cool air washing so much exposed skin. Loving even more the look of appreciation in Xinot's eyes. "How come I'm naked and you're still dressed?" She turned and knelt beside him, and then gently pushed her fingertip against the middle of his chest. He toppled over, but he took Lizzie with him. She sprawled across his powerful body, more aware of her petite size and feminine curves than she could ever recall.

And much too aware of the curve of his erection tenting his pants. She ran her fingers over his flat belly, following the narrow trail of dark blond hair that started at his navel and dipped beneath his waistband. Wrapping her fingers around his thick shaft, she squeezed him just enough to get his attention.

He groaned and arched into her touch.

"Make the pants go away," she said. He laughed and Lizzie decided it was a lot easier to shove them down herself, over his lean hips, down his long legs. When she pushed them past his feet, he kicked them off. "Grab the headboard." She placed his hands on the oak bars and wrapped his fingers around them. "Do not let go."

He didn't say a word, but his intent gaze never left her face. She scooted down his legs and straddled his knees, leaned over, and nuzzled the smooth, warm skin beside his sac. All the Nyrian men she'd seen had created forms totally different from one another. Some had body hair, others didn't or, like Xinot, had very little. A touch under his navel, blond tufts beneath his arms and a dusting on his legs, but none at his groin.

Some of the men were dark skinned, others, like Xinot, were fair with an almost California surfer, blond-haired, blue-eyed look. All were large, well-formed men, just as the women were each uniquely beautiful. The one thing they all seemed to have in common was the subtle scent of vanilla and honey.

Lizzie inhaled as she pressed her lips against the side of Xinot's shaft and ran her tongue around the thick base. Not merely the scent, but the taste as well, and all of it addictive.

She tried to remember what she and Xinot had done when they'd been together, but it had been so crazy, having sex with more than one man at a time, her memories were a little scrambled.

Not in her wildest fantasies had she ever imagined what her Nyrians had given her in reality. It was hard to recall which of the four men she'd actually gone down on. Her mind was filled with delicious memories of so many hands and searching lips and thick, erect cocks. Never in her life had she done anything as remotely wild, nor had she felt so free and comfortable in her own body.

But of all the men she'd tasted over the past couple of nights, she didn't think Xinot was one of them. She wondered if his lovemaking would feel the same, if his ejaculate tasted the same as the others.

It shouldn't be all that hard to find out.

She ran her tongue along his shaft, all the way to the tip. His foreskin was partially retracted behind the dark, plum-shaped glans, and she ran her tongue beneath the soft folds of skin.

He groaned when she found the tiny slit at the end. She played her tongue around the tip and he arched his hips closer when she traced the smooth contours. There were a few drops of pre-cum there, and he was sweet, just as sweet as she'd imagined. She took him deep, sliding her lips over the thickly veined surface of his cock, grasping the base with her fist so he wouldn't choke her.

Some men she could swallow, but not this one. He was too thick, too long, too much.

But he tasted so good. She cupped his sac in one hand and lightly fondled his balls while she sucked, using her tongue and teeth and lips until his hips were jerking and his chest billowing up and down with each harsh breath.

It was Darc who had explained to her what sex actually felt like for the Nyrians. They'd taken the energy from fantasy—even from the stories Zianne had shared with them when she was first involved with Mac—and realized that it was unlike anything they'd ever known before.

But now, since they'd all experienced not only intimate fantasies firsthand, but the actual sexual acts themselves, the rush of real sex was beyond description. Power so rich, so pure that it fired their veins as if they'd absorbed the energy from an exploding star. Add that to the ability now to feel those sensations with their human bodies, and it was no wonder none of them could get enough.

Oddly, though, they'd not had sex with each other. Not unless there'd been one of the dream team arranging it. None of them really knew what to do without a human lover leading the way.

As far as Liz could tell, Xinot was proof that the Nyrians

would figure it all out soon enough. His hands came down on her head, holding her still. She raised her eyes and looked at him, smiling around her mouthful of his erection.

Bad boy. You're not supposed to let go of the headboard.

"I can't let you do this alone." His voice sounded much deeper than she recalled, and he had a frantic look in his eyes. "Turn around. I have to taste you. I must have my mouth on you."

She slipped her lips along the full length of his erection, freeing him slowly, and did as he asked. "I don't think I'm going to taste nearly as good as you do," she said. And she was actually sorry about that, because she couldn't wait to get him back in her mouth.

"I'll be the judge of that," he said as he wrapped his big hands around her thighs and held her over his mouth.

She leaned close and took as much of him in her mouth as she could, but this time Xinot was using his tongue on her, playing her as if he'd done this many times before. Every touch was perfect, each sweep of his tongue or nip of sharp teeth. Perfect.

Then she realized he would know what she liked, because he was taking her desire straight from her mind. Without hesitation, Lizzie slipped into Xinot's thoughts, found the pleasure she was giving him, and discovered what he liked best.

Her tongue slipping beneath his foreskin again, stretching the skin gently behind the broad crown. Her fingers rolling his hard testicles and squeezing him almost to the point of pain, tugging on his sac, running her fingers along his perineum and circling the sensitive ring of his anus. He liked that a lot, and she pressed against him, and then pressed again.

He groaned and the vibration traveled across her clit. She sucked deeper, pressed harder. He used his fingers to penetrate her sheath while his tongue did amazing things to her clit, and while she hadn't planned to come this way, the first tendrils of her burgeoning climax were growing, building upon themselves, until the sweep of his tongue and the thrust of his fingers, the sweet taste of his seed and the intimacy of touching him, tasting him, being touched and tasted was all too much, too intense.

His tongue speared her deep as Lizzie pressed against his sphincter and slipped past that tight ring of muscle with her middle finger. His muscles clamped down on her finger, his lips tightened around her clit, and his cock jerked in her mouth. She felt his cry against her sensitive folds and the harsh sweep of his tongue over a clitoris almost too sensitive to touch.

She wanted to cry out, but her mouth was filled with his pulsing cock and the sweet honeyed taste of him. She held on to his sac, squeezing none too gently but it only made him come harder. His hips bucked against her, his anal muscles clamped around her finger, and their minds linked in the midst of total sensual chaos.

With a final jerk, something opened up between them. A connection to another mind, so faint, so terribly far away. She could barely understand what was little more than a whisper, but Xinot cried out again.

Not in sexual ecstasy. Not this time. No, this time he cried out in fear and pain. Lizzie knew he'd connected with his brother.

Not with Bane, who was merely on the far side of the plateau. No, he'd linked with Tor, trapped aboard the Gar ship that was hurtling toward Earth, only minutes away from total destruction.

Body still trembling, the taste of Xinot still fresh on her lips, Lizzie rolled away from him and grabbed up her clothes from the floor. "We have to get to the dream shack. Somehow we need to get them off that ship."

Xinot nodded as he pulled his pants up over his hips. "I'm calling Bane and the others. We need them together. All of them. Women and men. We can combine our minds, share power that way. They're injured. One of the Gar managed to shoot them just as they disassembled, and it's disrupted their energy. They can't leave the ship without help."

"How much time do they have?"

"Tor said maybe ten, fifteen minutes at the most. They shut down at the last minute, but he's not sure how long they've been unconscious. They're locked in a service bay with the door blocked so the Gar can't get at them, but they're trapped by their inability to reach us. They lack the strength. Rodie and Nattoch are the worst. They're both injured but okay as long as they stay in their energy forms."

Liz grabbed her phone as they raced across the compound. Her cabin was at the front of the property, one of the farthest from the dream shack. The sun was down but the sky still fairly bright. She heard the staccato beat of gunfire echoing across the plateau, and the steady roar of the chopper down by the front gate.

A loud explosion rocked the night.

Lights across the entire compound went out. Liz jerked to a stop and looked out over the plateau, but there was no sign of smoke. She spun around. Flames leapt above the trees near the main road far below the DEO-MAP road, and a huge cloud of black smoke rose into the twilight sky. "What the hell was that?"

"Something that interfered with your power. Let's go."

"Lizzie! Wait. Any idea what happened?" Mac raced out of Cameron's cabin with Cam on his heels.

"Explosion was down there, near the main road. Power's out, so they must have taken out the main power pole just at the point where the wiring goes underground."

"Shit." Mac spun away, but Lizzie grabbed him by the arm.

"There's more. Xinot contacted Tor on the Gar ship. The

team's injured, trapped in the same service bay where they arrived. They need help to get home."

She glanced at Xinot, who stared blankly across the plateau, and knew he was contacting the others. "We're headed to the dream shack so we can try and reach them, give them a strong signal to follow back to Earth."

"There's no power. The satellites are worthless."

"We've got Nyrians, Mac. Pure power. C'mon." She grabbed Xinot's arm and they took off for the dream shack with Mac and Cam on their heels.

The helicopter buzzed by, flying low overhead toward the far side of the plateau. The front door to the lodge flew open and the Nyrians who had been hiding out in the basement shelter spilled out onto the deck and raced for the dream shack. The reporter, Carl Waters, was with them, though Meg waited on the porch with her hands clasped over her heart.

Tara threw open the door to the shack as Xinot and Lizzie reached it. Both of them slipped inside. Kiera was moving things out of the way, making room for the huge number of Nyrians and team members trying to squeeze through the door.

Zianne was still in the recliner, conscious, but barely appearing to register all the activity. Liz couldn't think of her now, couldn't worry about Zianne or Mac. Not now.

Mac stopped just inside the door and shouted for everyone's attention. "Has Xinot explained what's going on? Okay. First thing, we need to power up the dishes, but the terrorists have taken out the main line down by the road. I've got a generator, but it's not enough. We need power—direct power to charge the system here, to get the array back on line immediately. We're talking minutes if we're going to get them off the ship in time."

Kiera's guy, Sakel, raised his hand. "I'll organize power to the antennae. Teev, you can help. Mac? Where's the main line?"

"Power panel is behind the dream shack." Mac was already headed out the door. "Follow me."

Teev, Sakel, and most of the women quickly left the shack and followed Mac. The helicopter swept in overhead and landed in the open area in front of the lodge.

Dink leapt out with the camera under his arm. Nick shut the chopper down and ducked out the other side, then raced around the machine beneath the still spinning rotors with his head low.

"Dink!" Lizzie waved him over. "You guys need to go behind the shack and film this. The Nyrians are going inside the electrical system so we can power up the satellite antennae."

Dink hardly broke stride before spinning away from the door and heading around the back, with Nick right behind. Bane and the others who'd been working along the fence line—Aza, Jesat, Dake, and Ankar—appeared inside the dream shack as glowing energy and immediately took their corporeal forms.

Bane went straight for Xinot and the brothers embraced. "Tor? You've spoken with him?"

Xinot nodded. "Briefly. He's injured. They've all had their energy disrupted but they can't risk taking human form. Rodie is injured, but they're not sure how badly. So is Nattoch. When they were shot, all were in the process of disassembling."

"That's the worse time, when they're most vulnerable to injuries to their human flesh and energy disruption of their energy form. What do we do?"

Gunfire erupted just outside the shack. Dink, Carl, and Nick raced through the door as a large-caliber bullet hit the frame beside the open door and chipped a big chunk of concrete off the wall. The door was made of thick metal. Dink pulled it closed and locked it behind him.

Everyone had converged on the dream shack; while Lizzie and Xinot filled them in, the gunfire grew louder. Only Ralph and the four security guards remained near the boundary of the plateau, with instructions to take cover and just lay low if their area was overrun, but they had plenty of ammunition, good cover, and the knowledge they had to hold on only for a very short time before the mission either ended in success or failure.

After that, Mac had sent instructions to Ralph and the others that Roberts could do what he damned well wanted, as far as Mac was concerned. If the mission failed, there was nothing else they needed the satellite array for.

His team members aboard the Gar ship would die, and Zianne's soulstone would be lost. Yes, the other Nyrians had been saved and the Gar attack on Earth stopped. Their rampage through space, the deaths of untold worlds would end, but Lizzie knew that, right now, Mac wasn't thinking of his successes so far. He wasn't counting anything but what they'd not yet accomplished.

She watched as he walked slowly over to Zianne and knelt beside her. Took her limp hand in both of his and held it against the side of his face. She rolled her head to one side and stared at him, but there was no light in her eyes.

Lizzie grabbed Xinot's hand and prayed to his goddess. Nyria had to help them now. They were so close to success.

Much too close even to consider failure.

12

Darkness had an unusual quality when you perceived it through a disassembled consciousness rather than seeing with eyes. Finn concentrated on the fascinating differences of perception, rather than the reality of his rather precarious situation.

He certainly still perceived pain, but the shock of it had softened until it was almost bearable. Almost.

Damn, but this was not how he'd expected to die, not with his disassembled molecules spinning in a sluggish circle in a dark service bay on an alien spacecraft far from home. He'd always sort of pictured himself getting shot by a jealous husband, or maybe a nice, clean aneurism while trying to make it with a beautiful young woman when he was, oh, say, about ninety.

It might not have been quite as depressing if his energy at least sparkled, but his colors were all wrong. Of course, Rodie's and Morgan's weren't any better.

In fact, Rodie's were worse, but she'd been badly injured. He wished he knew exactly how badly, but there was no way to tell unless she shifted to her corporeal form.

Duran had cautioned her. Actually, he'd told her quite

bluntly, she was fucked if she shifted and discovered she was hurt too badly, because she might not be able to disassemble again and then she'd end up bleeding to death. Besides, there was no way to get her home if she was solid. Nattoch wasn't in any better shape. He'd thrown himself in front of Rodie to protect her when the guard fired on them. It had been a brave and selfless act, and he'd taken the brunt of the charge.

His molecules barely moved at all.

He won't die, Finn. At least not from the Gar weapon.

Of course not. Finn knew that. They were all going to get blown to bits when the ship imploded, but he kept his frustration to himself when he replied to Duran. *Nattoch has always seemed so powerful, almost omnipotent. I hate seeing him this way. Not merely because he's injured. For a man who is always so powerful, it feels wrong.*

I know. I'm not used to it, either. He's always been the strongest among us, the one who's held us together when we've weakened. I pray to Nyria that he survives. That we all do.

Duran's mental voice sounded so depressed, Finn wondered if there was more bad news the Nyrian wasn't telling them. His energy was at a very low ebb as well. All of them had been weakened by that damned shot. The guard must have had the weapon set on its highest charge—a killing charge. Even Tor admitted they were lucky it hadn't killed them, because they'd been totally unprepared for that kind of attack.

They'd had no idea the Gar weapons were capable of so much destructive power. In hindsight, underestimating the enemy— one capable of killing off entire worlds—had been foolish. Foolish enough that it might have doomed all of them.

It still might.

But Tor had connected with his brother and even now the dream team was working on getting them home. Firing up the satellite dishes, creating a powerful link, one strong enough for all of them to ride back to Earth.

If only time didn't seem to crawl when he was in this form. The fact that their energy moved so very fast made everything else seem to take forever.

At least Tor had been keeping track. He said they had ten, maybe fifteen more minutes before the ship's systems began to fail. Within half an hour, life support for the Gar would degrade and the race as a whole would die.

That might have bothered Finn at one point, but not anymore. Not after their impromptu tour of that disgusting meat locker—one of many, according to Duran. The Gar's deaths would be much easier than what their victims had suffered. Row after row of gutted bodies, the agonized expressions on so many dead children, on the adults. No, he'd not be mourning the Gar.

Shortly after the Gar died, the ship would reach a critical point where the internal atmosphere could no longer stabilize the massive outer hull of the structure. It would collapse in upon itself and implode.

As to what would happen to Finn and the others with him? They didn't need atmosphere in this form, and they wouldn't be affected by the degradation of the ship's systems, but that final explosion would do them in. Arnec appeared to be the scientist in the group, and while he'd tried to keep his explanation simple, he'd still managed to lose Finn along the way.

Not an easy feat for any man. Finn was impressed. He was also scared to death, not something he'd expected, but he'd never really faced death before. It was one thing when you were actually fighting to stay alive, the way they'd done earlier when they'd actually fought the guards.

It was another thing altogether to be stuck here, spinning around in helpless swirls of disconnected molecules, waiting for something to happen. He had way too much time to think. Too much time to feel regret for things not done, words not said.

So much he wished he'd said to Lizzie. He felt as if they were just beginning to connect, and he could call it friendship as much as he wanted, but there was something more. Something deeper.

Now he might never find out what that was.

He glanced at Rodie, worried how she was holding up. Morgan had melded his energy with hers, and the two of them did look stronger. He wanted them to make it, wanted Morgan and Rodie to get that happily ever after that none of them had ever expected.

He'd gotten a taste of it with Tara and Duran, and it tore him apart, thinking of Tara without her man. She loved Duran so completely, just as Duran loved her. Talk about your forever love. They'd been together since before there'd been life on Earth. It was flat-out wrong that it should end here, in such an unsatisfactory way.

Stuck aboard a starship, waiting for the sucker to blow.

Lizzie's face filtered into his thoughts. He couldn't seem to stop thinking of her. Young, fresh, and filled with life. Board-straight brown hair framing a pixie's face and brown eyes twinkling with mischief. A friend without benefits—so far—and who would have thought she would come to mean so much to him in such a short time?

Patience had never been his strong suit, but damn it all, he wasn't ready to die. And somehow, some way, he'd have to make sure that didn't happen.

Another of the Irishman's errant thoughts flitted through Morgan's mind, and if he wasn't so pissed off right now, he might have enjoyed Finn's frustration. But Rodie was hurting and they had no idea how badly she'd been injured.

He really didn't think this was the end for them. It couldn't be, not when Rodie had Zianne's soulstone safe in her little fanny pack and they'd gotten everyone out of the engine room.

All they had to do was get off this fucking spaceship before the sucker imploded.

No big deal, right?

Bolt's cloud of energy moved closer until he'd wrapped the two of them within his personal sphere of power. It felt almost like a hug to Morgan. A strong, warm hug. Bolt was stronger than either Morgan or Rodie, and he'd missed the worst of the blast, though he didn't have enough energy to return to Earth. Not the way he was now.

Nattoch had caught the worst of the Gar attack, poor bugger, and his energy was barely visible.

Bolt? How's Nattoch?

Alive. If we can get him to Earth, get him to one of those who can heal, we can save him. How are you doing?

Morgan thought about that for a moment. How the hell was he doing? He was used to depending on his physical strength as much as his mind. Worrying about no one but himself, and here he was, reduced to a slow spiral of tired molecules with his entire focus on the woman he'd wrapped within his own fading energy.

And yet, he'd not given up. He still felt as if they had a chance, which was unlike him. Normally he'd be totally freaking out by now, to have so much out of his control. The truth was, he really wanted to hit something—or someone—but that was out of the question.

It would certainly make him feel better.

I'm doing better than I probably should be, considering. Rodie's alive, but she's not conscious. In a way, I'm relieved that she's not alert because I'd be worried about her worrying about what was going to happen. Now it's just me, worried about Rodie. Period.

I'm worried about her as well. This way, we can share our strength and hold on until rescue comes.

Do you think it will come?

I do. Tor is stubborn, but his brother Xinot is even more stubborn. And Bane? The third brother is the worst of all. Plus, there is your dream team. And Mac. Mac is a very stubborn man. Twenty years chasing a dream? He won't give up. Not as long as there is hope.

Morgan couldn't believe Bolt was actually laughing. After a moment, the Nyrian managed to share what he'd found so funny. Morgan realized that maybe they did have something to smile about.

Rodie has Zianne's soulstone. There is no doubt in my mind they will bring us home. Mac will allow nothing else. He is a man who has spent his entire adult life and a fortune by any world's standards to follow what most would call an impossible dream, and that dream is all wrapped up in his love for Zianne. He will do what he must to save her. We have no need to worry, Morgan. He's not about to quit.

The dream shack rocked with the concussion as another explosion thundered across the plateau. "What the hell was that?"

"Forty-eight to go, Cam. They just blew another satellite dish." Mac answered the kid's question with as much control as he could, but it wasn't easy when he'd put his entire life into this project and the bastards were blowing it up, dish by dish.

Grumbling, Cam stood off to one side and stared at the door. He was bare chested and still covered in paint. They'd rushed over here with Liz when the power failed, but those amazing paintings were still in Cam's cabin. So far, the terrorists hadn't come this far across the plateau, but Mac hoped like hell no one torched the cabins. Losing Cam's work would be a tragedy.

It might be the only record of what happened on the Gar ship if things continued to degrade. Hell, nothing was going the way he'd planned. They had emergency lighting here and in the safe room under the lodge, courtesy of the big generator that took over when the power went out, but it wasn't enough to power the entire array. It did, however, keep the dials on the control panel lit. Two of those denoting satellite dishes had now gone dark. They couldn't afford to lose many more.

He checked the clock. Seven minutes had already passed since he'd learned of the danger his team was in on the Gar ship. They could have no more than three minutes left; they might have as much as ten. Maybe more, maybe less, it didn't matter. Any way you looked at it, they were running out of time.

And that meant Zianne was running out of time.

There was a sparkle of light in the shack, and his heart practically leapt out of his chest, but it wasn't one of the guys from the Gar ship.

"Dake!" Kiera shoved past Mac and grabbed the big guy's hands. "Are you okay? What's going on?"

"We've almost got the power grid ready to go back up—it's taking time because we have to adjust our output to the correct type of current—but the idiots are blowing the dishes. Ralph says he thinks they've got explosives on a couple more. We can't afford the interruption to the signal once we link to the ones on the ship. Aza, Jesat, and I are going back out to see what we can do. There are enough of the others to power the grid. It took just three of us to run the whole damned Gar ship, so there's no problem with our going to help Ralph. You need to be ready to link your minds and reach for the ones on the ship."

He leaned close and kissed Kiera one more time. Then he quickly stepped around Mac, walked over to the recliner where Zianne lay as if she slept, and took her hand. Energy glowed around her body for just a few seconds, then seemed to soak directly into her pale skin. Dake turned and put a big hand on Mac's shoulder. "She is close to death. Hopefully, that will help her hold on a bit longer. I don't know for sure. I'm afraid to give her too much. None of us has ever gone without their soulstone for such a long time. I wish I could be more positive, Mac. Zianne is a heroine to all of us. We don't want to lose her."

Mac nodded as Dake dissolved into light and disappeared. He'd already known he was losing Zianne. Her life force was difficult to find. She'd been a constant presence in his heart and his mind when they'd been together so long ago.

Now, there was barely a whisper. He'd found himself praying to Nyria throughout the day. Zianne believed so strongly in her goddess, and he was a desperate man. He'd beg anyone he thought might save her.

But it was just as important that he save the array. Mac grabbed his cell phone and called Ralph. "What have you got?"

Nothing good, that was for sure. Damn it all. He rested his forehead in his palm while he talked briefly with Ralph, but after a moment he ended the call. At least he'd let Ralph know that three of the Nyrians were returning to help where they could. It wasn't much, but it might slow the attack.

Ralph and the other guards had taken refuge in a sheltered area where they could see what was happening and report in, take an occasional shot when Roberts's men got sloppy, but stay out of sight.

The whole fucking plateau was overrun with domestic terrorists. The local sheriff's department had taken a hands-off approach, which meant no help whatsoever. Mac hadn't heard back from his contact at the Pentagon. Whatever happened was entirely up to his small force of security guards and the Nyrian men who were able to help. The whole thing sucked, big time.

He raised his head and looked across the dream shack. Dink stood silently against the wall, holding the camera, recording everything as it happened, but just his presence alone meant more to Mac than Dink would ever realize.

He wasn't doing a live feed right now. Nick was running the interviews Carl had done earlier, feeding them directly to the station, which was broadcasting on both network television and the Internet. He'd set up a small desk in the tiny kitchen area just off the main room here in the shack, sharing whatever they had he hoped would build more sympathy for the Nyrians.

They'd collected quite a bit throughout the afternoon and early evening. Stories of the women talking about their lives before the Gar destroyed their planet, tales of the many worlds that had been left in ruins. Of the Nyrians' own world, totally destroyed. Their quiet, heartfelt tales were gaining sympathy and the world was beginning to understand that the alien ship approaching Earth was not one they should welcome with open arms.

It was too late for that, anyway, because, whether Zianne lived or died, whether his team made it back in time or not, the Gar ship was dead.

Right now, it was hurtling through space, coming closer by the second. He had no idea how far away it was, but he hoped that when it blew, it didn't take this world with it.

And then he had a totally selfish thought, one he immediately regretted, that if Zianne died, did it really matter?

Yes, damn it. It mattered because he knew that Zianne would never wish for such a thing. It wasn't in her nature to be cruel.

He watched her and wondered if she were sleeping or maybe even unconscious. She was so pale and listless—none of the spark he'd always associated with her. She'd always been bursting with so much life, so much to live for.

Overhead lights went on in the dream shack. The control panel lit up and those lights blinked, dials and gauges flickered as full power coursed through the system. Mac spun around, blocking everything but the job at hand. He checked the readouts, made a few adjustments to a couple of dials, and reset all the software.

He waited, ticking off seconds as the system rebooted and came back up online. "Cam? Liz and Kiera? We need to link minds. Dake said we have to concentrate on sending our thoughts directly to the ones on the ship."

Cam grabbed the mesh cap Lizzie handed to him. She and Kiera slipped theirs on. Mac opened a drawer set aside from the others and found his own cap. He'd had it made to test the system—he'd never imagined actually needing it.

Kiera sat on the floor next to Cam while Lizzie perched on one arm of the recliner beside Zianne. Mac carefully lifted Zianne and sat in the chair himself, then held her in his arms. Her head lolled against his chest, but her eyes blinked open and she focused on him. "Bring me into the link. Open to me, Mac. I can find the ship for you."

He nodded. It might kill her, expending that much energy, but he could never deny her anything. Especially not this. He leaned forward and touched a small switch on the control panel. "This allows us to synchronize. It connects the input from all of our minds and focuses our thoughts through the array. We've never done this before, a group link like this, but Zianne knows how to direct our signals to the ones on the ship. Sweetheart?"

She smiled at the endearment. The love in her eyes made his throat tighten. "We're going to ride you all the way to the team," he said. Then he kissed her. "Let's go." He flipped the switch.

Power. Pure, euphoric power, bursting into his head, surging in a chaotic maelstrom of fiery energy. Kiera, Lizzie, Cameron— their minds so strong, so pure, so totally honest and free of anything beyond the desire to save the lives of their friends, both Nyrian and human.

He tried to direct them, to force them into compliance. This energy had to go through the array, needed to ride the signal away from Earth, but it was almost beyond him.

Pandemonium when he needed order.

Demanded order.

Mac. Relax. Let me. You're fighting them. Do not lead. Share the energy, share the burden. Use that beautiful mind of yours to stabilize the link. Strengthen it, don't fight it.

Zianne's soft words soothed the chaos and calmed the bedlam. Mac relaxed, following her lead, and watched in amazement as their minds clicked together into a solid stream of pure mental energy.

A whispered "oh" from Kiera. A breathy sigh from Liz and a muttered "holy shit" from Cam, and he knew they'd done it. Knew they'd created a link that would reach from here to the Gar ship as it hurtled through space.

Now all they had to do was connect with one of the team members on board.

Totally focused on the link, Mac blinked in confusion when another mind joined theirs. Without moving, he knew it was Bane, who hovered beside him. His energy swirled and pulsed, and Mac felt the gentle intrusion as Bane hitched his energy to the link.

Followed the link through the array.

And disappeared entirely from the shack.

Zianne's fingers wrapped around Mac's and squeezed just before he felt another presence. Tara. Again, the link was subtle, the sense of their joining a sensual caress, but Mac and Zianne, Lizzie, Cameron, and Kiera held the link steady. Tara's energy disappeared as well.

Risking their lives to save their loved ones? The ship had to be close to imploding. They were willingly going into danger, risking everything, just as the ones who'd joined Ralph out on the plateau were taking risks.

Holding Zianne in his arms, connected so intimately to Cam, Liz, and Kiera, Mac finally, fully accepted the wonder of what they'd accomplished. What they would accomplish, because he refused to accept failure.

Not with these amazing people on his team. The connection they'd all formed—not only his dream team, but Zianne, Dink, and his reporters, the guys on his staff here at DEO-MAP—all of them working toward the same goal to protect a people they hadn't even known existed.

So much of their strength came directly from the Nyrians. People from not only another world but another time, and yet they shared the same sense of honor and duty to one another as Mac's team. The same love, the same sense of commitment.

It was a humbling experience to see love in action. Holding the mental link, he turned and made eye contact with Dink. His oldest friend, his lover, the one he could always count on. It was right that Dink was here tonight. Right that he shared this whole experience, no matter how it ended.

Mac smiled and then turned his attention to the link pulsing among the five of them. It felt strong and true, and he only hoped it would last long enough to bring their people home.

Finn sensed a change in the ship, almost as if it spoke to him, and he wondered if what he felt was the deaths of the Gar. He no longer heard the thrumming power from within the walls. Life support should be gone by now. There'd been no light in the service bay since they'd come here to escape the guard, but the sense of the darkness felt different somehow.

Arnec? Any idea what's going on now? Something's different.

The ship is dying. What has allowed a ship this large to exist is the pressure within keeping the outer hull rigid. I feel the walls flexing, as if the pressure has finally slipped beyond what the structure of the hull can withstand.

How long do you think? There was no need to be specific. They were all attuned to the final, dying gasps of the ship.

Not long. I have no idea what this will be like. I prefer to see it as an adventure, maybe?

One I'd prefer to do without. Finn glanced toward the area where Morgan and Rodie slowly spun in mingled energy. Morgan's looked a bit brighter, as if he might be recovering from the blast. Finn checked out the others. Tor looked almost normal. Nattoch was still sort of muddy and dark, but Duran and Bolt were brighter as well.

A blast of energy flashed into the service bay. He couldn't tell who or what it was, and then a second flash of light shot rays streaming to all corners of the darkened room.

Duran cried out. *Tara! What are you doing here?*

I'm taking you home. Why are you still here?

Nattoch is injured. Rodie, too. We couldn't leave them. Bolt, Morgan, and Finn were caught in the blast.

So you were just going to die? Idiot. Bane, how many can you carry?

Rodie, Morgan, Nattoch. Tor is strong enough to go on his own. Arnec? You, too? Good. How about you, Tara?

I'll get Finn, Duran, and Bolt. We have to hurry. The ship is dying.

Finn sensed the slight pressure as Tara drew him into her energy field. He felt Duran and Bolt coming with him, and then they were streaming through the walls of the vessel, moving along a beam of energy so powerful it was actually visible in the emptiness of space.

Streaking closer to Earth, following that amazing beam of power, sensing Cam and Kiera, Mac and even Zianne. And Lizzie. He sensed her energy, her pure spirit calling him back, and he felt his own energy grow and strengthen. Knew he had somehow reached out and touched the threads that were Lizzie's.

The air around them pulsed in ripples of heat and a horrible concussion almost knocked them from the beam. The ship imploding, collapsing in upon itself, and the shockwaves buffeted them even as they passed through Earth's atmosphere, moving at the speed of light, hanging on to that beam that was pulling them straight back to the dream shack.

Just before they reached the shack, the beam ended. Cut off as if it had never been, but they were so close and the array was still powered up enough that Tara and the others took them all the way in, directly through the cinderblock walls, into the small building that was the center of Mac Dugan's amazing project.

They entered together, a spiraling mass of energy. Bolt took form, and Finn and Duran as they slipped free of Tara's energy. She reformed as well, the four of them stumbling in the sudden switch to human bodies, to gravity, to clean, fresh air filling their lungs. Tara threw her arms around Duran and cried loud, broken sobs of relief.

"Finn!" Lizzie shot across the room and grabbed him. Still wobbly, wondering if he'd ever get enough clean air to breathe, he wrapped one arm around her shoulders and held her close. Arnec and Tor reformed next. All of them glancing around, looking for the others. No one said a word. Finn shot a quick glance at Mac, but he was holding Zianne close against his chest and Finn was almost sure the man was weeping.

Too late? No. It couldn't be. He spun with Liz clinging to his side, looking for the others. For Rodie with Zianne's soul-stone.

Kiera glanced this way and that, her brows knotted, but Tor was reaching for her, pulling her close and wrapping his big arms around her, speaking softly, rocking her back and forth as they held each other close.

Where the hell was Bane? He had Rodie, Morgan, and Nat-toch—where were they? Finn turned and stared at Arnec, but he was staring wide-eyed at the ceiling, at the massive blast of light visible through the skylight.

Finn grabbed Lizzie's hand, shoved his way past the others,

and raced outside. Dink followed with the camera and then a few of the others, all of them staring at the roiling fire in the sky, at the meteors streaking through the twilight as the remnants of the Gar ship hit Earth's atmosphere and burned up, leaving spectacular burning trails in their wake.

Had Bane been trapped in the explosion? Finn was almost certain they'd gotten out in time. But what if they hadn't? He glanced at Lizzie, looking up at him with a stricken expression. She hadn't said a word, but she knew.

He kissed her quickly, turned away from the death of the Gar ship, and walked back inside the shack. Whispered to Lizzie, "Just a minute," and then went to Mac and knelt beside the chair. He touched one of Zianne's hands resting on Mac's arm. "It was Zianne, wasn't it? She was the one directing that beam we followed home."

Mac didn't look at him, but Finn caught the slight nod of his head. "It just went away, right before we got here. Damn it, Mac. It wasn't supposed to happen like this. I can't believe we're too fucking late to save her. Not after she saved us. I'm so damned sorry."

"It's okay." He raised his head and, holding Zianne close against his chest, stared at Finn through tear-filled, red-rimmed eyes. "She got what she wanted. What we all wanted. The last of her people are safe." He looked past Finn and then at the others in the shack. "Where are Morgan and Rodie? And what about Bane? He went after them. I didn't see him come back."

Finn shook his head. He couldn't make eye contact with Liz or Kiera. Not with Cam, either. "Bane had Nattoch, Rodie, and Morgan. Rodie and Nattoch were injured, but they all left with Bane at the same time we did. He should be here. The ship exploded as we were leaving. I don't know if he got caught in the blast or what happened. Shit, Mac. Rodie has Zianne's soulstone. It recognized her name when Rodie went into the vault to get it, but she's not back. I can't believe they didn't make it."

He was rambling. He knew he was rambling, but it was so damned hard, kneeling here and trying to talk to Mac while the tears ran down the man's face and dripped off his chin. While Zianne lay pale and lifeless in Mac's arms.

The ones in the shack fell silent. Light continued flickering through the skylight as pieces of the Gar ship fell to Earth in long, burning trails across the heavens.

Then Niah raced into the shack with Mir just behind her. "Where are they?"

Finn turned and stared at her. "Where's who?"

"Rodie and Nattoch. Bane told us to meet him here, that they needed healing."

"Bane? You've heard from him?"

"Yes. Just now. He's . . ." She smiled. "Here they are."

Energy spiraled through the ceiling. Niah disassembled and a moment later she was back in her human form and helping to lay Nattoch on the floor of the shack. He was bleeding profusely from a deep slice running across his shoulder and chest, but Niah disassembled once again and disappeared inside the man.

Finn realized that Mir was helping Bane lay Rodie beside Nattoch. Like the older man, she was bleeding from deep wounds, but hers ran diagonally across her thighs. Mir brushed Rodie's hair back from her face as she checked for more injuries, and then flashed into energy and disappeared inside the unconscious woman.

Morgan knelt beside her, gasping for each breath. His hands shook badly. He fumbled awkwardly with the clasp on her fanny pack, finally loosened the strap and tugged it off her. The nylon bag was scorched from the Gar's weapon, but he unzipped the pouch and dug around a bit before pulling out her small digital camera. It appeared to be in one piece.

Morgan wrapped his hand around the thing and bowed his head over Rodie, as if he prayed. Finn put an arm around Morgan's shoulders and gave him a quick hug. "She'll be all right, Morgan. You got her home in time."

Morgan nodded, but he didn't move. His entire focus was on Rodie, on the way the deep wounds in her left thigh was already beginning to close. Fascinated, Finn watched for a moment before he noticed the soft glow of Zianne's soulstone in the bottom of Rodie's open pack.

He reached in and wrapped his fingers around the glowing diamond. It filled his hand, a warm, living stone that held Zianne's soul. What would happen to it, now that she was dead?

Cupping the stone in his palm, he carried it to Mac and opened his hand. The stone glimmered—an egg-sized diamond so perfect, so brilliant, it almost looked alive. "This is Zianne's. Mac, I'm so sorry."

Mac held out his hand and Finn set the stone carefully in his palm. Mac stared at it a moment, blinking away tears before he turned and looked at Finn. "How did they put the stones inside themselves? I want her to have it, even if it is too late. It belongs with her."

"The others retrieved their stones while they were still energy. They just seemed to absorb them. The stones disappeared inside. Here. Like this." He wrapped his hand around Mac's and turned it so that the stone touched Zianne between her breasts.

The diamond flashed and then it was gone. Mac flattened his hand over the spot where it disappeared inside her, and bowed his head against Zianne's. Finn backed away. This should be a private time. He didn't want to intrude on the man's grief.

Cam walked to the door and stared outside. "The shooting has stopped. I wonder if the ship exploding convinced them to leave."

Finn stood beside him. "I doubt it." As he watched, most of

the lights around the compound flickered and went out. "What's going on?"

Cam nodded toward the back of the dream shack. A group of Nyrians were coming around the side of the building. "They've been running the array and everything else on that line. Bart Roberts's group blew the power poles down on the main road and knocked us out. The generator runs emergency lights, but the Nyrians powered up the array so we could send that energy beam to you."

Finn shook his head. "I had no idea you'd lost power. If Tara and Bane hadn't come when they did, we'd all be dead. We were shot by one of the guards, and his weapon was a lot stronger than we expected. Nattoch and Rodie are the only ones with visible injuries, but the charge fried our energy levels. No one had enough strength to bring the wounded home."

Cam stared at him a moment. "You mean there were Nyrians who could have made the trip on their own, and they stayed because of the wounded?"

Finn nodded. He hadn't given himself time to really think that through, but it had truly been an act of both bravery and compassion when those who could have left chose to stay. "I know Tor and Arnec could have made it. Probably Bolt and Duran as well, but they never mentioned leaving without the rest of us. Bane and Tara arrived just in time. The ship's hull started to fail as we left. We just caught your stream of energy and followed it in."

"What was it like up there, Finn? My head was filled with images. Horrible images of bodies. Not human, I don't think, but there was such a terrible feeling about it."

"It was bad, Cam. Really bad." He glanced at Mac, still holding on to Zianne's body, his face buried in her long, black hair. It made him ache to see such grief. He shook his head and touched Cam's shoulder. "Later. When we're all together and we can share the story with everyone."

Cam was watching Mac as well. He glanced at Finn and nodded.

Lizzie stepped close to Finn and wrapped her arms around his waist. "I'm glad you're back, Finn."

He looked down at her. She was such a tiny little thing. Tiny, and yet so damned strong. "Me, too, Lizzie." He sighed and hugged her close. "Me, too."

13

Mac raised his head. He thought everyone had already gone, that they'd left him alone with Zianne, but then he heard Morgan's voice and realized Morgan was standing right beside him. Turning his head, Mac frowned. He really had been alone with Zianne, as far as he was concerned. Why was anyone still here?

"Thank you, Mir." Morgan went to his knees and scooped a barely conscious Rodie up in his arms. "I really can't thank you enough. She looks a lot better now, but I know she's exhausted. I'm going to take her to my cabin, let her get some sleep."

Mir stepped back and bowed her head, almost as if she was honoring Rodie and Morgan. Fascinated, Mac watched the interplay between the humans and the Nyrian, but it was hard to make sense of what was happening.

It was hard to make sense of anything. He rubbed his cheek against Zianne's dark hair. He knew he should take her over to the lodge, maybe lay her body in one of the rooms until they could deal with her burial, or however her people wanted to handle her death, but he wasn't ready to turn her free. Not yet.

Voices again, interrupting his thoughts. What was Mir saying? He focused on the beautiful Nyrian. She'd certainly done a great job when she healed Rodie's injuries. There was new, pink skin showing through the burned areas of Rodie's jeans—healed skin where deep burns had crossed her thighs. Why in the hell hadn't any of them been able to heal Zianne?

Morgan held Rodie cradled in his arms, as if she were a precious child.

The way Mac held Zianne.

"Morgan," Mir was saying, "you and Rodie and Finn risked your lives to save ours, an alien species you've only known a few days. I would do anything for you. We all feel the same way. No one has ever shown us such selfless love. All of you will be forever in our hearts, a part of us. Be well." Mir brushed her hand over Rodie's tangled hair. "She will need to eat before too long. Disassembling stresses these human bodies. We're all learning they have to be fed."

"I'll make sure she eats when she wakes up. How is Nattoch?"

Mac frowned and dropped his gaze lower. He hadn't realized the older Nyrian was still lying on the floor. Satza and Corin sat beside him. Mac thought Niah might be the one healing him. He remembered seeing a huge, gaping wound across Nattoch's chest, but it was almost entirely closed now.

"His injuries are serious," Mir said. "Much of his blood remained on the ship. Niah is trying to stabilize him for now. Is there a bed where we can take him? A quiet place to heal?"

Morgan answered her. "Rodie's cabin. It's empty and I'll be keeping her at my cabin for a while. If you can move Nattoch now and want to bring him, I'll show you the way." He turned and glanced over his shoulder at Mac. "Will you be okay, Mac? I don't like to leave you alone."

He wanted to shout that he wasn't alone. He had Zianne, but she wasn't really here anymore, was she? He pressed a hand to her chest, to the spot where her soulstone had disappeared.

Maybe part of her was still here. Her soul. Thank Nyria, Rodie had found her soul. She'd almost lost her life to bring it back. "I'm okay," he said. "Take care of Rodie." Morgan jerked his head in a sharp nod. Shifting Rodie's weight in his arms, he walked toward the door.

Niah slipped free of Nattoch in a burst of gold and blue energy and took corporeal form. The four women easily lifted the comatose man and followed Morgan out of the shack.

Finally. He was finally alone with Zianne.

Selfless love, Mir had called it. Zianne's love had been selfless, and now she was dead. It wasn't right.

He heard a helicopter make a low pass overhead. Maybe Dink was off filming something else. He knew Nick—the pilot—had slipped out a bit ago. Mac wondered where everyone had gone, what was happening with the terrorists. Then he wondered if it really mattered.

Not really.

Nothing mattered anymore. Nothing but holding Zianne close to his heart for as long as he could. He gazed up at the skylight. The emergency lighting in the shack was dim, and he could see stars in the nighttime sky. Was Zianne's goddess out there? Did Nyria understand what Zianne had lost, even though she'd followed through on her promise to save her people?

He had a feeling that last mental link had been too much, that by joining Mac and the others, Zianne had given up her own chance at survival. But by doing so, she'd saved all the others.

He choked back a curse. It wouldn't change a thing, but maybe a prayer? If the goddess was really out there, it certainly couldn't hurt, could it? He stared at the stars.

Nyria? If you're out there, will you please watch over my Zianne? She gave everything she had. I don't know how I'm going to go on without her, but I don't want to think of her alone, of her soul wandering. Please take care of her.

He wasn't sure what he wanted. Some kind of sign that

Zianne's elusive goddess had heard his prayer? He got nothing. Not a damned thing, which was really all he'd expected.

He was so tired. Twenty years working toward this goal, and even though it had been mostly a success, his ultimate failure would haunt him forever.

He was holding his failure in his arms.

He gazed at her, wishing for one more chance to see into those brilliant amethyst eyes. One more chance to tell her how much he loved her, hear her whisper the same words back to him.

"Damn it all, Zianne. I love you. Finn's right. This wasn't supposed to happen. Not like this. Never like this."

He needed to take Zianne to the lodge.

In a little while. For now, though, he really felt a need to close his eyes. Maybe take just a few minutes to rest.

To sleep with Zianne in his arms one last time.

Dink watched the sheriff's department helicopter make a low pass over the array. The big spotlight swept right to left and back again, lighting up the huge white dishes. A few men scattered beneath the beam of light, but there were more deputies on the ground, rounding them up like cattle.

They'd brought a bus in, parked it down on the road that led into Roberts's land, and they were arresting all the idiots they could catch and loading them in for the trip to town. They'd all be booked on myriad charges—enough to keep everyone out of Mac's hair for a while, at least.

There were no more gunshots. A few shouts, some cursing, but the battle was over. Help had come too little, too late, but he told Nick to keep the camera rolling. They were back to a live feed now, sending real-time film to the station in Sacramento. The crew there was editing, making it clean enough for broadcast, and they kept asking for more.

The Nyrians' story had gone viral. It was currently on all

the networks and cable stations. Short blasts showing up on Twitter and links to YouTube film on Facebook. Reporters from every major network and cable news show and all the tabloids were converging on the DEO-MAP site.

No one was getting in, not while Ralph and his men guarded the front gate.

That decision had been an easy one. Not yet. Not with Mac still in the dream shack holding Zianne. He owed it to both of them to give Mac this time to mourn. Dink couldn't allow himself to think of her. Not yet, if he wanted to do his job, but he refused to let anyone intrude on Mac's grief.

"Excuse me. I'm looking for MacArthur Dugan."

Well, shit. Dink turned quickly, signaled to Nick to continue filming, and grabbed the deputy sheriff's arm, leading him away from the camera. "Can I help you? Mac's really busy right now. I'm Nils Dinkemann, New World News." He held out his hand.

"Ted Alvisa." The deputy shook hands but his raised eyebrows told a story all their own. "Mac's bigger than I thought, if he's got New World's top reporter running interference."

Dink held on to his temper, barely. "Power has nothing to do with it. Mac's been a good friend for a long time. And, for what it's worth, anyone who knows Mac Dugan would do anything for him. Which brings up a salient point—where the hell were you when we were under attack?"

"Point taken." The deputy cursed under his breath. "The board of supervisors pulled rank. Wouldn't let us provide help. Said that Mac was leading an alien attack against the U.S. and called for military backup to shut you down."

Dink folded his arms over his chest and waited for more.

"Look, I came by to tell Mac I'm sorry. I'm probably going to lose my job over this, but while they were dicking around figuring what channels to go through to call in a strike on a civilian operation, I got together enough of my deputies, deputized a few others, and started arresting the jerks coming up here to help Roberts blow up the array."

He stared out across the plateau. "I don't know what Mac's got going on here, but he's always been straightforward with me, and his project has poured a hell of a lot of money into a very poor county. Money he's spent here with no strings attached. I want him to know I'm doing what I can, and I'll keep doing it."

Dink glanced at the helicopter still making low, slow sweeps across the plateau. "I take it the chopper's one of those things you're doing?"

Alvisa nodded. "It is, though from what we heard on our way up here, someone at the Pentagon has been on the horn to the local board, wondering why you're not getting any support, so I'm hoping authorization will come through at any time. I'm really sorry. Roberts has a lot of pull around here. He's put money into a lot of pockets, but Dugan's put even more money into the hands of people who really need it. I hope our inability to provide service didn't harm anyone."

Dink glanced toward the shack. "Only one," he said softly. "Just one."

"Hey, Dink?"

Dink looked over his shoulder. Cam walked across the open area, still dressed in those torn sweats, still covered in paint.

"Yeah? What's up?"

"I've got the paintings finished and set up in order in the dining hall. You said you wanted to do a recap of what's happened so far. They're ready to go when you are. My work's pretty rough, but should give viewers a visual of what's been going on."

"Thanks, Cam. I'll get Nick and Carl, and we'll be right over. Will Mir and Niah be available to help explain what we're seeing?"

"Niah's still working on Nattoch. He was pretty badly hurt, but Mir will be there. So will Tor, if I can get him away from Kiera." He laughed. "And Finn. He said he'd show up as well, so we'll have a pretty good narrative to go along with the visuals."

Cam gave Dink a cocky salute and headed back toward the lodge. "You'll have to excuse me, Deputy." Dink shoved his hands in his pockets and stared at the few stragglers still heading toward the lodge. "Unless you want to come see what's happened here tonight. Cameron's done some pretty explicit sketches and paintings of what we've been dealing with, both here and on the Gar ship before it exploded."

Alvisa stared after Cam. "I thought that kid looked familiar. That's Cameron Paisley, right? The artist?"

"You've heard of him?"

"Hasn't everyone? The guy's world famous. I had no idea he was part of this project."

"Mac preferred to keep things low key."

The deputy chuckled. "Well, he did a hell of a job. At least until tonight. Blowing an alien spaceship within sight of half the population of Earth is pretty high profile."

Dink merely nodded as he stood there with the deputy, watching the helicopter continue its slow sweep of the plateau and the surrounding countryside. He couldn't escape the hollow feeling in the pit of his stomach, no matter how much had been accomplished tonight. For him, personally, none of it really mattered as much as the one big failure they'd had.

Zianne hadn't survived to see any of this.

He really wanted to go to Mac. Needed to share his friend's grief, but there was a world awaiting news. A world of humans who would have to adjust to aliens living among them. And that was his job, wasn't it? Giving individual faces and personalities to the twenty-seven Nyrians they'd managed to save.

Twenty-seven out of twenty-eight. Not bad when you

looked at the numbers, but it really sucked when he thought of the one they'd failed.

With a sharp nod to Deputy Alvisa, Dink gestured for Nick to follow, and headed to the lodge.

Dreams were so strange. Mac knew he was dreaming when he suddenly felt cool grass beneath his bare feet and the strong grasp of Zianne's hand in his. They walked through a brilliant green meadow speckled with unfamiliar wildflowers and an even more brilliant blue sky overhead.

"It's not real, is it?"

"It's as real as you want it to be." Zianne stopped walking and grabbed his free hand, holding both his hands as she faced him. "This was Nyria as I remember it. I wanted to share it with you. I will always love you, Mac. And we did it. We saved all of them. Even Nattoch is going to make it, despite the old fool thinking he was ready to die. I'm so glad he didn't."

"But you did." His eyes were swimming in tears and he wondered if he'd ever be able to think of Zianne or dream of her without tears.

"I have my soulstone, and while I'm here in your mind, I certainly don't feel dead." She shrugged. "I don't know if a Nyrian can ever die if she has her soulstone. Remember, the body you're holding in the dream shack is merely a construct. It's one I created from your fantasies. Have you forgotten already?"

"It's not the body I love, Zianne. It's the spirit inside. I can't feel your spirit anymore. You're here in my dream, but the woman in my arms is growing cold. The life is gone from her."

"Dream me again, Mac. Bring me back. Nyria wouldn't have even suggested this if it weren't true. She is happy, now that you've saved her people. Did you know that if we'd all died, she would have died as well? Our gods and goddesses only survive because we give them life. Our faith enables them."

"Are you saying that my faith will enable you?" He grasped her arms just above the elbows, realized he was squeezing her much too hard, and loosened his grasp. "Can my faith give you life?"

"I don't know, Mac. It might. We can hope." She leaned close and kissed him. Her lips were warm and soft against his and the sweet scent of honey and vanilla made his head spin. And he just kept on spinning, farther and farther from Zianne.

Blinking, Mac opened his eyes. He was still in the dream shack, but his arms were empty. The body he'd been holding was gone. He looked around the small room, but there was no sign of Zianne. It was empty. The few lights on the control panel glowed without blinking. He stared at the skylight, at the dark sky speckled with stars, and he lay there, thinking of the dream.

Of Zianne. What exactly had the dream meant?

He had absolutely no idea. Was it real? Had she come to him, or had he merely created a fantasy where she could ease his heart?

Slowly he crawled out of the recliner and stretched. His bones ached. His muscles were tight and his arms felt like lead. His head hurt, and he realized he still had the stupid mesh cap stretched over his skull. He ripped it off. Tossed it on the console.

Then he glanced at the tote bag against the wall. Even the squirrel was gone. Would that tiny creature have understood that she was no longer needed? She must have escaped to the outdoors when Zianne died. Sighing, his mind spinning and heart heavy, Mac stepped outside. The night was quiet. The news helicopter sat like a large dragonfly, squatting in the open area between the shack and the lodge.

Deputy Alvisa's SUV was parked beside the lodge and all the lights were on around the deck, so it appeared the sheriff's department had finally showed up, the generator was still running, and everyone was probably in there celebrating.

As well they should be. They'd done what he'd asked them to do. More, in fact, since he'd never expected having to put any of his team in such danger, hadn't considered any of them going aboard the Gar ship.

But they'd done it without question. And they'd saved the remnants of Zianne's people.

But Mac really didn't feel like celebrating or even talking to anyone right now, so he went around the back way and took the private stairs that allowed him to bypass the main dining room on his way to the upper floor. Slipping quietly into his bedroom, he gazed at the mess he'd left in here. At least it was barely visible beneath the low voltage emergency lights.

In fact, the crappy lighting left the worst of the clutter in shadow. Clothes and blankets still on the floor, a half-empty bottle of Jack Daniel's sitting on the bedside table, sheets and bedding all twisted and tumbled after hours of sex—all of it a poignant reminder of the last time he'd been in his bed.

He hadn't been alone. He almost wept with the sweet memories of making love with Dink and Zianne. A lifetime ago.

Zianne's lifetime.

It was barely eight. He'd gone without sleep much too long, but as exhausted as he was, his emotions had gone through the wringer, his mind was still mired in grief, and his body thrummed with tension. He grabbed the bottle of Jack and carried it over to the window. All he could see was his own reflection, so he flipped off the lights and gazed across the moonlit plateau at the satellite dishes shimmering beneath a pale moon.

Then he upended the bottle and took a drink. The first big swallow went down rough. He coughed, blinked against the harsh burn, and tried it again. The second wasn't much better. By the time he got to the third, it was going down a little easier.

He took another, and then one more, closing his eyes against the burn but enjoying the pain all the way to his gut. When he upended the bottle again, only a couple of drops hit his tongue.

So much for getting blind, stinking drunk. He tossed the empty bottle at the wastepaper bin. It went in, but the weight took the bin over and it rolled a couple of feet before hitting the wall.

Papers scattered across the floor, adding to the mess, which seemed totally apropos for the way he felt.

Staring around the dark room, his gaze finally landed on the bathroom door. He really did stink. Showering first sounded better than crawling into bed reeking with the stench of the last thirty-six-plus hours. Especially when the bed still carried Zianne's sweet scent. Sacrilege, really, to foul his last memories of the woman he loved.

Unbuttoning his shirt on the way to the shower, Mac stumbled and fell against the wall. The room slowly spun. The whisky had hit him harder than he'd expected.

"Too fucking tired," he muttered. "Can't hold my booze." He planted his hands against the wall and pushed himself upright. "Nothing worse than a cheap drunk, is there, Zianne? This time, it's all your fault. Damn but I miss you. Miss you so much."

Good lord, but he'd been so drunk the first time Zianne came to him. So, so drunk that night after hanging out with Dink. Drunk and depressed and pissed off at life in general.

He almost laughed. Sort of how he felt now. Stumbling over his own feet, he made it to the bathroom and sat down on the toilet lid to pull off his shoes and socks. He almost fell off the pot, trying to get his pants off his butt and down over his feet. The shirt was easy, once he just ripped the buttons off rather than trying to get them through those stupid little holes, but he was glad he was already sitting.

Standing up again? Not so good, but once he was on his feet, adjusting the shower controls wasn't too difficult. Finally he crawled in under the steaming spray, his mind spinning with too much whisky and too many memories of that first night. She'd been so damned beautiful. So perfect, kneeling there in front of him, her violet eyes staring up through lush, black lashes clumped together by the spray. Full lips playing over the tip of his cock, and long, perfect fingers wrapped around the base, stroking his balls.

Her long, black hair had slicked over her shoulders, down her back, and over her breasts with the force of the spray, covering her so completely that only the dark rose tips of her breasts peeked through.

Hair like black silk, spilling over her lean body.

Her lips had been . . . dear God, they'd been perfect. Clasping his sensitive glans, nipping and kissing, her tongue . . . exactly. Just like that. He sighed and leaned his head against the tile as she loved him. Her fingers stroked his taut sac and cupped the weight of his balls and her mouth was the perfect sheath, hot and wet, closing on him and drawing him deep.

So perfect. She'd been only teasing him, hadn't she? She'd not really died. Not Zianne. He opened his eyes, fully expecting to see her, but the only thing staring at him was his dick, standing hard and tall and all alone. His knees almost buckled, but he leaned against the slick tile and set his grief free, tears flowing, mingling with the pulsing shower.

He'd never imagined losing her. He'd worried the Gar might hurt her, but never in his worst nightmares did he imagine finding her and losing her again.

Not when they'd come so close. But long minutes later, when he opened his eyes, praying that he'd see her, he was alone in the shower stall and the steam was rising all around.

Well, shit. He grabbed the soap and a washcloth and scrubbed away the stench. When he finally rinsed himself off, he felt an emptiness where his grief had been.

She wasn't coming back. No matter how much he wished for her, how badly he wanted her, she was gone.

All he had left were his memories. Memories and dreams.

Finn stood off to one side, his arm draped lightly around Liz's shoulders, as Duran talked about their mission aboard the Gar ship. The Nyrian spoke eloquently, without drama or pretense, speaking to the camera in a comfortable, almost intimate manner as he explained exactly what had happened. He easily used Cam's paintings to illustrate their mission, but when he pointed to the one of the bodies hanging in the meat locker, he raised his head and stared pointedly at Finn.

"I want Finn to tell you what Rodie discovered. It's not that we Nyrians lack empathy for the victims of the Gar, but after so many years and so many deaths, we could no longer allow ourselves to feel, or even to see them as sentient beings. Those who could not shut down their emotional reaction were driven to madness and death. The ones of us who survived are not the best witnesses. I fear we lost much during our servitude to the Gar. Much that we hope someday to regain."

Finn gave Liz's arm a squeeze and stepped up to the front of the group. A number of the sheriff's deputies had entered the lodge and now stood toward the back, but most of those here were Nyrians and the security guards who'd finally been pulled in when the last of Bart Roberts's army had been captured and hauled off to jail.

Finn looked at the now familiar faces and nodded, but as Duran had done, he spoke to the camera. To those who would be learning this story through his words, through Cam's paintings.

"Duran already told you how I'd been interrupted while

trying to disable the elevator. To avoid discovery, we raced back to the corridor where Rodie and Morgan were still hiding. Rodie had found a latch that was hidden in the wall—hidden from us, at least. I'm convinced the Gar had a lot of things on their ship coded in colors our eyes didn't register, though we'll never know.

"Anyway, Duran hasn't mentioned the stench, but the three of us humans were well aware that the air on the ship reeked. We were cracking sick jokes about 'essence of roadkill.' The air was thin, so we had to breathe deep to get enough oxygen, but we hated thinking of what we were drawing into our lungs. So Rodie found a door, and being Rodie, she opened it. The smell from that room almost knocked us over."

He realized he was swallowing just the way he had when they'd stepped inside, hoping like hell he wouldn't puke all over himself. Swallowing and sweating, only now he had a camera and worldwide television audience to worry about. He wiped his hand across his forehead. "The lights went on as soon as we stepped across the threshold. Luckily, Morgan was right behind Rodie and got his hand over her mouth before she screamed, but it was all I could do not to scream along with her.

"Cam's done a good job of capturing what we saw—row after row of frozen bodies, hanging from meat hooks." He paused while the cameraman moved closer to the painting. "They'd all been eviscerated—from the expressions of agony on their faces, I think it was done to them while they were alive and conscious. We're talking thousands of people, and when I call them people, I mean just that. Yes, they were alien, but some of them still had clothing on, some of them wore jewelry. They were humanoid. Rodie had her little digital video camera and got a lot of film."

He glanced at Dink. "Morgan's got the camera. We'll get the film to you later." He sucked in a deep breath as images he knew he'd never forget flashed across his mind. "I couldn't get over the children. So damned many kids, all sizes, from infants to what were probably the equivalent of teenagers. The women had two sets of breasts, which made us wonder if that was because they had multiple births, but we were just guessing." He shuddered, shaking his head, remembering. "All of them dead, frozen, hanging there like gutted beef."

He glanced at Duran. "We asked Duran about the fact this meat locker was down on the lower level, so far from where the Gar lived, and he said it's probably because they weren't as tasty to the Gar as other species. They were probably kept more like emergency rations, in case the Gar ran out of the good stuff."

He raised his head and looked directly at the camera. "That Gar ship was headed here. They were obviously planning to take all the edibles off our world first. Maybe we would have been tastier than the people in that meat locker. Who knows. It didn't happen because the Nyrians had already made the decision to commit suicide rather than allow the Gar to plunder another planet."

He walked over to the larger, dark and terrifying painting Cam had done before they actually left on their mission. "See this? Cameron said this came to him very suddenly. He painted it in almost a dream state and has no idea who or what gave him this particular visual, but when he showed it to the Nyrians, they recognized it.

"It's a planet they remember destroying long before there was life on Earth. If it looks at all familiar to you, that's because this is Mars. It was Mars. It's been a dead planet for as long as we've known about it, but Nyrians live a long, long time, and they remember when this planet was destroyed, when its people were taken on board as food for the Gar, when the atmosphere was stripped, when the minerals were taken. That would have been our fate, so for those of you who thought of welcoming the Gar with open arms, just be glad the Nyrians were brave enough to stop them. Earth wouldn't have had a chance. No one here would be alive now if they hadn't stopped that ship."

Shaken by the emotions roiling through his head, the sense that what he'd experienced was never really going to go away, Finn walked back to stand beside Liz, while Duran went on to describe the rest of the mission.

Finn didn't want to hear any more. He was so damned tired. Exhausted and heartsick to think that Zianne hadn't made it.

Tara was sitting beside Duran while he talked, and love was written all over her face. Finn had already found them a room upstairs and told them they needed a night alone together, time to get used to their human bodies and maybe even try making love. Just the two of them. He figured they should learn to generate their own energy. They hadn't argued with him.

He leaned over and breathed deeply of Lizzie's sweet scent. "I'm beat," he said. "I'm going to head back to my cabin and get some sleep."

She reached up and cupped the side of his face in her hand. His five o'clock shadow was more like a nine o'clock, and he rubbed his coarse whiskers against her palm.

"I'd like to come with you."

Frowning, he turned and kissed her palm. Stared into her steady gaze for a long time, wondering if that was such a good idea. "But what about your guys? Shouldn't you . . . ?"

Interrupting him, she shook her head. "They're exhausted, too. Xinot is still recovering and I think all the guys are a bit shell-shocked. The two women, Reiah and Seri, got dibs on my bed, and the men are planning to sleep on air mattresses and the couch. I've got their bedding already set up." She shrugged and a dimple he'd not noticed before popped up on her right cheek. "You see, I really don't have anywhere to sleep."

Finn slipped an arm around her waist and hugged her close.

"Yes, you do." Quietly, they slipped out of the lodge. Together, the two of them walked through the moonlight to his cabin.

Mac crawled beneath the rumpled sheets, and just as he'd hoped, the sweet scent of honey and vanilla filled his senses. At least tonight he'd still have her close. Grabbing the pillow Zianne had used, he shoved it under his head and buried his nose in her soft cotton pillowcase.

Sleep claimed him, but so did dreams—dreams that came so clearly, so quickly, he hadn't been aware of slipping into sleep. Once again he and Zianne were walking through that greener than green meadow with the brilliant blue sky overhead. Holding hands, just walking through tall grass that brushed against his bare feet. This time, Zianne wore a long, flowing skirt and a white peasant blouse that left her beautiful shoulders bare. Neither Mac nor Zianne spoke, but he was almost preternaturally aware of her beside him—her warmth, her sweet scent, her amazing vitality. He took comfort in the softness of her touch. The warmth of their clasped hands.

She'd been so cold when he last held her. So cold and still, and then she'd been gone. There was a tree ahead and he led her there, sat in the shade, and pulled her down so that she tumbled into his lap. Her long arms wrapped around his shoulders and she leaned her head against his chest. He felt her warm breath against his throat, heard the soft, steady drum of her heart, and felt more at peace than he could recall.

If this was all he could have of Zianne, it would have to be enough. He'd make it work for him, even though he wanted her so badly he ached. She raised her head, he lowered his, and their lips met. So soft, so absolutely perfect.

He ended the kiss, brushing his lips across hers. Inhaling her scent. "What could I have done differently, Zianne? Is there any way I could have held on to you?"

He felt her sigh and hugged her even tighter. "I've dreamed of holding you like this for so many years. Imagined how it would feel to have you in my life for all of my life, and it was always so perfect. I imagined Dink coming to visit and the three of us together. Other times I dreamed of you and me—just the two of us—alone up here at the site, once all your people were safe."

"I need you, Mac. I need you to want me, to hold me, to make love to me." He felt each word, whispered against his throat. The movement of her lips, the soft puffs of air. Felt loss the moment when she pulled away from him, but it was only to tug the blouse over her head, to slide the skirt past her hips. She spread her full skirt out on the thick grass and it was more than enough to make a bed for the two of them.

With almost frantic haste, he kicked off his clothing and, naked, kneeling beside her, ran his fingers along the curve of her breast, then cupped the soft weight and reveled in that satiny skin resting in his palm. Leaning close, he took the taut peak of her nipple between his lips and sucked until she moaned, arching her body against him. She was satin and silk and strong, lean muscles. Soft breasts and the sharp jut of hipbones, the curve of a perfect thigh and the long, slender stretch of her legs.

Every part of her he'd committed to memory, every part he loved. She lay back in the folds of her colorful skirt and Mac knelt between her thighs. Lifting them, he hooked her legs over his arms and held her up to his mouth, drawing in a deep breath perfumed with her sweet scent. Then he dipped forward to taste her amazing flavors.

He could feast on her for hours. In fact, he'd done it more than once years past, so lost in her addictive taste, in her moans and cries with each release, he'd felt no need to do anything more than give her pleasure.

Pleasuring Zianne pleased him, but that's what love was all about, wasn't it? Pleasing the one you love. Giving them all of you, everything you have, making that one person smile for the same reason you smile—because you're together. Because you love.

"Now, Mac." Her breathless cry made him smile against her sweet, feminine folds. "I need you inside me now." So demanding.

He gave her one last lick and she whimpered, so he leaned close and kissed her mouth, tangling his tongue with hers, connecting on so many levels. When he finally pressed close with his thick, hard cock, when he pushed through her folds and slipped inside, she was wet and ready, so swollen with arousal, with need and desire that her body trembled. He seated himself deep inside, and it was as if he'd finally come home. Finally found the perfect place where all was as it should be.

They rocked together, not in wild passion but in a slow, sensual loving, bodies and hearts connected, and the reality of death and loss forgotten for now. All that mattered was this moment, this place, this miraculous dream. If that was all he could have, Mac would take it. If Zianne could return and hold him close, only in his dreams, he would have to be content.

He felt her tense, sensed the tiny ripples in her vaginal sheath, but he didn't speed up, didn't press harder or deeper. No, this time he merely loved her. Slow and steady as if they had all the time in the world, the two of them finally reached their climax together, a sweet, almost tender connection.

Mac felt no grief. No sense of loss, not even the anger he'd experienced earlier when he realized she was gone. She wasn't entirely gone. Not really. Not if he could have her like this, could connect on this level. It wasn't enough. It would never be enough, but if this was all he could have, he'd damned well take it and be happy.

He stayed buried deep inside, holding his weight up on his

elbows, his body tightly lodged between her legs. He was still hard, still wanting more, but she'd drifted off. Her eyes were closed and there were dark circles beneath them.

He kissed first one closed lid and then the other. Could the specters of dreams actually grow tired? She looked exhausted, as if this dying had been as hard on her as it had been on Mac. Such a strange concept. An exhausted figment of his imagination. He pulled her into his arms and rolled over so that Zianne sprawled across him. And lying there in the tangled fabric of her cotton skirt, Mac drifted off to sleep in that strange dream world, with the blue sky overhead and Zianne sleeping soundly, her long, lithe form sprawled warm and trusting across his chest.

14

Dink rubbed a hand across the back of his neck. It was late, but at least it appeared everyone was settled. He'd found a room for Carl and Nick in the workers' barracks. All the other rooms were taken up with Nyrians, most of them sleeping two or three to a bed. No one wanted to be alone tonight.

Including me. And yet, he was the only one left in the dining hall. Deputy Alvisa had taken his men and gone almost an hour ago, and the DEO-MAP site was finally quiet. They'd have to go over the place in the morning to check for damage, but a canine patrol had done a sweep of the entire area around midnight, looking for bodies. They'd found a couple of injured, but no one appeared to have died.

Surprising, considering all the gunshots and heavy explosives, but he knew Mac would be pleased. Dink was, too. He'd seen enough bloodshed over the years, from Bosnia to Iraq and Afghanistan, not to mention the semipermanent wars in so many parts of the African continent. So many pointless deaths. He was glad they'd not added more to the number tonight.

One had been more than enough.

The last ones to leave the lodge had been Kiera and her Nyrian, Tor. She'd been teasing him about sharing her bed with a couple of other guys, but Tor didn't seem to mind the idea a bit. Dink couldn't remember their names. Too many names to keep track of. Not too many people, though. Not enough.

He thought of Zianne, but only for a moment to indulge his grief before pushing her memory aside. Later, when he felt as if he could actually deal with her loss.

He worried about Mac.

Of course, he'd always worried about Mac, ever since they were little kids. He figured that worry was wired into him, until now it was part of his DNA. At least he was used to it.

After turning out lights, Dink headed up the stairs. He hoped Mac didn't mind sharing, but his was the only bed available.

He paused in front of the door to Mac's room. Images of how he'd spent last night in this same room, the same bed, threatened to choke him. Whether he wanted it or not, he had the feeling it was going to be a long time before he could think of Zianne without weeping.

The door was unlocked, and he stepped into the dark room. Moonlight cut a pale swath across the bed. Mac lay in the middle of it, arms and legs sprawled, his face buried in the pillow.

He was such a beautiful man. Dink loved him so much it hurt, but then he'd always loved Mac. He knew Mac loved him back, in his own way. It would have to be enough. Hadn't it always been?

Quietly, he stripped off his clothes and left them where they fell before ducking into the bathroom for a quick shower. Mac's clothing lay in a pile on the floor in front of the toilet.

What a couple of slobs they were! Zianne had teased them unmercifully about their "bad man habits." And they, in turn, would remind her that she seemed to like her men bad. Still, it appeared her complaints were well deserved.

Standing beneath the spray, he thought of the conversation he'd had earlier with the president. Mac was going to love it, but what an experience. Dink had met the president before at news conferences where he'd been but one reporter in the crowd, but a personal phone call to check on their "new citizens," as the commander in chief referred to the Nyrians, had been amazing.

Rodie's little camera had accomplished what all the words in the world couldn't—those images of gutted aliens hanging in what was essentially an interstellar meat locker had flashed around the world. Combined with NASA's film of the massive Gar star cruiser exploding just beyond Earth's atmosphere, of the burning chunks of the thing hurtling toward the ground, and the story of the Nyrians' decision to sacrifice themselves rather than be responsible for harming anyone or anything on this world had convinced the people of Earth that Nyrians were the good guys.

From what he'd seen and the Nyrians he'd met, they were a hell of a lot better than some of the folks who'd been born here.

Yawning, Dink turned off the tap and dried himself. Then he crawled into bed beside Mac. He had to shove him a bit to clear up enough space, but Mac merely grunted and rolled aside. Dink lay beside him, staring at the ceiling.

What was going to happen now? Mac's entire focus for the past twenty years had been all about saving the Nyrians and rescuing Zianne. Having Zianne forever. Dink rolled over on his side and studied his old friend. His lover.

He'd dreamed of Mac as his lover for so long it didn't feel real even now. Mac must have felt his steady gaze, because he slowly blinked and then opened his eyes. Turned his head and frowned briefly, before a slow smile spread across his face.

"She was here, Dink. Here, with me."

"Zianne? But how?"

Mac shook his head. "I don't know. It was a dream, but too

real to have been nothing but fantasy. We talked, we made love, we walked in a world that she said she'd imagined, one that was a copy of Nyria. If that's all I can have of her ..." He sighed. "It's not really enough, but it's better than nothing."

"Do you think she's real? Is she alive, but maybe in a different reality? On a different plane?" Hell, he was willing to believe anything after the last couple of days.

Mac chuckled. "I don't know. She said something about my faith giving her life, but when I woke up, she was gone. Maybe that's just wishful thinking, but I'll find out more if she comes back." He pushed himself up and leaned against the headboard.

Dink was in the process of sitting up beside him when Mac asked, "Did anything happen after I left?"

"Oh, shit." Laughter was not what he was expecting, but once he started, Dink couldn't seem to stop. "Mac, you have no idea!"

"What? C'mon, Dink. Pull it together. What the fuck happened?"

"Let's see. The sheriff showed up with a shitload of deputies, a helicopter, and a canine unit. All of Roberts's men have been arrested and hauled off to jail. A couple of injured will be locked up once they're patched up. We did a live feed of the whole operation here at the site with the helicopter and the canine units, and then a full-scale show-and-tell with Cam's drawings and paintings. Duran, Tor, and Finn did the color commentary, and they were great. Rodie's film of gutted aliens aboard the Gar ship has gone viral, and people all over the world are hailing the Nyrians as heroes. Oh, and the president called and said they're all considered U.S. citizens, since they chose to come here first."

He shrugged and grinned. "But other than that, nope. Nothing happened." He burst out laughing. "Shut your mouth, Mac. You'll catch a fly."

"Holy fucking shit." Mac flopped back against the headboard. "That's better than anything we could have hoped for. How are the Nyrians? I can't believe I missed all of that."

"They're all good. All of them. Even Nattoch, though Niah said he's still weak and will take a while to recover. And don't worry—everything's backed up and you can get all the coverage later. Ya know, Mac, the thing I keep thinking is that Zianne would love the way this is all working out."

"She will love it, Dink. I'll tell her as soon as I see her." Then Mac leaned over and kissed him full on the mouth.

Dink had figured he was too damned tired to even think of sex, but it appeared he'd been wrong. Arousal surged through him with the force and heat of lightning. His dick stretched and lengthened, going from tired and flaccid to so hard he ached. Mac kept kissing him, sliding his hand down Dink's belly, finding his dick and squeezing it.

Dink moaned, arching his back, pressing himself into Mac's hand, and then they were slipping over and around each other, turning almost desperately so that Mac could take Dink in his mouth and Dink could return the favor. Before he was able to position Mac, Mac had one hand on his balls, the other around the base of his cock, and that hot, wet mouth of his was taking Dink down deep.

Groaning, he locked up all his muscles just to keep from coming at the first strong suction, the first hot lick of Mac's tongue. After a moment, he finally felt as if he had some control, enough to nuzzle Mac's groin, to take a deep breath and inhale what should have been that familiar male musk that was all Mac.

Except that wasn't what he smelled at all. His senses were shocked with the rich scent of honey and vanilla. He dipped his head and took Mac's thick cock in his mouth, but the flavor was all Zianne, not Mac. Zianne, as if her sweet honey still coated Mac's erection, as if he'd recently made love to her.

Really made love to her. The thought slammed into Dink, turned him on even more. He used his tongue and teeth, his lips and his fingers to take Mac to the brink and hold him there.

The same thing Mac was doing to him. They each sucked and nuzzled, licked and nipped until Dink slid one long finger behind Mac's balls, found the tight pucker of his anus, and pressed. Pressed again, reveling in Mac's soft moan vibrating his cock before pressing hard enough to gain entrance, to find that small sphere that was much too responsive to Dink's touch.

Mac thrust his hips forward and Dink took all of him. Sucked him deep, took his seed and swallowed it down, licking and sucking until Mac's penis finally softened between his lips, until his erection was merely a sweet memory and the taste of Zianne no longer lingered on Dink's tongue.

Only then did he let himself go. He groaned against a surge of pleasure so sharp it hurt. Almost whimpered as Mac squeezed his sac just the way he liked, and cried out when Mac swallowed Dink entirely, taking his cock down his throat where the strong muscles of mouth and throat compressed and released and threw him almost painfully into orgasm.

It seemed to go on forever, that rhythmic pulse and release of climax. Mac licked and sucked, taking everything, every drop, nuzzling and laving the full length with his tongue, running his lips along the softening length of Dink's shaft.

Long minutes later, the two of them lay side by side, bodies replete, thoughts held close. Finally Dink rolled to his side so he could look directly into Mac's eyes. "I tasted Zianne on you. You really did make love with her tonight. It wasn't a dream. Your cock was covered in honey and vanilla." He laughed, and it was a harsh sound in such a quiet, dark room. "You've never tasted that good before, by the way."

Mac swallowed, and the sound almost echoed in the dark. "Can you explain it any other way?"

Dink shook his head. "No. And I don't really know that I want to."

"Me, either, Dink." His voice broke. "Me, either." He leaned close and kissed Dink. Then he rolled away and buried his face in his pillow. He didn't make a sound, but his shoulders trembled and his misery was a third presence in the bed.

Unwilling to intrude on Mac's private grief, Dink lay there for a long time before sleep finally claimed him.

Finn lay in his bed, staring at the ceiling. It was late, he was exhausted, but he'd not been able to sleep. He'd blame his arousal, but it wasn't merely that. It wasn't even the fact that Lizzie slept so peacefully beside him, her slightly parted lips a hairsbreadth from his left nipple.

She wore one of his T-shirts and nothing else, and he hadn't laid a finger on her. That alone worried him. He'd been wondering if he was falling in love with Ms. Elizabeth Anne Connor. The fact they'd spent hours talking without sex, and then she'd just curled up against him like a trusting kitten and fallen asleep, almost had him convinced that was his problem.

He'd never been in love before. The closest he'd come had been Tara and Duran, but the two of them needed time alone together, time to explore their love from the standpoint of their new, human bodies. He hoped they'd made love tonight. Hoped that natural human instincts had come with their corporeal forms.

He figured he'd find out in the morning, but that was another thing about him that had changed. He was never unselfish, and yet he'd sent Duran off with Tara when he could have gone with them, and he'd brought Lizzie back to his cabin because she'd asked him to. Not for sex so much as to get to know each other.

And he'd had a wonderful night with her. Talking, teasing,

and telling her about going aboard the Gar ship, promising to teach her how to disassemble when she was ready. Not once had he tried to convince her that sex with him was part of the deal. Yes, he'd been aroused. He was still hard as a post. He doubted any man alive could spend time with Lizzie and not want to make love with her, but holding back, holding her . . . now that had been special.

He closed his eyes and tried to sleep, but the damned visual of all those bodies kept coming back. Would he ever be free of that? The mission aboard the Gar ship had changed him. Accepting that he might die, seeing the fragility of life, realizing what the Nyrians had lived with for eons—he would never be the same.

He didn't want to be the same. He wanted to be better. Worthy of love from a woman like Lizzie. He'd never in his life worried about being worthy. He'd spent his life taking so much for granted—his intelligence, his decent looks, the way women flocked to him. He'd never questioned why they didn't stay. He'd always thought it was his choice, but that wasn't it at all.

They hadn't stayed because there was no reason to. There was no substance to him. He was nothing more than a good time, and for the past thirty-odd years, that had been enough. It wasn't anymore. Not when he held a woman like Lizzie in his arms and realized she was too good for him. That he didn't want to sully someone as pure and good as Lizzie.

That he didn't want to let her go, either.

She raised her head, eyes sleepy, hair tousled, and shook her head. "You're wrong, Finn. And, yes, I've been eavesdropping. Shamelessly, I might add, but angst doesn't suit you."

"How do you know?" She was so damned cute. And young. Eight years younger than he was. Made him feel jaded and worn. "I might be the king of angst."

She yawned. "I don't think so. Make love to me, Finn. I need holding tonight. Specifically, I need you. Need to know you're safe." She rose up on her elbows, leaned over, and kissed him. Her lips parted, her tongue swept across his mouth, and he opened to her. Welcomed her in.

After a moment, she pulled back, rolled away to sit beside him with her legs crossed, and glared at him. "Do you have any idea how worried I was today? How afraid that you wouldn't come back? But I didn't feel as if I had a right to be open about my worry, because no one knows how I feel about you."

He frowned right back at her. "I don't know how you feel about me, either."

She grabbed the hem of his borrowed T-shirt and tugged it over her head. Finn couldn't even speak. He'd never seen such perfect breasts, such an amazing body on an absolutely amazing frame. Where the Nyrian women were all tall and lean, Lizzie was more compact, still lean, but not much over five feet tall with the body of a goddess.

Flat stomach, perfect little dark thatch of curls between her thighs, and the world's most beautiful breasts. He realized he was staring like an idiot. Licking his lips and staring.

She lifted her breasts and stared down at her tightly puckered nipples. "Well, my girls only stand up when they're really interested. What do you think?"

He couldn't have stopped if he'd wanted to. Leaning forward, Finn took first one nipple between his lips and then the other, sucking each of them hard, tugging just a bit and then releasing. "I think they're absolutely perfect." His voice cracked and he cleared his throat. So much for playing it cool. "I think you're absolutely perfect."

The smile spread slowly across her face. "Good. I sort of think the same thing about you, and that's just weird."

"Why? Do you think I'm weird?"

She laughed. "Well, I thought you were really a jerk when I first met you. So did Kiera, if you'll recall."

"I remember." And he did. Would he ever forget the fantasy

they'd given him on the long ride up to the DEO-MAP site that first day? He'd thought it was his own fantasy, tied hand and foot to a tree overhead and the ground beneath with both Kiera and Lizzie having their way with him. It had been absolutely amazing, at least until Lizzie shoved an imaginary purple dildo up his ass.

It wasn't until then he'd realized both young women had directed every single part of that fantasy, but he'd come so hard his dick hurt. The worst part was riding the rest of the way up the mountain in shorts sticky with his own spunk.

"I still want to know where the purple dildo came from."

She crawled across his legs and stretched out on top of him, and if she thought he'd be able to keep his hands to himself, she was dead wrong. "No idea," she said. "Will you ever forgive me?"

He cupped her face in his hands, leaned close, and kissed her. "I forgave you the moment it happened. I deserved it. Deserved worse, actually. You were really quite forgiving, considering how I'd been acting."

"I know. But you've changed." She shook her head and her long silky hair brushed his chest. "I like the guy I'm seeing now. A lot."

"Enough to let him play with your girls?" He lifted one eyebrow and focused on her breasts.

"Oh, yeah." She scooted down his legs until his dick was standing there between them as if it had a mind of its own. "As long as I get to play with this guy." She leaned over and licked the sensitive glans. His hips jerked and he clutched the bedding to keep from grabbing Liz.

Then she raised her head and winked at him, bent over, and slowly sucked his rather sizeable length and girth much deeper than any woman had ever attempted.

His jaded, totally cool response was little more than a whimper. She was such a minx! Maybe she looked about six-

teen and came across as a first-class nerd when they got to talking science and computers and all the stuff she excelled at, but
her outward innocence hid the heart and soul of a truly adven-
turous vixen.

And with that single, sexy, adorable wink, Finnegan O'Toole
fell.

Hard.

She wondered if Finn knew she'd never gone down on a guy
in her life, not until she'd met her first Nyrians. She was such a
fake, but she must be doing something right because she could
swear Finn's eyes just about crossed.

She'd read all the books and even watched more than her
share of porn, but it was totally different, doing this for real.
The Nyrians had tasted different, almost like cookies, but Finn
had a musky, male scent and flavor that reached her on a totally
visceral level. She couldn't get enough of him, and damn it, but
she really liked the guy.

He wasn't the predator he'd said he was. Maybe he had
been, but like the rest of them, he'd changed. She knew she had.
She'd learned more about herself over the past few days than
she'd ever dreamed. She was stronger than she'd thought. Sex-
ier, and much more self-confident.

And she'd discovered that she really, really loved sex. The
Nyrians had taught her that. It was easy to be uninhibited with
them, knowing sex would help save their lives.

Maybe it was time to save herself—and Finn. She swirled
her tongue around Finn's penis and teased the tiny eye at the
top. He was already leaking those first, pearly drops, but unlike
Xinot and the other guys, his tasted salty, almost bitter—and
somehow absolutely wonderful.

Suddenly he had his big hands on her arms and he was lifting
her away, rolling her over and holding her flat to the bed with

his fingers tangled in hers. He loomed over her, all muscle and tousled hair, his chest heaving with each breath and those gorgeous green eyes glittering like chips of emerald.

His cock was so hard that it rose up against his belly in a graceful curve, all shiny from her mouth. She wanted it inside her. Now. So much it was hard to breathe for wanting him.

Finn tightened his grip on her hands, holding her still. He let out a big breath and his nostrils flared. "Lizzie, I've been trying my damnedest not to push you. You're so young and I had you pegged as sweet and sexy but a little too innocent for a guy like me. I didn't want to hurt you, but girl, that's not how it is at all, is it? You are sweet, and for all your bravado, I think you're still pretty innocent, but I'm afraid that if anyone's going to get hurt, it's going to be me. Do you have any idea what you do to me? How much I want you?"

Her eyes filled with tears. So not cool, but he looked so desperate and even a little afraid, and that was more touching than anything she could imagine. "Actually, Finn, I do know. I want you just as badly, and you do things to me I never imagined. I didn't see this coming, did you?" She laughed, but the sound broke on a sob and left her sniffing and wishing she could wipe her eyes before the tears spilled.

Finn leaned over and kissed the tears from the corners of her eyes. Kissed her lips, her throat, her breasts. Then he turned her hands free and slid down between her legs. He took his own sweet time about kissing his way from her knees, along her inner thighs, around all the important stuff to the slight swell of her belly.

She arched her hips and he grinned at her, but then he lowered his mouth between her legs and she started crying for real. She'd never experienced anything like this. Never, and it was beautiful and sweet and scary because he made her feel things she hadn't expected.

Made her want even more. Her first climax rolled through her and she clamped her knees against his shoulders, but he kept licking and sucking until he took her over again. She'd barely caught her breath when he backed away, grabbed his cock in his hand, and aimed it directly between her legs.

Damn, she wasn't even close to being a virgin, but she'd never taken anything this big in her life. He filled her, stretched all those tender places, and she cried out because it was so damned good, so perfectly beautiful to have him deep inside and to be looking into those glittering eyes and know she'd done this to him. She'd taken this totally sexy guy, expecting to have some good sex, and she'd gotten so much more.

She felt her third climax building, but she didn't want to go alone. She clutched at his buttocks and pulled him close, digging her nails into the taut muscles. He sped up, thrusting hard and deep in short, fast strokes, taking her with him, taking both of them over the top. As she hung there, suspended for an interminable period of time, she felt his thoughts clinging to hers, felt the need and the love and the amazement that they should be this good together.

And then, as quickly as they'd connected, she joined him in free fall as they tumbled over together. The connection faded, but it couldn't be denied. More than their usual telepathy—this was something altogether unique.

Long minutes later Finn got up, went into the bathroom, and came back with a warm washcloth. He sat on the bed beside her and gently parted her thighs. Embarrassed, she tried to press them together. He stopped her with a gentle hand on her belly.

"Let me do this. Please?"

Heat flooded her chest and face, but she nodded, and he carefully bathed her, washing away the sticky remnants of his ejaculate, treating her as if she were some delicate porcelain doll. When he was finished, he carried the washcloth over to the hamper and tossed it in. Then he crawled into bed beside her and tucked her close against his shoulder.

"Thank you, Lizzie." He took a deep breath. "I didn't expect that."

"Expect what?"

He shrugged. "You. Me. That amazing connection. I felt something similar with Tara and Duran, and it blew me away. This, with you? It was even more powerful. Sorta scary, you know?" He leaned over and kissed her.

"I know," she said. She was glad he'd admitted that, because it was scary. Because she didn't know what it meant, but she fully intended to find out. And that was good, too. It was all good. Then she had a weird thought. "Have you ever made love with a friend before?"

He shook his head. "Until Tara and Duran, I'd never made love. Had a lot of sex, but never made love. You're the first, Lizzie. The first real friend I've ever made love with."

He kissed her again. Slowly. Softly.

"Me, too. You. Me." Damn. She laughed. "I are a good talker, huh?" He chuckled softly and she licked her lips. Tasted him and decided it was a really good taste. "You're the first time for me, too, Finn. It makes everything . . ." She shrugged, still at a loss for words. "Special. Really, really special."

She was still thinking of all the good in her life when she finally fell asleep, wrapped in Finn's arms.

Mac blinked, vaguely aware that the sun was up and it was shining directly into his bedroom window. Squinting against the brilliant light, he stretched—and bumped into Dink. He rolled his head to the side and grinned. Hell, Dink even looked good asleep. He tried to remember if he'd dreamed of Zianne, but he'd slept the night through.

Damn. He was really hoping that those dreams would become a regular thing. She'd come to him the first time because of fantasy. Why not now? And then he remembered that first time he'd had sex with Dink over twenty years ago, how they'd awakened the next morning, he'd rolled over and . . .

He rolled over, and found himself gazing at the most beloved face he'd never thought to see in his bed. *Zianne?* He tried to say her name, but no sound came out. He reached for her, wanting to wake her but afraid he'd discover she wasn't real.

Damn, but he couldn't stand the suspense.

He stretched his fingers out to touch her hair, and his calluses snagged in silken strands. Carefully, gently, he ran his hand over her dark hair, along her shoulder, following the line of her hip. She groaned softly and stretched, and then she turned to him and opened her eyes.

Amethyst eyes. Perfect violet eyes, framed in lush, dark lashes. "Mac? Am I here? Really here?"

He nodded, almost afraid to speak. "How?"

She shook her head, obviously confused. "I was so weak, so depleted, that even with my soulstone I couldn't maintain any form. I remember Nyria, and making love with you, but I wasn't strong enough to stay."

"Will you stay now?"

"I think so. I feel . . ." She held up her arms and turned her hands this way and that. "I feel good. Like me again. I think my soulstone needed time, but I'm whole, now." She looked past him. Raised up on her elbow. "Hello, Dink. You're here, too!"

"I am." His voice rumbled in Mac's ear. "And so are you." He kissed Mac on the shoulder. "This reminds me of another time, another place, when we all awakened together."

Mac chuckled softly. He pulled Zianne into his arms and held her close, loving her so much he ached, but he couldn't stop laughing. The tears were merely incidental. Dink wrapped his arms around both of them and the three of them lay there in the big bed, hugging one another, laughing and crying at absolutely nothing.

At everything. Her people were safe. The world was safe, and he had the woman he loved. He had Dink at his back, and Zianne to hold, and life couldn't get any better.

Then he felt Dink's fingers trailing along the crease of his ass. Zianne stroked his shaft and cupped his balls, and he decided that, yes, it could get better. A lot better.

It already was.

Dink, Zianne, and Mac were the last ones into the dining hall. Mac glanced at the buffet table and grinned. Meg had outdone herself, and there was enough food for an army. Of course, with all the Nyrians here for breakfast, they just about had an army of their own.

The moment the three of them reached the bottom of the stairs, every single person in the dining hall came to their feet. The applause embarrassed him, but he was touched, too, by the way everyone rushed them when they realized Zianne was alive, that she'd made it after all. She was hugged and kissed and passed from person to person until she finally ended up in front of Nattoch.

He was still too weak to stand, and she knelt at his feet, wrapped her arms around his waist, and hugged him. Mac walked over and gently rubbed Nattoch's shoulder. "How are you doing today? Are you feeling better?"

Nattoch stroked his hand over Zianne's hair, but he didn't answer Mac for a moment. Finally, he raised his head and wiped tears from his face with a paper napkin. "I am still learning to work with the emotions that appear to be a part of this body." He laughed softly. "As a creature of energy, I felt them but had no way to express my deepest feelings."

He glanced up at Mac. "This body expresses everything, all

too easily. It will take me many years of study before I feel I know it well, but I am well, thanks to your people. We are all well. All alive." He slipped his fingers beneath Zianne's chin and raised her face. "This one is alive, thanks be to Nyria. I worried we were too late."

Zianne turned her lips to the elder's hand and kissed his palm. "Nyria lives, Nattoch. While I lingered between life and death, she came to me. She's been helping us as much as she could, all along. She told me she gave Cam his visions so this world would know how evil the Gar were. She helped me find my strength after Rodie brought my soulstone back. Then Mac's love brought me home."

Zianne smiled up at him and then broke into laughter. It was a sound Mac thought he'd never hear again, but her words opened an entirely new set of possibilities.

"Nyria is still helping us. In a few more months, once our bodies have adjusted to life as humans, we will be able to have children. Children who carry our Nyrian heritage." She turned those beautiful amethyst eyes on Mac. "Sons and daughters, Mac."

Stunned, Mac was still trying to assimilate what Zianne had just said when she squeezed his hand and returned her attention to Nattoch.

"Nattoch, I am so glad you survived. I was angry with you! You were much too ready to sacrifice yourself."

"As were you, child. I've discovered that you and I have much in common. We also have much to live for. So much."

Mac's head spun with possibilities, with dreams he'd never dared as he helped Zianne to her feet. She leaned close to Nattoch and gave him a kiss on the cheek.

"Be well, Nattoch."

She straightened, and Mac grabbed her shoulders, forced her to look at him. "Do you mean it? We can have children?"

Slowly, she nodded. "Not for a while. Nyria says we're too new in this world, but soon." She stretched up on her toes and kissed his chin. "She'll tell us when. You would like that?"

It took him a minute to find his voice. "I would. Very much." Little girls with amethyst eyes and brilliant minds like their mother, little boys who had to take things apart to see how they worked. He raised his head and caught Dink staring at him. Imagined a son with Dink's blond hair and silvery eyes. Possibilities. So many possibilities he'd never allowed himself to consider.

Zianne held Mac's hand as they turned away from Nattoch. "Look, Mac!" Tugging him along, she walked quickly over to a table where Rodie and Morgan sat with Bolt, Kiera, and Tor. Sitting in the middle of the table was the little gray squirrel, munching on peanuts.

"She came back." Zianne ran her finger over the squirrel's sleek back. "If not for your generosity, I might not have survived." The squirrel chattered, stood up on her hind legs, and wrapped her tiny paws around Zianne's finger. Then she turned around and went back to her pile of nuts.

Morgan nudged Rodie. "Well, we know what she prefers."

Rodie leaned against his shoulder. "You know women. We're all fickle." Morgan kissed her while the others at the table laughed.

Mac tugged Zianne's hand and they walked over to the buffet. Dink was already filling his plate, but he paused a moment and they gazed about the crowded dining hall, at the men and women who had been creatures of energy as well as the ones who were merely ordinary humans with extraordinary abilities.

Zianne touched the side of his face. He turned and gazed at the face of the woman he thought he'd lost forever.

"You did it, Mac. I hoped, but never did I believe that all would be saved, that the Gar would be stopped forever." Her eyes filled with tears. "That I would have the chance, finally, to love you."

She reached around Mac and grabbed Dink's hand. "And you, too, Nils Dinkemann." She tugged him close, kissed Dink, and then wrapped her arms around Mac's neck and kissed him soundly.

There was no doubt in his mind. She was real. She was alive, and she was his. He wasn't sure what the future held for any of them—the world knew all about the Nyrians and would soon know more about their abilities.

He hoped they'd be welcome. He hoped the Bart Roberts of the world could be kept under control. He'd promised his team six months here at the DEO-MAP site, and he hoped they all planned to stay. There was a lot left to do, but considering what they'd accomplished in less than five full days, his dream team had proved they could do whatever they set their collective minds to.

There was so much the Nyrians needed to learn about humans and humanity, and even more that the human race needed to learn about Nyrians.

And then there was Dink. Mac felt as if he'd rediscovered what they could be to each other. He'd mentioned that to Dink, that he didn't know how he was going to handle it when the newscaster returned to his work and life on the opposite side of the country.

Dink had merely smiled and said not to worry. He had a plan. Of course, Dink always had a plan, but maybe this time it would bring him closer, not take him so far away.

So many things to think about. So much going on. So many possibilities. Mac's mind spun glorious circles with plans for the site, for the dream team, for their new batch of American citizens.

For Zianne and Dink and Mac.

For children—a dream he'd put aside so many years ago. A dream Zianne had simply and suddenly resurrected.

"Mac?"

He gazed into Zianne's twinkling violet eyes. "Yes?"

"You can make plans later. Right now, we need to eat."

"Ah." He glanced about the room. Everyone had gone back to their food. The room was filled with laughter and chatter, and it reminded him, in a way, of the student cafeteria so many years ago when he was still in college. He'd dreamed big then, too.

He'd made those dreams come true. There was no reason to cut back on any of his dreams for the future. He grabbed a tray at the long buffet table, and as he was loading his plate with bacon and eggs and fried potatoes and all the things a man his age probably shouldn't be eating, his mind went to more mundane things.

Finishing breakfast, a walk around the plateau with Dink and Zianne to check out the site, maybe a return call to the president of the United States. Then he paused to savor the most important item of all—enjoying the first day of a lifetime to come with Zianne.

The phone call could wait. After so many years, Mac finally felt as if he had his priorities straight.

Turn the page for a special preview
of the first book of
Kate Douglas's brand-new series:

DARK WOLF

Featuring the next generation of Chanku,
from the wildly popular and long-running
WOLF TALES series.

A trade paperback on sale May 2013.

1

Crickets chirped. An owl hooted. A dusting of starlight shimmered faintly against granite peaks, but here at the forest's edge, all was dark. Shivering slightly in the cool night air, Sebastian Xenakis stood beneath the gnarled oak, just one more shadow among many. With great humility and as much confidence as he could muster while standing naked in the darkness, he raised his arms, drew on the magic coursing through his veins, and called on the spirit within the tree, humbly asking for her strength.

Nothing.

"Damn it all." He exhaled a huge blast of frustration, stared at the massive tree towering overhead, and then methodically emptied his mind of all thoughts, all distractions. He put aside anger and frustration, fears and hopes, leaving room for nothing but *here* and *now*. Focusing everything within, he opened his heart to possibilities, and waited.

A few long, frustrating minutes later, he felt her warmth envelop him. An unexpected frisson raced across his bare shoulders, along his arms. It caressed his naked buttocks and swirled over his belly, lifting the dark line of body hair that trailed from navel to groin. Then it slithered along his thighs, circled his calves, and tickled across his bare feet.

Sliding away as soft as a whisper, the intimate sense of touch, of sentient communion, bled off into the damp loam and returned to its source through thickly tangled roots. Sebastian sighed, a shuddering acceptance of sensual pleasure, the gift of contact with such a powerful force.

Ancient beyond belief, her thick and twisted branches spreading far and wide, the mother oak had stood here, a silent sentinel of the forest since long before the dawn of modern history. A few heavy branches had fallen over time, but he knew her roots were strong, her branches healthy.

As if challenging time itself, the graceful beauty and symmetry of the tree remained.

He remembered the first time he saw the oak, recalled the sense of life, the sure knowledge of her power.

It was on that day he'd learned his father wielded the kind of power Sebastian had quickly begun to crave.

Standing just beyond the reach of the great branches, unsure of his relationship with a man he barely knew, Sebastian had watched Aldo Xenakis call lightning out of a clear, star-filled sky—call it and control it with the deft hands of a master.

He'd been seduced so easily, so quickly by that flashy show of power. So thoroughly he knew he might never break free of its siren call.

Might never break free of the man he'd consciously sought, despite his mother's warning. Now, it was much too late, and he was almost glad his mother was dead.

Glad she couldn't see what he'd become.

Sebastian quickly shoved thoughts of his moral weakness and his failures—and his father—aside. There was no need to mar the beauty of this night. He took a deep breath and then, almost as an afterthought, drew more power to him. Pulled it from the earth, from the sky, from the water of a nearby stream. The fire must come from within, but he called on that as well and felt the power build.

Then he buffered the swirling energy with the strength of the oak until it was entirely under his control. Until he was the one holding the power.

Unlike his father, unwilling to display such arrogance, Sebastian turned and bowed his head toward the oak, giving the tree's spirit his grateful thanks for her help. Then, spreading his fingers wide, he consciously breathed deeply and opened himself to the energy flowing into him from all directions. A brilliant glow surrounded him, but it wasn't lightning that lit the dark night.

It was power. Raw power he'd pulled from the earth, from the air and water. From the fire burning in his soul.

Within seconds, the light blinked out. Gone as if it had never existed at all.

As did the man. In his place, a wolf darker than night raised its head and sniffed the air. Then it turned away and raced into the forest.

"Lily? Have you seen this morning's news?"

Lily Cheval fumbled with the phone and squinted at the bedside clock in the early-morning darkness. Blue numbers blurred into focus. Her best buddy looked at her out of the screen on her phone. "Alex, it's six fifteen in the morning. On a Sunday. What can possibly be important enough to . . ."

"There's been another one. Just inside the entrance to the park this time."

Lily bit back a growl and sat up. The last body, discovered less than a week ago, had been found along the highway leading into Glacier National Park. The one before that on the outskirts of Kalispell. "What have you got?"

Alex sighed and wiped a hand across his eyes. Poor Alex.

How he'd ever ended up as the pack's liaison to the Flathead County sheriff's department was beyond understanding. He might be brilliant and charismatic, but he was not cut out to deal with—much less deliver—bad news, especially early on a Sunday morning.

His eyes looked bloodshot. She wondered if he'd even made it to bed the night before. Alex did love his social life on a Saturday night.

Even in Kalispell.

"Same as the last seven," he said. "Young woman, beaten, brutally raped. Throat torn out. Just like the others, probably killed somewhere else and dumped. A park ranger found her body beside the road."

"Shit. I hope you've got an alibi."

She hated having to ask, but with public sentiment the way it had been heading . . .

"I was with Jennifer last night. I got the call on the way home."

Jennifer. Poor choice of woman, but at least she could account for Alex's time when the attack occurred. Frustrated, Lily dug her fingers into her tangled hair and tugged. Anything to help focus her thoughts. "Let me know what you find out. Check with the pack, see if they've got any new leads. I'm stuck in San Francisco until after the reception, but I'll try and get up there by the weekend."

"Okay. Be careful. Whoever's behind this, they've hit the Bay Area just as hard. I'll find out what I can. Thanks, Lil."

Quietly, Lily set the phone back in the charger and leaned against the headboard. Another young woman dead. Another murder with all the signs of a wild animal attack—except for the rape.

Just like the other seven.

Eight young women, dead by a combination of man and beast. Five in or near Glacier National Park. Three in the San

Francisco Bay Area. And where were the largest populations of Chanku shapeshifters?

"Glacier National Park and the San Francisco Bay Area. Shit." A chilling sense of premonition shuddered along Lily's spine. If they didn't find the one behind this, and find him soon, someone was going to be hunting Chanku.

The sharp click of Lily's heels echoed against the pale gray walls of Cheval International, one of the more profitable branches of Chanku Global Industries. She walked quickly toward her office, wishing she could ignore the tension headache pounding in sharp counterpoint to her footsteps.

Her father insisted headaches were purely psychosomatic—according to Anton Cheval, Chanku shapeshifters were impervious to human frailties. "Tell that to my head," she muttered, timing the steady throbbing between her eyes against the click of her heels.

Damn. She did not need a headache. Not on a Monday, not with a full day of meetings ahead, including lunch with the mayor and a one-on-one with the head of security.

Resentment of the long-lived Chanku shapeshifters had been simmering for years, but the recent series of attacks against young women had brought that simmer to a boil. It didn't help that a local celebrity had taken a very public stance against the Chanku, blaming them for everything from the current downturn in the economy to the vicious rapes and murders.

Aldo Xenakis had been a thorn in Lily's side ever since she'd assumed leadership of Cheval International. Recently, his verbal attacks had taken on a frighteningly personal slant.

It didn't help that he owned a massive amount of land that abutted her father's vast holdings in Montana. It was bad enough he was stirring up resentment here in California, but Montana was home. Having longtime friends and neighbors turn against them hurt Lily and the rest of the pack on a much more personal level. They'd worked hard at being good neighbors, at integrating themselves into the community.

Now this.

"Good morning, Ms. Cheval."

"G'morning, Jean." Lily paused in front of her secretary's desk. "Have you got today's calendar?"

Jean nodded. Gray-haired, round-faced, and very human, she'd been Lily's secretary since she'd been named CEO of the company seven years earlier. And, while Jean continued to age, Lily still looked as youthful and fresh as the day she'd walked out of Berkley with her MBA.

One more reason for humans to resent shapeshifters, though she'd never noticed any resentment at all from Jean. Considering the good pay and generous benefit packages all CGI employees received, she didn't expect it to become an issue.

Lily glanced over the daily calendar Jean handed to her. The morning wasn't too busy, but . . . "Why have you got a question mark by my lunch date with the mayor?"

Jean shook her head. "Her office called a few minutes ago. When the mayor's schedule went out to the media yesterday, they forgot to black out your lunch appointment. Reporters know when and where you're meeting, and the mayor said she'd understand if you decide to cancel."

The pounding between her eyes got worse. Goddess, but it had been too long since she'd shifted and run. Right now, Lily really wanted to chase down something furry and kill it. "Not necessary," she said, rubbing her temple. "We really need to talk. Maybe I'll wear a disguise."

Jean grinned as she gave her an appraising look. "Don't think that would help. You're hard to miss."

Lily raised her eyebrows and glanced at Jean. "Thank you. I think." She grabbed the mail Jean handed to her and headed toward her office, but paused at the door. "I'm expecting a call from Alex Aragat. Be sure and put him through even if I'm on something else."

"Okay." The phone rang, but before answering it, Jean added, "You'll find a list of the calls you need to return on your desk. Uhm, more than a few from your father." She laughed.

Lily just shook her head when Jean added, "He wanted to remind you not to forget the reception Thursday night."

"I wish," she muttered, but she turned and smiled at Jean. "I won't. And even if I wanted to, dear old Dad would make sure I got there on time."

Lily shut the office door as Jean took her call. She glanced at the clock over the bookcase. Seven thirty, which meant that, with any luck, she'd have time to get her desk cleared before lunch. Her head was still pounding like a damned jackhammer, but she flopped down in the comfortable chair behind her desk and read through Jean's messages. All were carefully organized by importance. The stack from her father—and damn, but how many times had the man called?—was set off to one side.

She knew he'd be up. Might as well check in with the boss first. The phone rang as she reached for it. She glanced at the caller ID and sighed. "Hello, Dad. I was just getting ready to call you."

"How's your headache?"

She frowned at his smug image. "How do you know I've got a headache?"

"Because I've been trying to mindspeak all morning and I know you're blocking me."

"Oh." No wonder her head hurt. She'd developed the habit of keeping her shields high and tight since she was just a child, but that never kept her father from trying. "Well, if you knew you were giving me a headache, why'd you keep pushing?"

No answer. Typical. She was convinced he heard only what he wanted to.

"You've talked to Alex."

Not a question. He'd know, of course. Anton Cheval knew everything. "Yes. He called first thing Sunday morning, but he didn't have any details. I expect to hear more today. Have you learned anything else?"

"How well do you know Aldo Xenakis?"

"Not well at all," she said, used to her father's non sequiturs. Amazing . . . her headache was gone. She almost laughed. Her father'd been the cause of it all along. "Why do you ask?"

"His son will be attending the reception Thursday night. I want you to meet him."

"He has a son? Since when? I thought Xenakis lived alone."

"The younger Xenakis has stayed in the background. From what I've learned, he didn't even know Aldo was his father until a couple of years ago. When the boy's mother died, he traced Aldo through her private papers."

"Interesting. Why do you think the son's important?"

"He's been staying at his father's home up here for the past month. You know where the house is. It's a few miles from our place, though our property shares the southern boundary. Tinker thought he smelled an unfamiliar wolf near the edge of our holdings night before last. He traced the scent to a ridge on the Xenakis property. The wolf scent disappeared, but he picked up the trail of a man and followed it to the house. The only one there was a young man who appeared to be Xenakis's son."

"He's Chanku?" Now that would be interesting, considering how xenophobic the father was.

"We don't know. The elder Xenakis has powerful magic. If the son inherited his father's gift, he could be shifting by magical means, not natural. I want you to get close enough, see if you sense anything."

"Do you think he's our murderer?"

"I don't know, Lily. But women have been killed near Kalispell and in the San Francisco Bay Area. Xenakis has homes in both places, and his son spends time at both locations.

I've got Alex looking into his schedule now, checking flight records, that sort of thing. Be very careful."

"One question. What's his name? How will I know him?"

"Sebastian. I don't know what surname he used before, but he's taken his father's name. Look for Sebastian Xenakis. Tinker says he's tall with dark hair. And really odd eyes. Teal blue, according to Tink. Not amber like most of us. And, Lily?"

"Yes?"

"I love you, sweetheart, but I have a bad feeling about this. Be very careful. We don't know a thing about this guy, but he's got my sense of premonition in high gear. No specific danger, just a strong feeling he will have some kind of effect on our family."

Lily stared at the handset long after her father had ended the call. The pack might tease Anton Cheval about his premonitions, but invariably he'd been proven correct. She flipped on her computer and typed in Sebastian Xenakis's name.

It never hurt to be fully informed about the enemy.

"Lily. So glad you agreed to meet even after my office screwed this up so badly."

"Well, hopefully the media haven't bugged the restaurant." Lily smiled at the mayor and shook her hand. "It's good to see you, Jill." Then she nodded toward the group of reporters gathered just outside the restaurant. "I was hoping they were here for you. It's been a while since I've run a gauntlet like that."

Mayor Jill Bradley shook her head as she reached for the menu. "It's the killings, Lily. We're doing everything we can to keep a lid on things, but . . ."

"I know." Sighing, Lily reached for her own menu. "I heard from Alex Aragat, our pack's law enforcement liaison in Montana. People are scared, and I can't blame them. My father's got every available resource working on this from our angle."

Jill shook her head. "My gut feeling is that it's not a Chanku killing these girls. I think someone's trying to raise public anger against shifters."

Lily had to agree. "Dad feels the same way, but until this guy is stopped . . ."

"Or they. DNA is inconclusive, but I've been told it points to more than one perp. Animal, definitely, but possibly more than one human committing the rapes."

The waitress reached their table before Lily could respond. Jill set her menu down to place her order; Lily closed hers and studied the mayor. Jill Bradley had held her post for almost five years now, and her popularity had yet to wane. She'd become a good friend and a powerful ally, a woman Lily would have liked and admired even if she hadn't been the mayor.

It never hurt to have friends in high places. Smart friends. The fact she had already considered what Lily figured was happening was a good sign. She glanced up and realized the waitress was waiting to take her order.

"Hamburger. Rare." Lily smiled at the waitress, waiting for the admonition that rare beef wasn't safe. Instead, she got a saucy wink. "You got it. Be back in a minute with your drinks."

"Did we order drinks?"

Jill laughed. "It's on me. I figured you could use a glass of wine. I know I sure can. Let's discuss the reception and your father's generous donation. The other topic is too frustrating when we don't have any answers."

"I agree. I think we're being set up, but I'm not sure it's more than one person."

Jill's dark brows drew down. "You'll let me know if you learn anything to substantiate that, won't you?"

"Of course. Alex is working on a couple of things, but at this point it's all supposition."

The waitress reached the table and opened a bottle of wine.

She poured a taste for the mayor, who sipped and quickly agreed.

"I'll have your meals in a few moments. Enjoy." The waitress smiled and left.

Lily tipped her glass in a toast to her friend. "Here's to the new wing at the museum. I saw it this weekend. It's turned out beautifully."

"Thanks to your father's generosity."

Lily dipped her head, acknowledging the mayor's comment. Anton Cheval had become a generous benefactor over the years, and Jill Bradley's status as mayor had benefited greatly from his many gifts to the city during her administration.

"Consorting with the local fauna, Mayor Bradley?"

Lily fought the urge to spin around and glare. Instead, she sat perfectly still, outwardly calm and relaxed. Jill set her wine on the table and glowered at the man beyond Lily's shoulder.

"There's no call for that, Aldo. You're interrupting a private lunch."

Lily twisted in her chair, at a disadvantage to the tall, elegant man standing much too close behind her for comfort. The hairs along her spine rose and she bit back a growl. She'd never met Aldo Xenakis in person, but the man was on the news often enough. Lately he'd made a point of baiting Chanku shapeshifters, and Lily Cheval in particular. She recognized him immediately.

Turning and standing, she enjoyed the satisfaction of watching him back up when he realized she met him at eye level. "Ah, Mr. Xenakis. A pleasure." She held out her hand. He stared at it a moment. Lily didn't waver. Reluctantly, he shook hands.

The frisson of awareness she felt left her wanting to wash her hands. There was something wrong about Xenakis. Something she couldn't place, and it wasn't her Chanku senses that left her skin crawling.

No. It was her magic, something as much a part of her as her Chanku heritage. Her innate power recoiled almost violently at the man's brief touch.

Lily surreptitiously wiped her palm against her slim skirt. She noticed that Jill wasn't the least bit welcoming. "Was there something you wanted, Aldo? Ms. Cheval and I were preparing to discuss some business."

"No." He stepped back and nodded. "I merely saw a beautiful woman sitting here and took a chance to say hello." He kept his gaze planted firmly on Jill and blatantly ignored Lily.

She remained standing, purposefully invading his space until the waitress arrived with their meals. Aldo stepped out of her way and then left without another word. Lily turned and sat, raised an eyebrow, and glanced at Jill.

Jill shook her head. The moment the waitress was gone, she took a sip of her wine. "I do not like that man. Something about him . . ."

Lily nodded. "Makes your skin crawl?"

"Exactly. Why? He's handsome enough. Well mannered."

"Rich and powerful." Lily laughed. "I bet he's asked you out."

"He did, and like a fool, I accepted. I couldn't wait for the evening to end."

"Did he make a pass?"

Jill shook her head. "Nothing so obvious, but he makes me very uncomfortable. Just a feeling I wasn't safe with him."

Lily took a bite of her very rare hamburger and swallowed. "You sure you're not Chanku? You've always got good intuition."

"No. Not a drop. I was tested. Took the nutrients for two weeks. Not even a hint of a need to howl." She shrugged and turned her attention to her salad.

Lily used her French fry as a pointer. "I'm sorry. I think you could have given the guys in my pack a run for their money."

Jill sipped her wine. "I still can. I just have to do it on two legs."

They both laughed, but at the same time, the fact she'd tried the nutrients meant Jill had hoped she was Chanku. Lily was sorry for her, for the fact that her friend had wanted something badly enough to go for it, yet failed.

It was something Jill had to accept she could never have. Lily wondered what that would be like, to want something that was totally impossible, something forever out of reach.

They concentrated on their food for a bit. Then Jill set her fork down. "You know, Lily. I think the world of you, and I really love your folks. You're good people. All of you, and your mom and dad especially. They give generously whenever there's a need, and they've done a lot for this city, even though they don't live here. I don't want to see these killings hurt any of you, but if we can't find the killer, I don't know how we're going to keep the anger under control."

Lily glanced toward the crowd of reporters waiting at the front door. The questions they'd thrown at her as she walked into the restaurant had been pointed and ugly. In their minds, shapeshifters were committing rapes and murders and she was just as guilty as the ones actually doing the deed.

The sudden jackhammer inside her head had her gasping.

"Lily? Are you all right?"

Jill reached across the table and took her hand.

Lily pressed fingers to her skull. "Just a minute."

Her father's voice filled her mind.

There's been another killing, Lily. A woman's body was found about ten minutes ago in Golden Gate Park, not far from the garden your mother designed so many years ago. If you're in a public place, you might want to find somewhere private to fin- ish your lunch with the mayor.

"Shit." Lily took one more quick bite of her burger and tossed back the last of her wine, taking a moment to consider the consequences of her father's words. She focused on Jill. "My father just contacted me. There's been another murder. The body was found about . . ."

The mayor's cell phone rang. She answered the call, but her gaze was glued to Lily. With a soft curse, she asked a couple of questions and then ended the call. "That was the chief of police. I'm needed back at City Hall." She stood up. "I'm sorry, Lily. I'll do what I can."

"I know. Thank you. Go ahead. I'll get lunch."

Jill was reaching for her handbag. "That's not—"

"Go. Call me later."

"I will." She slipped the strap to her purse over her shoulder and gave Lily a quick hug. "Later. And thank you."

Lily watched her walk away. A pleasant-looking woman in her early fifties, Jill Bradley looked like someone's mom, not like the head of one of California's largest, most diverse cities.

She walked as if she didn't have a care in the world, passing through the throng of reporters with a quick smile and a friendly greeting to the ones she knew.

Lily wished she had that kind of grace under fire. She handed her card to the waitress, signed the tab when it came after adding a sizeable tip for that perfectly prepared, almost-raw burger, and walked toward the back of the restaurant.

There was no way she was going to try to get through the reporters. Nope. She'd take the coward's exit, through the kitchen and out the back.

And the first thing she'd do when she got back to the office was call Alex. The last murder had been in Montana, but this latest had happened barely a mile from her office.

She wondered where Sebastian Xenakis had been last night.